A HANDFUL OF SAND

A
HANDFUL
OF SAND

Marinko Koščec

Translated from the original Croatian by
Will Firth

English-language edition first published in 2013 by
Istros Books
London, United Kingdom
www.istrosbooks.com

This book was first published in Croatia as *To malo pijeska na dlanu*
(PROFIL INTERNATIONAL, 2005)

© Marinko Koščec, 2013
Translation © Will Firth, 2013

Cover image and artwork by Roxana Stere
© Roxana Stere, 2013

The right of to Marinko Koščec be identified as the author of this work has
been asserted in accordance with the Copyright, Designs and Patents Act, 1988

ISBN 978-1-908236-074

Typeset by Octavo Smith Ltd in
Constantia and Franklin Gothic Book 10.25/13

This project has been funded with support from the European Commission. This publication
reflects the views only of the author, and the Commission cannot be held responsible for any
use which may be made of the information contained therein.

Education and Culture DG

Culture Programme

This publication was made possible with the help of the
Ministry of Culture of Croatia.

The man had been absent for so long
that he finally ceased to exist for the woman he had left.
The woman was so torn by that thought
that the man finally really did cease to exist.

Jacques Sternberg, *Absence*

＊　＊　＊

It's snowing again; it must have started during that time where the night takes a break from its tormenting and delivers me to uniform blackness. You don't hear it but you feel it behind the glass, and the noises from the street are softer, as if through cotton wool. The first bus came whining by at exactly five fifteen, picked up two frozen figures that embraced to maintain their uprightness despite the alcohol in them, snorted as if in disdain at such a modest morsel of humanity, and went grumbling off up Victoria Street. The rubbish containers were emptied at half past five. A snowplough went past, pushing the powdery snow from the road into piles which would later be taken away on trucks. Cars began to trickle by until they filled all four lanes heading for the inner city, like monstrous bees swarming in to drink at a source of poison; their humming would only gradually die away around midnight, together with the roar of the aeroplanes taking off and landing every fifteen minutes; so close that you can read the names of the airlines, one more exotic than the next.

It falls night and day. After an hour or two's break it starts floating down again, calmly, thoroughly, only letting through enough sun to remind you it still exists. People say they can't remember such a cold winter; when the temperature goes up to minus fifteen you feel like going out in short sleeves. I still haven't seen the Canadian soil, that thin layer they conceive maps on, beneath the crust of snow. The lake is frozen up, too; last weekend I took a bus down Red River and went for a walk alongside it, though it could only be sensed beneath the monotony of the white, white plain thanks to the wild geese

7

shifting from one end to the other, riveted by memories or because they couldn't think of anywhere else to go. Smells, too, are imprisoned in the ice, everything is sterile, white and muted, like a cold room in which we, both geese and people, wait for our autopsy.

Every morning I wake up at five. A jolt, the beating of my heart, and then all I can do is stare into the same painful thoughts in the darkness; as soon as my conscious mind switches on, they're there. For months they would at best recede a little to the demands of work, but never for an instant did they stop trampling me, digging away inside me and crushing me into ever smaller pieces. Yet things have improved since I arrived in Canada. My body has become hard and numb; when I'm stabbed, I'm able to smile. There's nothing funny about it, but why not, we laugh. Why shouldn't we have a beer and share a vulgar joke or two, ride on the underground, grill sausages, go to a museum or a strip-joint. *Sure,* I said, when Jeremy suggested we celebrate my birthday after I'd blabbed that I was born exactly thirty-three years before, to the day. He said that to please me, no doubt, and I didn't want to disappoint him. Something told me he'd never seen a woman's naked body before, let alone touched one. That just added to his mystical aura.

While I sit writing at the kitchen table, Jeremy lies in his room eternally immobile like a mummy, all two metres of him lying lifelessly on his back. He has fifteen minutes more until his alarm clock rings. If it was the weekend, he'd stay there till noon. I don't know exactly what makes him a mystic, but I have no other name for the harmony which emanates from him, for the feeling that he's achieved absolute equilibrium, plenitude and well-roundedness within his own body in a way known to him alone. At first glance you'd feel sad at the sight of him lying paralysed – this giant of a man made of nothing but muscle with a basilical frame and a blond ponytail down to his belt; the felling of a centennial oak is more heart-wrenching than when an ordinary plum tree hits the ground. But there's no need for sadness; he's completely at peace with himself, smiles back at every glance, both at home and at work. Never once have I see him ruffled or heard him raise his voice. As conscientious as he is contented, as if it were exactly the way to attain nirvana, he demolishes walls with a jackhammer. At breakfast he stirs oatmeal in a pot until it turns to porridge, then he meditates over every spoonful. He answers questions gently and benignly and never asks any himself. Nor do I; he could hardly have found a more compatible flatmate. I don't bring home visitors, I'm not loud, in fact I hardly make any noise at all, but here I am, without a doubt – at least physically. And he lets me know in his discreet way that he notices and appreciates that.

Saturday the twenty-ninth of December: frying-pan hamburgers and pre-made chips with sachets of free ketchup, then an odyssey into the Winnipeg night in Jeremy's rattly Chevrolet through the cosmopolitan quarter which has grown up near the airport, a labyrinth of fifteen-storey buildings with subsidised rents. And on through the tunnel formed by the aluminium monsters lining the road, or rather their outlines which faded away beneath neon aureoles and columns of thick smoke, and then through the ice-sheathed wasteland. And at the end a low, log cabin with the sign *Nude Inn*, adorned outside and in with long lines of little twinkling lights bulbs for the New Year. Here Jeremy and I celebrated my birthday and alternated in buying each other beers. He got the first round, then me, and then it was take turns once more. Each time we said cheers, exchanged significant glances, and in between were mostly silent. He looked towards the stage, but the expression on his face made you think of a rippling mountain stream and a fawn drinking from it. The girls performed their acts, alone or in pairs, wrapping themselves around metal bars or one another and demonstrating ever greater gymnastic prowess. In the break he said something in my ear, but the music was too loud and I was too tired. On the way back he added that we'd had an excellent table, and I agreed.

The next day, and that was the only time, he told me a few words about himself, with the same softness in his voice and the same impassive smile. He'd recently moved here from a small town fifty miles further north after the firm he'd worked for went bankrupt and the aunt he'd grown up with died, as well as his twin brother. His aunt never married; she'd developed multiple sclerosis long ago and been immobile for the last twelve years of her life. His mother had been taken away when he was five by the hand of his father – or an axe, to be precise. He'd never seen his father sober. After prison, he saw his son now and again in the house of the widow with whom he started a new life, but he soon lost that too, in a fire caused by smoking drunk in bed. And his brother had died just last year when a hunting rifle blew up in his face. Jeremy liked it here in Winnipeg and was completely happy with his job.

I went out before lunch, into the flaying cold. After fifteen minutes of rocking from foot to foot, the train arrived empty. The doors opened and closed pointlessly at the stations until the train dipped underground, signalling its approach to the city centre. A handful of people got in, muffled from head to toe, and rushed to huddle up on one of the heated seats. I got out at Yong Street. There were still a few shops open in China-town. Steam emerged from a bakery, through cracks in the dilapidated windows. I went in and bought a bag of crab and pineapple crackers from a shrimp of a man who didn't stop thanking me even after I'd left; waving to me once more through the bedewed window pane. The only thing I remember about that afternoon is that I spent some time leafing through books in the subterranean shopping mall which had sunk into apathy after the fever of Christmas, although neon promises were still blinking that all our wishes would come true in 2006.

The day dragged on until it was finally time for dinner. A handwritten board solicited me with Taiwanese delicacies at a special season's discount. The restaurant was at the bottom of the court, squeezed in between a flower shop and an undertaker's. A reception desk almost as high as me rose up immediately inside the premises, with a hotel bell which you had to ring for service. A frighteningly broad female face appeared and observed me from below for several seconds over the desk; for a moment I thought it was a gimmick – a carnival mask they put on as a welcome. *Eat one person*, she said with an intonation probably supposed to indicate a question, descended from her throne and beckoned with her finger for me to follow her into an empty hall. Where exactly to seat me still demanded some thought; she took me to a table in one of the compartments for couples behind a sumptuous screen of plywood embellished with a jungle of imitation carved tendrils of vibrant red, green and gold. The whole place was smothered in vivid opulence, gold paint and plastic. Every table was dominated by a bouquet of artificial flowers. Imitation candlesticks and a plethora of Oriental abstract art hung from the pink-painted walls, while polychromatic paper dragons with protruding tongues dangled from the ceiling, or rather from the canopies hanging low over my head. As a counterpoint to that colourful exaltation, a bloodless female voice oozed from the loudspeaker for the duration of my stay in the establishment. It was so dirgeful that even the carpet would have started to cry if it understood Taiwanese, and was accompanied contrastingly by a rather irritating piano, which at times sounded like a French chanson, at others like a salsa. A piercing hum sporadically drowned out the music.

This went on and on, and my food still hadn't been served. But the smell of frying issued from the kitchen, heavy and abundant, and the hasty rattle of utensils intimated that a large family was rushing to serve a sudden throng of guests, although not another soul turned up the whole time I was eating. Still, the proprietress finally brought me the clams I had ordered and ceremoniously presented them together with a bowl of rice and a bottle of tap water. They tasted like pork. *Not eat much* she commented when returning the change, as concerned as she was disappointed. I replied with my best imitation of a Taiwanese smile and bow.

For all the abundance of Winnipeg's gastronomic attractions, there is none I've visited a second time. Yesterday, at a Japanese restaurant, the decor was exactly the opposite: rectangular and austere, with reproachfully clean lines and a minimum of colour, pale yellow and black; the lighting was subtle, attenuated by rice-paper screens; and there was no music. The owner, his wife, and two boys, evidently their sons, stood in line at the entrance. All of them, one after another, called on me while I was eating to ask *Everything OK?* or to fill up my water glass. I ruminated on their credo engraved in a little plaque in the restroom: *Who comes as a friend, always comes too late and leaves too early*. I have always firmly believed in a friendly attitude, and it was with such that I went to see them; yet this adage informed us that every hope is futile – it's always too late, if not too early.

At the table next to me, two Japanese businessmen were conversing quietly between mouthfuls. They understood each other perfectly, after just a syllable or two; as soon as one started to speak the other would nod, and they filled in the pauses by both nodding. The men were restrained, their manners refined, and they fitted flawlessly into the setting. But during the course of dinner they gradually shed their veneer; a second bottle saw their jackets thrown over the backs of the chairs, their tie-knots loosened, and the ties then rolled up and pocketed; they talked ever more loudly, smiled from ear to ear, laughed spasmodically and wiped their sweat-beaded foreheads on the tablecloth. A group of Asian girls turned up from somewhere – teenagers, probably on an excursion. They clustered around five joined-together tables and immediately started chirping in a language the waiters didn't understand, full of long ascending tones. Negotiations were conducted in slow and painful English: one of them interpreted for the others, translating the name of every dish on the menu, which led to lively debates. Finally, a huge shared platter arrived, noisily greeted with shouts and clapping, and was immediately attacked with cameras. They took snapshots of each other hugging or fraternising with glasses of water. Not one of them drank any alcohol, but they were soon seized by rapture and the place was inundated with a mood of collective inebriation. The businessmen were joined by the owner, pretty pickled himself, who started an exchange with one of them about something very funny; they burst out laughing together, slapping their thighs and showing all their teeth. The other businessman tittered with his head on the table as his eyes wandering off and he hummed to himself intermittently. All this proceeded quite naturally and anything could have happened; we were just a hair's breadth away from all bursting into song together and dancing traditional dances on the tables as we welcomed fire-eaters and trapeze artists accompanied by giraffes.

The flirtatious glances the girls were casting my way, at first coy, became very open and inquisitive, accompanied by whispers and giggles. The atmosphere inspired me and I was tempted to move to their table, almost convinced that I would swiftly bridge the language barrier, racial and age differences, perhaps some distinctions in world view too, socialise freely with them all, and head off home with them arm in arm, wherever that may be.

But in the end I went outside: into the awful, crusty cold, amidst the snowflakes which were dancing again, this time in a horizontal *danse macabre* borne on a marrow-biting northerly wind, and I dragged my bag of bones slowly through the graveyard of ghostily extinguished glass-and-steel giants.

It's not masochism which draws me to such restaurants. On the contrary, there's usually a beneficial, liberating turn of events: my accumulated grief is stirred up, grows to unbearable satiety and bursts out in bouts of hysterical laughter, before morphing into a diabolical euphoria; this subsides into an ease which I take away with me, almost floating. In the hours that follow, everything is rinsed out of me, everything is gone. I'm damned wherever I am and whatever happens; I'd give my last piece of clothing if someone asked, or calmly watch my inner organs be excised.

And in the morning, on the dot of five, it starts all over again.

* * *

Exactly three weeks later they started jumping. There had only just been time for me to acclimatise and for the aggression of unfamiliar smells to stop. Time for the spirits of the former tenants to disperse – that residue of messy, broken lives; that concentrate of misery. And time for me to attain at least a fragile peace with this space, without any ambition to feel it would ever be mine.

The living room became my studio; there was a bathroom, a kitchen with a dining corner, and a tiny closet of a bedroom. And as much light as I needed, thanks to the generous windows: fortunately with bars. Call it paranoia if you like, but being alone in the basement flat, I was glad they were there. I soon learnt that dogs raised their legs at the windows, even those which were kept on a leash. I had always wanted to have a dog, or at least its bark. Like the yapping which the neighbour has to guard his flat, three or so floors up. The windows were also pissed on by beer-soaked football fans after every match, since the stadium was just one hundred metres away. They always came in groups and yowled their *Dii-naa-mo* or *We are the champions, Croa-a-atia!* There was a cramped parking area in front of the windows, and in the middle some of the tenants heroically maintained a little island of greenery with signs like *Don't kill the plants, God is watching you!* Opposite there was a house which a religious community built for itself. They had evening gatherings several days a week, and also on weekends. You didn't see the people arrive, you just heard the strains of a song, barely audible but borne by an ever greater chorus, and ever more imbued with His voice. When they really whooped it up, I opened the windows and fired back with industrial noise.

Or with the folk singer Sigfriede Skunk, from her Satanistic phase which ended in her being put away in the loony-bin. That didn't discourage the faithful vis-à-vis, but at least it struck a kind of balance in the sound waves. I also heard my upstairs neighbours very clearly whenever they had sex, or when they argued and started smashing the furniture. Once I tried to signal to them that my ears didn't want anything to do with it by banging the broomstick on the ceiling. They took this as a wish to participate, as if I was flirtatiously egging them on, and replied with an identical tock-tock-tock before going on to groan even more heartily and fuck each other with a vengeance.

And then a lady threw herself off the twelfth floor. I was sitting on the windowsill with my millionth cigarette; without a thought, except perhaps for the warmth of the autumn night and the intensive quivering of the stars as I sieved the sky in vain, searching for the angel of sleep. All at once, behind my back I heard a sound like a breath of wind. I just managed to turn my head slightly, enough to glimpse an unnaturally twisted lower leg and a bare foot out of the corner of my eye. A split second later there came a thud, without an echo, as a heap of dead limbs hit the pavement and instantly pulped.

She'd been ill, they said: in the head and elsewhere, and old and lonely to boot. But why did I have to be part of her relieving herself of her suffering? Why did she have to spill it all five metres from my window?

Three months later it was the opening of my exhibition at the prestigious Gradec Gallery. On three levels, with TV coverage and the minister of culture in attendance, as well as all the significant acolytes of culture – twelve long years after my first exhibit in a suburban library. And there were flocks of tarted-up culture vulturettes, sighing and holding their hands to their hearts in front of the pictures and only able to stammer: *It's so... It's so...* Plus their strutting, parvenu husbands, square-headed and short-necked, who furtively noted the address with the intention of surprising their darling; their aesthetic interest was limited to the colours not clashing with the sofa. And then there were the perverts who merge with the crowd, unnoticed, but when they catch you alone in the studio there's no getting rid of them. First they inquire circuitously about your techniques, about the meaning of this or that, discover cosmogonic connotations, make ever bolder allusions, and the whole time burn with only one desire: to unzip their flies and show you their jewels. The place was chock-full, but I spotted two or three other female artists discreetly letting themselves drift closer and closer to the curators and gallery owners, while looking anywhere but at the canvases. Quite indiscreetly, two male artists were ogling them with delight and a discerning thumb and forefinger on the chin, whispering into each other's ears and bending double with laughter.

I trembled with fear, and also shame, under the spotlights and the shower of eulogies. Being presented like some kind of circus attraction, being photographed for people's private albums, touched and felt, and having a dictaphone thrust into my mouth was OK, that was part of it all. But my pictures – I felt as if I was now seeing them for the first time. The gallery walls bore the marks of the mourning which I had painted out on canvases day and night, for months, unaware of what I was doing. Now it screamed from the walls, showing me strung up in a hundred copies. I felt that everyone there in the hall must have noticed, that every last person saw me as I saw myself before them: not just naked but flayed alive.

Yet the words praising my work gradually reached me and sank in, something about a 'plunge into archetypical meanders' and 'the concatenated metamorphoses of points of departure', about the paintings' 'psychogrammatic texture' and the 'inter-secting of oneiric planes', and it finally occurred to me how wrong

I had been. There was nothing to be seen, either in me or the paintings. Now they belonged to the buyers, who could hang them wherever they liked. They were never mine anyway, but only passed through me. That brought relief; a huge burden left me, trickling away like sand through my fingers. At the same time, I rose up towards the ceiling and stayed there floating, invisible. I set off home, or towards what I had started to call home, in a stupor, even giggling a little. The bubbles of champagne converged to carry me down Vlaška and Maksimirska streets like on a cushion of air – even after I had noticed a commotion in front of the building, people wringing their hands and others running to the scene.

My reflexes always set in too late. Anyone with the slightest instinct of self-preservation would have interpreted the commotion as a warning to turn around and go back without delay. But I kept walking, hypnotised, until I found myself eye-to-eye, literally, with what I had first taken to be a football under one of the parked cars. Only after staring for an eternity did I realise that it was the most important piece of the woman who had thrown herself off the roof to land in front of my window with more precision that her precursor. As my new friend, the caretaker of the building, explained to me in detail, the woman's head had caught on a first-floor clothes line, rolled away and been hidden from the people who found the rest of her. Until I arrived, they'd been sure this was an unheard-of murder by decapitation.

There was a curious watchfulness in that pair of eyes, something which long thereafter observed me timidly from the dark; now it's with me to stay.

When I finally turned and went back the way I had come, back along Maksimirska and Vlaška, it was quite involuntary. Only at the intersection of Medveščak Street did I realise where I was going and comprehend that I had to spend the night at Father's. I ended up staying three days. He was attentive, cooked for me and brought the food to my room. I only left it to go to the bathroom and spent the rest of the time curled up on the bed. That at least enlivened him for a while. After such a long time, he noticed that I existed.

On the third day, the landlady located me. She was full of comforting words but above all worried about how to find another tenant under these circumstances.

'The caretaker has looked after everything,' she assured me, 'although she didn't need to take responsibility. I paid her well.'

'How do you mean *take responsibility*?' I asked.

'Don't you know that you left your window open, so part of the unfortunate person, or rather what was inside...'

At that point I hung up.

It took me a lot of effort to imagine myself in that flat again. I could have asked someone to collect my things and store them somewhere for me; anywhere would do. But perhaps out of spite, or perhaps because it was hard to resist an opportunity to hurt myself, I returned. The woman who had taken on the unpleasant job had done her very best. She'd washed the curtains, polished the furniture and even ordered the cutlery in the drawers. But she was getting on in years, had a tremor, and the finger-thick lenses over her eyes prevented her from being particularly thorough. For days, I kept finding reminders of the event between the fins of the radiator, on my paintbrushes and even on the oil paintings I'd left to dry. I must admit, after the initial shock those stains and little relief-forming chunks fitted in very well on the canvases. The jumpers, who I'll never know anything about (not that I want to) are sure to have had anything but that on their minds when they climbed up to the top of the building. But now they've become part of my art in a special way. That person deserves that their last traces be preserved, and at least they now hang in an ultra-swish dining room or the conference chamber of a big mobile-phone operator. In any case, their remains will serve to provide archetypes and oneiric points of departure for the art critics just as well as any stroke of my brush could.

That event served to bring me together with the caretaker, who lived on the second floor. In practice, our rapport was formed around her almost daily visits, carrying mushrooms picked on the slopes of Mount Sljeme. They were just about her only food, a fact she tried to conceal along with the other signs of abject poverty. She got up at dawn and walked all the way there and back to keep fit, she said. Her mushroom-picking was actually risky given her short-sightedness because a toadstool or two is sure to have ended up in her bag along with the edible ones. I can't stand mushrooms: I feel that living off decay is already common enough in the human kingdom. But the first time I accepted them in the name of friendship, and after that I communicated with that one person in the building. She saw that as her good deed, an opportunity to take care of someone. She'd let me make her coffee but would never have anything else, even when she sat for hours through to late lunchtime, telling me episodes from her life – stories sadder than sad. Although she did repeat them all several times, with considerable variation on each occasion. Her younger and only brother, for example, drowned as a child while trying to save a friend who couldn't swim, but the second time it was a lamb he wanted to save, and the third time round he was killed by the Ustashi, the Croatian Fascists. That makes your ear a little immune after a while. I didn't want to risk disposing of the mushrooms in our rubbish container, so I wandered the neighbourhood with bags of fungus. I hadn't yet found her rummaging through the bins, but the prospects were all too likely.

The title of caretaker helped her little in preventing a practical jokester from stealing the light bulbs on the ground floor as soon she replaced them. That, in conjunction with the front door's eternally broken lock, turned my walk down the corridor to my basement flat in the evenings into fifteen seconds of panic. And it would do even less to prevent people in this part of Zagreb who wanted to commit suicide from thronging to our building, which was taller than the others, now that a pioneer had demonstrated how well it worked. In a flash of inspiration I stuck a note on the front door: *To whom it may concern, the northern side is also good for suicide jumping.* The next morning my friend just gave me a strange, mildly reproachful look. She was right, it was childish, so I took it down again.

* * *

For as long as I can remember I've been a magnet for weirdos, both for those who are kept at a safe distance with that label, as well as people who live among us peacefully and pose no danger until something in them erupts, for no apparent reason, and seem to need my proximity when it starts. It's as if they recognise some kind of essential stimulus, like kindling needs a lighter; then afterwards they stop seeking me out and don't approach me again for years, if at all.

It began with Jelenko. I met him on my first day at school and immediately realised, with an instinct for danger like that innate to small animals, that it would be best to avoid him. He stared in front of himself, as pale as a ghost, almost transparent, obviously asking himself what he'd done to deserve such terrible punishment, as if he was carrying the world he'd been thrust into on his shoulders. Over time, this ceased to be dramatic and diminished to a melancholic resignation, but his air of absence never went away. He emanated it like a saint wears a halo – an absence so real that it was visible to the even slightly sensitive eye, as irrefutable as the body of a normal person.

He did much better at school than all the others, but you could tell how little it mattered to him, and you could forget about the earthly application of whatever brilliance he had. Therefore he didn't provoke any great envy or disappoint his parents' ambitions: everyone sensed he was useless for any practical purposes and left him in peace.

Jelenko's lyrical dimension, the ethereality of his being, was where we differed; I'm rooted in the ground and only achieved good marks with great effort. But I am able to listen, and from time to time he had to speak his mind; early in secondary school he started dropping in and meditating about suicide. I would listen carefully, in trepidation, neither agreeing nor attempting to dissuade him, aware of how much his argumentation set him apart him from the kind of teenager-ish ravings which make the enigma of death enticing, of how far he was from those who hang themselves because of a bad report card, breaking up with their girlfriend or being fat. Simply put, it was as if he'd been born not into this life but into an adjacent plane, which by some freak of nature turned out to be a dead end, and as such it was all the same to him if he was to cut his life short or wait for it to end by itself; he always had one leg in the other world.

He could discuss death endlessly. These were actually dialogues with himself, because I had nothing to say on the topic. Death is something certain and eternal, everywhere and at all times; it's damn hard to forget that but even today I don't have anything to add. Maybe he came to me with his endless monologues because no one else took him seriously; but how can you dismiss someone when they show so much passion, when they only seem really alive when talking about death?

One year after the summer holidays we had to write about an event we remembered fondly. Jelenko, in a solemn and moving voice, with a wealth of poetic detail, described the burial of his rabbit and the dignity and reverence with which his whole family consigned the body of this beloved being to the earth. While he read, and for some time afterwards, the classroom was oppressed by heavy silence, and the relief was almost palpable when the teacher stopped him from reading on, without a word of commentary.

Still, the next day she suggested that he round off his composition with a story about the rabbit – about the feelings which had connected them and those which the loss of the rabbit aroused in him, with the aim of entering him in a national competition. Jelenko gave her an anxious look, but she persevered, thoroughly mistaking his reticence for modesty, until he shrugged his shoulders.

In the extended version, the rabbit was an exceptionally sweet creature, hungry for love and capable of returning it. It hopped freely around the house, stood up on its hind legs and held out its little paws wanting to be picked up and scratched on the tummy; it even ate from a dish at the dining table. An albino with red eyes, it seemed to be aware of its own uniqueness and was only waiting for the day when it would start speaking. There was a special bond between Jelenko and the rabbit: it would always wait for him at the door and knew when he was coming; whenever Jelenko was sad, even if he was out of the house, it would curl up in its cage, no longer caring to be stroked or given any attention, and would fill the house with sadness. The composition made no attempt to explain why the boy decided to kill the rabbit, be it as an experiment or because he was deranged; it was simply presented as a fact. But the description of the act was exhaustive: when it proved too much to do it with a knife, he took a knitting needle and loosed it from his slingshot. He had to do this several times, but the rabbit didn't budge or utter a sound. It waited patiently, as if with relief, for its destiny. The description of the funeral ceremony which followed now appeared in a different light and no longer had much prospect in the competition.

After secondary school, Jelenko surprised everyone by deciding to become a priest. I personally think that, rather than 'hearing the call', he devised it as a way out – a ruse for avoiding both earth and heaven in a refuge halfway. In any case, he never got in touch with me after leaving for the seminary, and his family later moved away. I never saw him again.

Goran, by way of contrast, was every parent's dream: delightfully undemanding but not autistic enough for the psychiatrists. The kind of child you want to pat on the head, one to be seen and not heard. You could give him a lollipop and he wouldn't ask for anything else for hours. Disinclined to tantrums even in puberty, there wasn't a shred of rebelliousness in him.

We didn't have anything much to do with each other until we were sixteen. He called on me at home, shyly at first, with various pretexts, but soon he came every day and stayed for hours. What connected us was mainly that we didn't have any friends; each of us in his own way enjoyed the reputation of a freak. But our conversations went into just about everything sixteen-year-olds can talk about, mostly books, especially those which were too complicated for us or where we only knew the title. And about sex: insights into the best ways to bring a girl to orgasm, the most intriguing places to *do it*, the most exciting positions, the comparative advantages of a virgin or a mature woman, and the secret inclinations of brunettes and blondes. Having exclusively theoretical knowledge of such matters was no hindrance to us. In other things, too, Goran liked to go into juicy details, smacking his lips like a connoisseur and pausing after spicy remarks to leave space for my admiration. I was well on the way to accepting him, if not as a replacement for my father, then at least as an elder brother – a kind of spiritual leader.

And then, without any warning or any subsequent explanation, he broke into the Chinese embassy. At that time, I should emphasise, an ambassador wasn't someone you could just bump into on any street corner like in our Croatian metropolis today; you had to go off to the then capital, Belgrade.

It already exceeded the comprehensible that he got on the train one morning like he otherwise got on the tram to school, after one of the identical evenings we spent together, and I don't remember us then or earlier having ever, even obliquely, mentioned Confucius, Lao Tzu, Mao Ze or *feng shui*, or travelling to the end of the night, or an *acte gratuit*. According to the version which leaked through despite his parents' secrecy, he roamed the unfamiliar city until midnight, climbed the iron fence and silently crawled in through a window left slightly open, as if just for him. Today, the media would zero in on that act of pubescent stupidity and blow it up into an incident between the two countries, but back then one had to hide every eccentricity and white out the decadent blemishes on the moth-eaten garb of self-managed socialism. Besides, Goran hadn't given rise to any suspicions of spying; apparently he didn't touch a single document or try to open any of the drawers. He just sat on the floor and waited for the Chinese bureaucrats and then, without resistance, let himself be taken away by the police, who briefly and unsuccessfully questioned him before returning him to his parents.

Time stood still for Goran after that. He was briefly institutionalised and then discharged for treatment at home, which proved unnecessary; he never ran away again or was a risk to anyone. He neither went back to school nor engaged with the world any more, although a few years later he started leaving the house again. Today you can still see him when he goes out on his walks, twice a day, sometimes in the middle of the night: he's become the walking landmark of the neighbourhood. His walks are different to those where a person is accompanied by a dog, or takes a trip into the countryside, or has an issue to ruminate on. He's become a phantom with empty eyes and mechanical movements, and he stopped returning greetings long ago. Sometimes children throw stones at him. When he gets hit, he stops for an instant and a spark of surprise flickers in his eyes, a kind of smile, but then they disappear around the corner in a flash. The years have left their mark on him in a ragged beard which clings to his cheeks, and grimaces which distort his face, but sometimes it seems you could catch a glimpse of something enigmatic inside, perhaps truly Taoistic.

There were others similar to him, thank God, and I may mention one or two later. Them recognising me as one of their own was largely thanks to my mother. According to generally accepted opinion, she was one of the loonies of the benign sort whom people like to run into in the street because they're sure to come up with something interesting you can share with your family or flatmates and therefore allow all of you to feel better, more normal, and convinced that the Almighty has had mercy on you after all. You don't let people like that into the house, of course, but they only turn up on your doorstep rarely anyway, for example with the diabolical insinuation that you've poisoned their cat, which they don't dare to speak openly but just shoot at you with their crazy eyes. To shoo them away you just need to reply in a calm, ever so slightly raised voice: *Lady, just move along now*. You don't hold it against them because you're compassionate and will soon forget the incident; you'll continue to greet them on the street and inquire after their health, although you know more than enough about them already.

I've never seen a more good-natured, grateful creature in my life than the cat. I found her in the meadow which the neighbourhood children used as a playground and the households as a disposal site: a bristling black kitten with clotted, scabby fur, which for hunger and trembling couldn't even miaow. It opened its mouth in vain, crying out with its frightened eyes. Mother very nearly jumped out of her skin when she discovered her beneath my bed, but that was the first of only two things where I didn't give in to her so often extravagant demands: I wept and blubbered and rolled on the floor until I won permission for the cat to stay. *Cat* was her name because Mother refused to call her anything else, so in the end I accepted it. She slept on my pillow and brought me mice and little birds; I didn't know how to explain to her that I didn't want to share them with her. Periodically there was the problem of her offspring to deal with. The first time, while I was at school, Mother incinerated them in the woodstove. You can imagine what it must have sounded like because disconcerted neighbours called the police, and the rest was written in Cat's eyes. For days she whined softly on the floor by my bed and didn't care for the food I brought her. With the other litters, Mother categorically refused any discussion: *What am I to feed them with? What?!* she cried in such a desperate voice that I fell silent. At least she didn't burn them any more. But she took them away in a sack and I didn't dare to ask where.

It would have been an exaggeration to say that Mother ever took a liking to Cat. But when she was poisoned with something which made her vomit yellow mucous for two days before dying, she cried together with me. Cat used to visit the neighbours' houses, and she particularly loved children. A week before the event, our neighbour Mr Kruhek gave Mother a telling off: the *dirty animal* had given his daughters fleas, he said.

On my first day at school, Mother made a name for herself by introducing herself to the teacher as my father. Classical Freudiansm; those aware of the situation might have seen their theories confirmed. For others it served as my first labelling, an indication of what kind of family I came from.

Father was a concept bound to rear its head sooner or

later, precisely because it was so painstakingly suppressed, swept out of everyday use and pulverised – it was meant to lose all meaning. With exemplary obedience, I accepted Mother's explanation that I was the fruit of momentary weakness, what she called an 'adventure', with a *Gypsy* who had only been in town for a few days with his travelling orchestra. When I started asking questions as a child, that story seemed as convincing as any other, but over time I felt there was too much nebulousness in it to want to correct it. The neighbours also accepted it, although they knew full well what I found out ten years later: that my father wasn't a Gypsy at all but a man who had led an orderly life alongside them, had bought a little plot nearby and was building a house; but as soon as his wife's belly began to bulge he chickened out of both challenges overnight, never to be seen again. Mother's family – there was never any mention of the other side – had no ear for her version of the truth and soon all contact was severed; I didn't meet a single relative from one side or the other until my grandmother's death.

And so my mother's romantic inspiration gave me the nickname 'Gypo'. It was underscored by my astonishingly dark complexion, bristly black hair and deep, almost black eyes, which tended to arouse unease in people, the instinct to look away, more than the desire to explore what was inside. I was never ashamed of that nickname, least of all in front of those who used it to demean me and exclude me from their games; for the latter, in fact, I was grateful.

Mother's Gypsy was not merely a caprice, however, but also a form of penance. For reasons which were never elucidated, she blamed herself for her husband's disappearance and intended to expiate it. The collateral damage to me was of no concern to her. In one of her hysterical states, as frequent as they were arbitrary, she uttered with blithe ignorance of the consequences that I was a sorry case; she'd never wanted to have children and everything could have been different if she hadn't got pregnant; and me turning out the way I did – *the cross she had to bear* – was God's way of punishing her. Oh, the curse of my *behaviour*... That word embodied one of the root evils, which no gestures or avowals to the contrary could dispel. However much I tried to please her, and although my extreme self-consciousness in early childhood severed any inclination to escapades, her use of the term *your behaviour* designated my certain descent into a career of substance abuse and my predetermined, inevitable matricide.

God arrived in her life at the same time as me; until then she'd been involved in purely worldly pursuits, but thanks to my birth she found her God. From that point on she never missed Mass and worked tirelessly to equip the house with little holy pictures, statuettes and olive branches. She even lit candles and gave alms at church as soon she had a few coins to spare and our most pressing needs had been satisfied. At work she was rewarded for her spiritual zeal with a demotion – the Yugoslav state frowned on any religious fervour – although cause and effect were not spelt out. She was replaced as municipal cultural officer by the typist, a woman who never finished high school, and Mother was made her assistant. She bore that blow heroically, not flinching from her beliefs despite the objections of others. Her response was to opt out of any effective activity and spend the rest of her working life on go-slow, practicing quiet sabotage, until this was interrupted by the democratic changes in the early nineties; and her job was immediately terminated. Aged fifty-three, in the middle of the war, she found herself on the dole. The only other thing she could do, being a graduate accordion teacher, was to try and make ends meet by giving private lessons, but her skill was anything but appealing at that moment in history; in oh-so-refined Croatia, few things were considered as barbarously Balkan as playing the accordion.

Mother didn't even try to arouse my musical talent, but God was number one on the agenda. I went through the complete torture of confession, communion, confirmation, saying the Lord's Prayer before bed and going on pilgrimages to Marija Bistrica. The merciless woman even managed – undoubtedly through the magnitude of her sacrifice – to have me accepted as an altar boy. But that didn't last long, thanks to the unavoidable difficulties caused by my sooty black head jutting out of the angelically white habit and my dark hands wrapped around the candle – it reeked of a Satanic diversion.

When I think back to my childhood, my first association is with smoke, not only from censers but also cigarettes. Mother smoked so much that layers of haze constantly hung in the house, around one metre from the ceiling, which no airing could dispel; she always had at least one cigarette burning, frequently more. She would forget them in the rooms and light a new one as soon as she noticed she had one hand too many. She got up for a smoke at night, too, woken by the lack of nicotine. Smoking merged with her being to such an extent that you no longer perceived a cigarette in her hand as an object; it could only be seen as an absence in the rare moments she wasn't smoking – then Mother lacked something.

Towards the end of her religious phase, her devotion escalated to the point that she toyed with the idea of bequeathing the house to the Jehovah's Witnesses. That was the second and last time I stood up to her, threatening that I would go away and that she would never see me again. But soon afterwards she broke with churches and all taints of religion; it being a time when people started pushing and shoving to get in the front pews, when those who had once persecuted the Lamb of God now eagerly held their mouths up to it at communion, and religious devotion shifted from being a reactionary stigma to a guarantee of virtue and patriotism. Ostensible piety inundated Croatia to such an extent that even garments, massage chairs and luxury yachts were renamed with a Christian epithet. The Jesus figure on the cross at the bottom of our street repented for our sins day and night; his fans soon had him gilted and put up a little tin roof so he wouldn't get wet. Really, hardly anyone had taken any notice of him before, and now almost no one passed by without instinctively crossing themselves: not even the drunkard who lived somewhere near the top of the street and left his bicycle there every time his heroism only sufficed to lug himself up the hill, nor the other Jesus fan, a tea-totaller who beat his wife so badly that she had to be rushed to hospital on at least two occasions.

After the changes, new traffic regulations were introduced in our quarter and a one-way sign was put up next to the crucifix, not a metre away. It's at exactly the same height and has an arrow showing which direction to drive. I don't know if the local authorities and their staff are aware of how fraught that semiotic combination is. Coincidental or not, you have to admit the message is powerful: passers-by are confronted with a crucifixion – a drastic reminder that the rules of the road are to be observed; and immediately next to it, following the stick-and-carrot principle, is an upward-pointing arrow showing what is in store as a reward for obedience.

* * *

Christmas was designed as a punishment for those who don't experience a sense of unification with God's love, or their own love. It's supposed to be the culmination of cheerfulness and hope for an even more cheerful afterlife which they've been beavering away for all year, a sentiment now represented by baubles and angels dangling from a dead conifer. I can't decide what makes Christmas more unbearable: the warm putrefaction of this year or the usual soppy snowflakes.

That evening I dropped in to see Father. I could see from the street that it was dark in the kitchen, which was enough to trigger the darkest forebodings. I rushed breathless up the stairs. The TV set suffocated the living room more than casting it in a bluish light. It took a few seconds for me to make him out on the couch: one hand hanging to the floor, his head thrown back, and his mouth wide open. From up close it was clear he wasn't breathing. I was stunned and my heart felt as if it would break. I grabbed him by the collar, shook him, and he opened his eyes. He gazed through me for an instant and then choked up, gasping for air. This happened to him from time to time – he would stop breathing when he fell asleep. But never before had he so staunchly, so pedantically, staged a respiratory shutdown.

I gave him his eye drops. His cataracts were growing diligently. Sooner or later he'd need an operation, but for the time being he brushed the prospect aside. The good side of it was that his impaired vision didn't bring any major disadvantages; there were no longer any particularly precious sights for him in this world.

When I told him I was moving out, exactly fifteen months ago,

33

he didn't have any objections. Or if he did, he didn't dare to state them. If he'd had a sliver of lucidity left, he would have seen what his *condition* had done to me. It had penetrated me to the core and turned me into a black hole. But he just kept on going, perhaps aware of what he was doing to me but powerless to prevent it. Unable to help himself and to accept my attempts to help him. No one can help anyone. That's easily said, and I knew it all those years; but still I let myself be fettered, remaining in the embrace of his sorrow. As we know, time heals sorrow. His responded well to the treatment, was tamed, and grew over time into our own domestic monster.

Mother died in the summer of ninety-one when I was eighteenth, less than a month after Father's appointment as a minister in the Government of Democratic Unity. That came about due to the Reconciliation: ex-Communists and Catholic conservatives alike welcomed a Jew in the cabinet so they could demonstrate their inclusiveness. He himself didn't give a damn about reconciliation and the blossoming of democracy. He was already weary, preoccupied with his untimely ageing. But the offer flattered his vanity and he accepted the position like a medal awarded at retirement for sufferings endured. It's safe to say that no one remembered his time as minister, and the Jewish bit was a half-truth at best. Religion was never mentioned in our family, let alone practiced – his 'Jewishness' and my mother's nominal Orthodox Christianity existed purely on paper. That was almost the only thing I ever agreed about with my parents.

After all, I didn't consider them capable of any sensible conversation, nor did they show even the semblance of a desire to comprehend where I was at. We lived under the same roof but on different planets. At least up until the day when Father, eavesdropping on my phone conversation, learnt that I'd lost my virginity. I was fourteen. *I heard that*, he growled, dashed into the room wild-eyed and laid into me with fists and feet. Mother didn't lift a finger or say a word to stop him. When the 'lesson' was over, she took my head in her lap and stroked it until I'd cried my very last tear. Then she quietly closed the door behind her.

Still, her death probably would have well and truly crushed me if Father hadn't made it there first. It was already hot and sultry in the morning, that July Sunday. Around four in the afternoon, I heard a smashing of crockery in the kitchen and then a despairing *Oooh, oooh*. Father was kneeling on the tiled floor, his face grotesquely twisted. Between the palms of his hands he held my mother's face; unlike his, it was calm and almost serene, more beautiful than ever.

A face so different to mine that people viewed us innumerable times in disbelief: her soft, fair hair, blue eyes and milky complexion, and me downright swarthy. She had especially large, doe eyes. At forty-four, her beauty was fully intact and easily interrupted ministers' conversations, turned heads 180 degrees, and caused nervous grimaces in other women. Allegedly it was the cause of one broken marriage and a broken skull before she married Father. He, in turn, was a striking man with austere features, of lean yet athletic build – an esteemed architect, broad-minded and cultured; although sixteen years her senior, he probably had no trouble hunting her down to put in the showcase among the other trophies he had won. He thought highly of competitions.

And then, all at once, she lay there on the kitchen floor, and he above her, with horrible cries which couldn't bring anything back. By the time the ambulance arrived, it was too late. The clot had whisked her away. Now she lay on their double bed, and he didn't stop hugging her, and choking on his tears and cries for help. The scene dried up my tears within a few minutes. I shoved him out and spent the evening with her alone, then I

35

showed in the coroner and the woman we paid to do her up. I spent the night there by her side, following my father's uneven breathing in the living room and wondering if it too would cease. My mother's mouth hung slightly open. I was obsessed by the ghastly thought that, if my vigilance slackened for just an instant, the flies circling up near the ceiling would get inside her. In the morning her mouth still looked completely alive, as if it was about to tell me something important she'd been thinking of all her life.

I had to make the arrangements with the undertaker, choose the coffin, look after the epitaph, the wording on the wreath, the obituary notices in the papers and the details of the funeral protocol, as well as take care of catering for the condolence bearers, all by myself. The very mention of these things made Father's eyes flow. However, he was only seized by hysteria one more time: when they were carrying Mother out of the house, like a log wrapped in a sheet; he fell to his knees and clung to the coat of one of the medics, a boy my age, whom I stared at in astonishment, wondering how he could have chosen such an occupation. Over time, Father calmed down and spent most of his time staring out the window. For him it was like Jim Jarmush's window drawn on the prison wall, not one intended for looking out of.

It hurt to watch him diminish like that, both mentally and physically. He became bent and wrinkled, ridiculously small for the couch which was his prison; he devoted his days to the window and in the evenings hovered in the grey zone between the TV chat show and dozing off. For several months they *took* him to work, a bit like they cart away domestic rubbish. He resigned before the end of his term of office and before reaching retirement age, 'for health reasons'. But these weren't just of an emotional nature because all the ailments which had already been gnawing at him now gained momentum. Diabetes, gout, high creatinine levels, prostrate problems, painful joints, cardiac arrhythmia, a duodenal ulcer, insomnia, corns and cataracts: he was a gerontological showpiece. But he contributed to all that himself with intensive concentration, which he could direct depending on the acuteness of the problems and above all by *groaning*. With every step he took in the flat, and also when he went out to walk in the courtyard, he let out the sound of his suffering, such that until I moved out I was able to follow his every step as if he was carrying a beeper. Just recently he admitted that he groaned on purpose, self-therapeutically, in the hope that things would hurt less. Since pain can't be seen, it's easier to live with suffering if you hear it. Whatever.

Apart from shuffling to the corner shop, for years now he's only been leaving the house to go to the Health Centre (is the sarcasm of that term intentional?) and the cemetery. He trudges back with his bags as if from martyrdom, groaning three times louder. When I cooked for him he only stabbed listlessly at the food, and the slightest criticism made him get up from the table, offended: *This is the death of me, can't you understand that?!* He'd never been of the jovial kind. No frivolities interested him, not even spending time with friends. When Mother died, the rest of humanity passed away for him too. To those who phoned with words of encouragement or just with a conventional enquiry as to his health, he always replied with the same *To be honest, I'm not well* and never asked anything back. Oh, how many times did that *honesty* make me want to get up and strangle him just to cure him of his misconception that being *honest* like that was the best he could do, in fact the only thing he could do, for himself and others.

I never stopped missing Mother, but at the risk of sounding harsh, I also missed her when she was alive; a mother with human blood in her veins, whom you wish to confide in. Sometimes I feel the need to go to her grave, light a candle and sit for ten minutes. Not that I feel more of her presence there, but it's soothing.

I never let my sorrow break the surface – because of Father more than myself. I felt that he hung from me like a thread. Today I know that was mistaken because he's essentially been dead all this time. The fact that he can still take a few steps, and groan, doesn't mean anything. I sought in vain for something to at least reanimate him a little. No antidepressants or psychotherapy, no pensioners' excursions or stays at rheumatic clinics, not even his favourite pastries mother used to make or my quasi successes in life could evoke even a semblance of liveliness in him. At the same time, however dead he was, he cried out from the depths of his unconscious to share his suffering with me and for me to be part of it. It didn't overly concern him that his need was also a hand dragging me into the grave. But I couldn't muster enough self-respect to decide that it wasn't my problem any more. And so, on the threshold of my own life, I became a mother to my much-lamented father.

Yet I couldn't replace Mother or do anything for him. We'd lived alongside each other for so many years, separated by a vast sea of silence. I had pangs of conscience, but I gradually gave up trying to contrive words. All of them were destined to fall into a deep well. He didn't even try and pretend that what I said meant anything to him, to wipe that *nothing-matters-any-more* look off his face for at least a second. We both knew very well how much harder it would be for him if I wasn't around. So ever more often, when I left the study to check how he was doing, I would just stand at the door. He'd raise his eyes and we'd look at each other in a silence no words could unlock.

*   *   *

Although she accepted the blame, Mother didn't consider the deadening of the woman in her, her sexual being, to be one of the forms of penitence. I don't mean to say she was *putting out* or showing the world she was eligible; on the contrary, she cultivated an arrogant air of self-reliance and a neurotic gruffness in communication. But when the widower Gabriel came along and started to circle in on her, she didn't need much convincing. Uncle Gabrek, as I had to call him, worked at an insurance company as a specialist in motor-car collisions and traffic-accident premiums. But the only thing which really interested him was fishing; he lived for the occasion – and that was almost every non-working day – to cram his deluxe fishing paraphernalia into the car and to drive off to a body of water, which if you were lucky was just twenty or thirty kilometres away. His expeditions were far from fruitless; he came back with bucketfuls, sometimes even with prize specimens. He liked to take me along as well, and I was too submissive to show what I really thought; he showed peculiar persistence in teaching me the secrets of the trade, the subtleties of choosing the right bait and position, the habits and psychology of different species of fish, etc. Mother prepared them in all imaginable ways, and he didn't fail to admire her skill, most often with the words *You can't taste the silt in it at all, can you?* If I was accompanied through to adulthood by incense and cigarette smoke, those two years with Gabrek owe their uniqueness to the reek of swamp water and fish entrails.

I was twelve when we moved in with him, after he'd called by at our house for months with his broad smile, smart suit, waistcoat, tiepin and slicked-back hair. He would tousle mine as a sign of affection, produce a bag of toffees from his pocket, and once even tried to take me on his lap. I never liked toffees, but Cat did. Cat, in fact, turned out to be a bone of contention when Mother was set to be married because she didn't fit into Gabrek's vision of a happy family; but just then the problem disappeared.

The period before their marriage was perhaps the only time when I felt something like happiness. I'd discovered books and knew their power to whirlpool me away into fictitious worlds. During the summer holidays I went to the library twice a day: in the morning for my daytime dose and again for my evening hit which would keep me in feverish vigilance and oblivion long into the night. I spent the rest of the time on my bike, which became Don Quixote's Rocinante, the Orient Express, or a Mississippi steamboat. That little blue, wobble-wheeled bike had been salvaged from the scrap heap after some boy in the neighbourhood had outgrown it, and now I pushed it up the steepest streets of our quarter for the matchless feeling of zooming downhill, pedalling to increase my speed and perhaps break my own record, trying to hold on for just a second longer with my eyes closed.

I cruised streets full of ghosts and bleak castles for hours as a lone rider and avenger. Gabrek's visits ushered in a Copernican revolution; Mother's obsession with my behaviour disappeared and she was understanding of my absences from home. One place I liked to ride was in the enclosed grounds of the psychiatric hospital which our part of the city is known for. I was able to zip in past the guard, no questions asked, and then cheerfully trundle along under the green of the grand old chestnut trees. Or talk with the patients who were out walking in striped pyjamas, sauntering about with their arms folded behind their backs or waving them in the air in lively debate with inner voices. Many of them were happy to chat, and they came up to me whenever I stopped for a break and daydreamed on a bench or by the goldfish pond. It was here that I heard some very interesting life histories.

One day I even plucked up the courage to approach Zoran and see what he was drawing. Day after day, I found him sitting on the same bench, preoccupied with the paper on his lap as if nothing else existed. He was so tall that I thought he must have been some kind of giant, albeit a little bent from always having to lean down; his grey hair, cut in a somehow feminine way, grew thickly above an almost boyish face; and he had enormous hands, elegant and well-manicured, with long nails on both little fingers. He was a good-natured giant, because he was always smiling and showing his handsome teeth, but with such feeling and ephemeral emotion that I would take a piece of it home every time and shut myself away in my room without a word. I remember clearly the smell of flowers that came from him. The patients at the hospital generally needed to be kept at an arm's length because hygiene at the hospital probably wasn't high on the scale of priorities. But Zoran radiated a vernal freshness, sweet and polliniferous.

I remember his drawings even more clearly. Each in its own way showed living labyrinths: scenes of teeming action, dense and compact, full of interlaced movements, collisions, rifts and transformations. They were covered from edge to edge in intricate patterns, calligraphic tendrils and arabesques which intersected and merged, plunging into one another, vanishing into depths and forming bizarre figures here and there with unbelievable, enchanting colour combinations. There wasn't a single empty spot. It was impossible to recognise anything from the earthly world from up close. But when I moved back a little, without realising what they were about, I felt a childlike sense of bliss – at the absolute tranquillity they emanated.

Even today I wouldn't be able to judge the artistic worth of those drawings, but one thing is for sure: neither before nor since have I seen anything more beautiful.

He'd once been a promising young nuclear physicist, he willingly told me, a university dux with offers of a career abroad, but he kept putting it off for the sake of a girl; he burned with love and waited impatiently for her to decide. Until one day she gave him a simple, dry *No*. And no question he could ask explained where it had all disappeared to so abruptly: all the warmth, the fusion of their souls, the moments of inconceivable tenderness... How could it be that he was suddenly deprived of all that mattered to him? Forget about physics – all he wanted was her and to devote his whole being to her happiness. For days he called and beseeched her, promising any sacrifice and even threatening to kill himself, but that only strengthened her resolve and added to her annoyance.

I've reconstructed the way he described things, but I remember the end of the story word by word. She agreed to another date, under her conditions, at the local football grounds. She met him in the middle of the pitch and said: *There, exactly where you're standing, I've fucked half the junior team. I had such earth-shaking orgasms that I thought my brain would explode, if you have even the slightest idea what I'm talking about. Have you got the point now? Is it enough for you to leave me in peace?*

It was. He turned and went; he didn't know where to, or how much time passed after that. The next thing he remembered was the hospital. He had only positive things to say about it: everyone was friendly, the food was fine, his parents often visited him, and they brought him all the paper and drawing supplies he wanted. It was only here that he felt the need to draw, and he didn't stop, from morning till lights-out. But when we returned a year after moving to Gabrek's, there was no trace of Zoran and I never heard of him again.

I wouldn't know what to single out from that year. I didn't make friends with anyone at the new school. There was nothing of interest at home; Mother temporarily overcame her hysterics, and overall she suddenly seemed to have got it all together. She got along fantastically with Gabrek, or at least that's how it looked; I don't remember a single quarrel, or one of them even raising their voice. An exceptional peace reigned in the flat, all the more seeing as Gabrek didn't allow television or radio. I didn't miss any programmes in particular, but his ban condensed the silence into something morbid. He only consumed the external world as printed on paper and spent most of his time reading the newspaper in the armchair. Apart from the rustling of the pages, you could hear him clucking with his tongue, like a clock emphasising significant seconds to the rhythm of its own inspiration; originally the clucks must have been substitute for a toothbrush, but over time they grew into a means of expression with a broad range of applications, from approval and surprise to disgust at what he had just read. He was mild-mannered, almost always in a good mood and happy to help Mother, but as soon as she left him in peace he would grab a newspaper and be consumed by it, and all that was to be heard were his clucking noises. The day Mother told me – without explanation – that we were packing our things, he only raised his gaze when the boxes had piled up in the hall.

But there was something of a *homme fatal* about him because the next year Mother announced we were moving back to Gabrek's and shrugged her shoulders at all my questions. The first move had been in the summer time. Now it was midterm and winter, which caused certain complications and under-standably provoked comments from classmates and the neighbours, who were even gladder when we returned, in exactly the same way as before, after less than a month. The good thing was that Gabrek never showed up again.

In the meantime, the house had gone to the dogs. We found it in a sorry state: the walls were green from moisture and a lasting chill had sunk in; it was full of holes, dead flies, mouse droppings and unimaginable smells as if to show us how much it had appreciated our care of it (or perhaps the totality of our existence as seen from inside). Mother actually cared very much for cleanliness and order; once, late at night, I found her in the bathroom trying to scrub something out from between the tiles with a toothbrush and grinding her teeth so fiercely that I returned to bed in fear. From early childhood I carried a feeling of guilt around with me because of my alleged slovenliness, which in my mother's eyes was a harbinger of delinquency, a path to certain ruin and failure. In fact, the fear of irritating her actually made me develop a pedantry bordering on the pathological, an intolerance of what people like to call *creative disorder*, everything unfinished and abandoned which was up in the air, including stray embryonic ideas; in other words, I had a precocious obsession with order worthy of a born bookkeeper. After that second outing, however, things stayed in their boxes for a long time, perhaps in anticipation of another journey in the opposite direction, or more likely because of the utter futility of any efforts to keep them in their right place.

The house weighed heavily on our minds. Mother heroically resisted its collapse, first by herself and later with my help, but this didn't bring about any lasting solution. The house, like our livelihood, rested on fragile foundations. Everything else; the cracks, the leaks and the never-mentioned but credible concern that the roof could come down on our heads in both a physical and a figurative sense, were the inevitable consequence. He, whose name wasn't to be mentioned (and his heavenly forefather, when we're talking about the collective structure of things) built it quickly, without a building permit, convinced of his inborn talent for architecture; plus the workers had syphoned off some of the material for more profitable purposes, my mother claimed. For lack of documentation, the house couldn't be entered in the land registry and so formally didn't exist, which in practical terms prevented it from being connected to municipal services. An electricity cable was installed thanks to the kindness of a neighbour, but his generosity didn't stretch to a water pipe. Mother liked to repeat his words, *No man alive is going to go digging up my courtyard.* Needless to say, his 'courtyard' consisted of piles of rubble overgrown with weeds and nettles.

For years I watched her from the windows, still too small to take on the chore of going to the water pump several times a day; in those days it used to be down by the crucifix, so that in the neighbourhood we called that spot 'at the cross'. Pumping water was strenuous, even for men, but for Mother it was a welcome opportunity to exchange a few words with the bleeder on the cross. Then she tramped back up the street carrying the full buckets, with a defiant fag between her lips.

In the mood of piety prevalent in the nineties, after the war, the municipal council had the inspiration of changing the name of our street to The Way of the Cross. But the insight prevailed that the name was too grand for a cul-de-sac which turned into a muddy creek, especially when heavy rain made the septic tanks overflow. But they did see fit to discontinue the free water from the pump. Fortunately, Mother was able to solve the problem beforehand; just *how*, she didn't want to say; but one day workmen turned up, dug a duct out to the street, knocked massive great holes in the walls, and the water flowed. It took much longer to patch up all those holes, and for years they let in the draught and the dust. Then Mother got hold of a loan and a 'Normalisation Project' popped up on our agenda, which meant doing away with all the gaps and blemishes in the house. Unfortunately, things got bogged down before the end. It would have been quite contrary to Mother's nature to have at least consulted someone when setting the priorities; one result was that the reinforcement of the load-bearing walls lost out to an extension of the upper storey. We also got a lovely new façade, it's just a shame that it started to crack so quickly and peel off. Our ground-floor ceiling was so unpleasantly low that you could touch it with your arm outstretched, though nothing could be done about that; it had already been dark inside because the windows were so small, and you needed to turn on the light during the day as well; but the result of the extension was polar night. The money from the loan ran out much faster than expected, of course. When making the major alterations, the tradesmen ingeniously found other small things that absolutely needed doing, so there was no money left for the new staircase up to the first floor.

'That's all right, I can wait, I've got a heart,' the contractor consoled us. And then proposed: 'Look, it's fine if you just pay me for the material...'

So, that same day, the workmen demolished the old staircase which led nowhere. But they didn't come the next day and no one answered the phone at the number given in the telephone directory.

As a temporary solution, we placed a ladder against the wall of the house. As with most temporary solutions, this one proved to be long-lasting. But Mother soon stopped using it after she lost her balance, fell and broke her arm. Not only did she no longer climb up to the upper storey, but from that day it ceased to exist for her.

When I started Year 12, she summoned the courage for the desperate step of joining a 'lonely hearts agency'. After several dubious offers, she hit a bull's eye: a retired German industrialist of Jewish origin by the name of Jakob Steinhammer. They began corresponding, facilitated by the agency, because Mother didn't speak German. The first letter was accompanied by a photograph of a greying gentleman with a neatly-trimmed moustache and metal-rimmed glasses on a slightly crooked nose. When he visited us, three letters later, we realised the photo hadn't been quite up to date and that Mr Steinhammer had made the acquaintance of Mr Alzheimer. But the wheels were turning and scenes of salvation spun before Mother's eyes.

Reduced mainly to smiles and gestures of mutual enthusiasm, the rapprochement didn't go smoothly. But soon a one-way ticket arrived nevertheless, and Mother didn't vacillate; the offer of marriage involved me joining the newly-weds as soon as I finished high school. Mr and Mrs Steinhammer settled down in a country house in green and peaceful south-western Germany. Mother wrote to me almost every day and soon showed great skill at inserting mangled German expressions into her sentences, which most foreigners take years to master. She enthusiastically described all the wonders of the house with its underfloor heating, gold-plated fixtures in the bathroom, wallpaper with life-size woodland animals, or the breakfasts they had at the nearby lake. Never mind the spelling; she evidently had enormous potential for assimilation. I must admit, I too started to feel I was becoming German.

All the more because all my clothes soon had German labels. Not one of the garments and pieces of apparel which arrived in the parcels, from shoes to sunglasses, would have been my choice in a shop, but I told myself it was a different country and a different taste, and I had to get used to it. Mother didn't choose them either, but rather Uncle Jakob, who was better informed about fashion in Germany, and even more importantly about the difference between quality merchandise and junk. Mother illuminated each individual item with an assurance of the quality of the material, its water-resistant qualities or the enormous saving made due to the excellent value for money.

Mr Steinhammer was unable to have children – a consequence of his internment in Auschwitz, but to have a son as an heir was his great unfulfilled desire. The death of his wife had left him alone in the world, since he'd lost all his relatives in the concentration camps together with the fortune his family had gained through manufacturing mine-shaft frames; but he was able to regain and redouble this fortune after the war owing to his business talent. Now he was looking forward to my arrival so he could enrol me in university. My studies, of course, would be to prepare me for a position in the management of the firm, because he remained its majority shareholder.

And no sooner had Mother settled in and got up the courage to leave the house by herself and was entering the local supermarket one day, than a frenzied dog came bolting around the corner and went like a projectile for her buttocks, as if it had been waiting just for her – as if it had been sent down to Earth with exactly that mission; it sank its teeth into her several times and disappeared again in a flash, just like it had come.

The wounds healed relatively quickly, but something in her heart shifted irreversibly. When they brought her back from hospital, she wouldn't hear a word about staying. No pleading and promises would help, nor pointing out the difference between what she had there and what she said she wanted to go back to, nor the fact that no such incident had been recorded in the area for decades. She interpreted this last aspect as a sign from God showing her where she really belonged. Until her last days she remained broken and timid, always more or less on pins and needles, but passive, forever awaiting the next blow of fate.

But rapid flourishing and abrupt end of the Steinhammer episode was nothing compared to what had happened a few years earlier, straight after we returned from Gabrek's for the second time. The boy I sat next to in class was called Božidar. Also an only child, from even poorer circumstances than mine, he had a hard time keeping up with lessons. I whispered him the answers in tests. We didn't meet outside of school, but since our way home was in the same direction we usually walked together. There was one hundred metres of poorly illuminated footpath down to the first intersection and compacted snow had turned it into a veritable ice rink that day. It was 24th December and the Christmas-tree vendors were selling off the last of their wares cheaply in front of the school. Božidar pushed off with one leg and skated in front of me to the very edge of the cross street, where he turned to wait for me. At that instant the cabin of a large truck and trailer appeared from behind the building on the corner. I only just managed to yell *Watch out!* before the truck, winding around the tight bend, collected Božidar with its veering rear end and sucked him under its wheels.

Even today, that is the only plausible version of the event for me. According to the forensic report, Božidar died from a skull fracture caused by a blow to the back of his head and can't possibly have been run over by the wheels because the weight of the trailer, loaded with sacks of potting soil, would have crushed his body. But I kept telling the investigators what I'd seen – an image which visited me for years afterwards, especially in the middle of the night: of Božidar being swallowed up by wheels bigger than himself and thrown out like a rag doll, and of him lying on his belly, eyes wide open, with the blood from his nostrils conquering the snow in a starlike stain. The only other thing I remember is the man who shook me and yelled to me that I should go home, which I finally did, still believing that Božidar would just blink, wipe his nose and get up.

That man, who had been at the other side of the intersection, was the only witness, and he stated at the inquest that he'd seen me and Božidar standing *together* at the curb. That was enough for different stories to spread through the school and the neighbourhood suggesting that I'd pushed Božidar onto the street or tripped him while he was running. And it was enough to make Božidar's father come to our door, distraught, with his distress further fuelled by alcohol. *What the hell are you hiding him for?* he cried and swore, *Let me ask him what bloody well happened!* Mother managed to stop him at the doorstep and send him away, with tears of both sympathy and determination to protect me, and threatened to make heavy weather to anyone who needled me by alluding to the event. Moreover, she stopped the investigators molesting me and taking me to court as a witness, and also prevented the psychiatrists from poking around in my head. She spent many nights by my bed watching over me in the months which followed.

From then on I always detoured Božidar's street as if it were cursed. The seat next to me in class remained empty until the end of primary school.

Father's condition was stable. That meant he couldn't think of a single part of his body which didn't hurt, but no pain was excruciating enough to make him forget the others.

It was incomprehensible that I'd lived with him for so many years. I would rather have gone to have a wisdom tooth pulled out than visit him, and yet the whole time I was rankled by an emptiness I seemed to have left there. So I forced myself to go once a week. I showed up, that was all I could do for him. That cheered him up, for three or four seconds. Then it would be back to moping. We don't hug, not even when we say goodbye. Basically we avoid physical contact. We're full of respect for the air between us and careful not to infringe it. We don't touch on difficult topics, in fact hardly any at all, because when he runs into a gap in his ever more impoverished vocabulary he doesn't know how to get round it. He stays all frowning and stares into that void – *oh what do they call it...* – until I help by changing the topic. He regularly reports about the rotten fruit they slip him at the market and the obligatory misunderstandings about the change. But medical issues are still the major topic, and if we leave them it's virtually only to talk about the weather. At this time of year, that boiled down to the remark that the weather outside was *nasty, really nasty*. If it was summer, it would have been nasty inside as well. *Unbearable*. I wouldn't have disagreed. We'd sit quietly by the TV for a bit because we haven't played ludo for thirty years or so.

That evening I happened to see a feature on the exhibition of a former fellow student from the Academy. Today he's a big-time artist, the gallery owner explained with a playful smile: not only intriguing as a personality but also dynamic in the market place. Then a critic spoke in front of one of his pictures about its inner necessity and about reality growing into an elusive fascination; the tangible vanished in the immeasurable yet gained new quantifiability through abstraction. He mentioned a shifting luminosity rising from the depths and crystallising in a seething turmoil, in wellsprings of resistance and reflection. Here we saw broad vision and deep resonance, a blend of abrasive energy and sweet intimacy.

I had to rub my eyes. The pictures were deceptively similar to those he'd begun to paint in the middle of his studies just for fun, as a way of mocking minimalism: each had two or three small squares or triangles, perhaps an arrow or a curvy line, a bit like Kandinsky for bathroom tiles. But their titles were long and enigmatic like *Bursting from their Blue Embankment, Bareheaded Brownies Behold the Beanstalk*. He made an intelligent impression, which the feature confirmed. Not only did he dazzle critics, the reporter noted, but his clientele was in the specific milieu of footballers and models. Art lovers of this calibre would willingly sacrifice *ten thousand kunas and more* for a picture, the artist himself admitted in the only original snippet we heard. The camera focussed for a second on a glass of champagne being filled.

Some are born with a champagne glass in their hand and sooner or later it will be filled. And whatever happens in life, they'll still have their champagne to sip. I have a little theory of my own which I'm coming to believe in more and more: that my father was born with a talent for suffering. Something big just had to come along to trigger that potential and really get him going. There had always been material in abundance, albeit scattered and subject to wear. But the real thing, the capital-E event worthy of full commitment, came in the form of my mother's death: he seized it with all his remaining strength and devoted himself to it entirely. But over the years, imperceptibly, it stole away once it had done its job and raised him into a state of permanent hypnosis. He mentions Mother less and less, and her grave is overgrown with weeds, because what he now sees is the very essence of suffering, cleansed of external substances.

My own substances and substrates didn't overly impassion me. Whatever made its way down to me through the genetic gutters didn't reach my erogenous zones. On my mother's side, there wasn't much to whet one's archaeological appetite anyway. All she inherited from her parents was the vocation of primary school teacher, which she gladly gave up for my future. Her family moved to the city after the Second World War from an area which had been outside the Independent State of Croatia and occupied by the Nazis – this was fortunate because the Germans didn't put them on an extermination list. They died fairly young of normal human ailments. We had them buried back in their village and visited their graves from time to time. In 1995, the sons of the Croatian Army's 'Operation Storm' thoroughly 'liberated' the ramshackle house and daubed a sign on the crumbling walls: OCCUPIED DO NOT BLOW UP. This was quite superfluous because no one intended to expropriate the ruins, but it did happen a few years later when the government presented its refugee resettlement programme.

Father's family tree was more ramified, but his parsimonious nature also meant that he was no storyteller. I only knew the basics. But in the middle of my studies, while going through Father's things, I chanced upon my grandfather's notebook. It wasn't intended for me or anyone else. Grandfather had evidently kept it in an attempt to clear his head. His aim had been to set down what was real and true amidst the mess of images and voices which besieged him towards the end of his life, taking complete control and deleting his life's present tense. The truth as laid down by Grandfather's hand was a hotchpotch of brainwaves jotted down as they came, without order and without concern for occasional contradictions. I needed this about as much as the girl George in *Dead Like Me* needed the toilet seat to come down and hit her on the head. Still, I showed a sensational, hitherto unseen ability to relate to the family's nitty-gritty. I adopted all those basics, integrated them into my foundations and took them along with me as life's luggage. Or rather, they adopted me and shaped me *a posteriori* to fit into an already tailored dress.

Grandfather's father grew up in a family of Jewish tailors, and later innkeepers, on German soil. The notebook didn't trace the family roots back any further. It mentioned a boarding house on the shores of an unnamed lake, which my great-grandfather lost at cards. Allied with alcohol, his gambling passion consumed all other real estate and even created debts which left him no other choice than to secretly relocate to some backwoods. In the chaos of the First World War, he managed to move with his wife and my very small grandfather. Zagreb played the role of backwoods impeccably. No one looked for him there and he was able to start afresh with the acquisition of property, and its squandering.

He found work with a textile dealer. As the years went by, he was allowed to manage the business and later bought the shop in Kačićeva Street. Apart from fabrics, he also traded in sugar, lard, coal and timber. He would often lose his stock to others in games of chance. He played cards almost every night, in German, Hungarian, Czech, Yiddish or a mixture of all those, soaked in wine. Great-grandfather learnt only as much Croatian as he needed for his transactions with local farmers. Games were broken off due to excessive drunkenness. Then they sang, retold their exploits and other's misfortunes, and let out animal-like howls. Some drunkards had to sleep the night on the floor until they were brought new clothes because they'd pawned everything down to their underwear. The apprentices would come in the morning and sweep everything out onto the street: sawdust, broken glass and dead-drunk bodies. They would take great-grandfather home in the horse-drawn cart and put him to bed.

He quickly realised the value of having a private wine cellar, so he set one up in the premises next door. Then he bought the whole house and extended his business to renting out rooms. Things happened here which mellow-mooded gentlemen are inclined to desire in the middle of the night. Women from the annexe were part of the shop's decor, tasked with topping up the glasses and sitting on customers' knees. Grandfather learnt to sit on their knees at an early age, the notebook boasted. He grew up quickly, married at eighteen and immediately had a son, and another on the eve of the war. The elder, my father, spent a good part of his childhood helping out in the shop. The basement of that so educational business complex is today a macrobiotic food shop.

Great-grandfather was more inclined to the nocturnal aspects of entrepreneurship than to dry, academic business. Until Grandfather came of age, the day-to-day management was run by the apprentices, who sometimes lined their own pockets. If there was a profit, my great-grandfather looked the other way; otherwise he sacked them regardless of their diligence. A fanatical follower of his own instinct for happiness, every now and then he zeroed the business results and was left without a single bale of fabric, sack of flour or barrel of wine. Then he started from scratch again. I ask myself if he perhaps did that intentionally or because of a subconscious instinct to undermine whatever he'd built.

He was a great admirer of the Teutonic spirit: its breadth and firmness, its cult of vitality and personal expansion. A self-taught philosopher, he particularly esteemed German idealism. And he loved music, above all else, especially Wagner's operas.

He rarely got up before noon, and until then all noise was banned in the house, including kitchen clatter and children's voices. But as soon as he opened his eyes he would start to sing arias from operas or military marches, whose words he would playfully, lasciviously change. That was a signal that one was allowed to talk at normal volume, and also for the beginning of preparations for the ritual main meal. He also sang while he shaved, then donned a fresh, starched white shirt which was waiting on the coat-hanger, while on the table was a little glass of *rakija*. *Kein Glas mehr!* he admonished, although rivers of wine had flowed the night before.

The house he bought in the Medveščak neighbourhood was soon populated. Along with three generations of my ancestors, there were also two Jewish girls who he took in as servants as much as out of compassion, and they also became part of the family. No problems were to be mentioned at the table, not even in the frequent periods of scarcity. Nothing was to spoil his mood or appetite. He had another child, a girl, in the early 1930s. He liked to caress her and both his grandsons in passing, amazed each time how much they had grown. Of this numerous household, Father was to be the only one to escape the concentration camps.

At first, it seemed that great-grandfather's connections would guard his back. Business partners and pals held high positions in the new government of the Independent State of Croatia. His friendships with them now became especially cordial, assisted by many a costly gift. But the neighbours were also enterprising and proved to be even better connected. One June morning in 1942, an extermination team turned up at the door. Within a few minutes the whole household was out in the truck, with bundles of sheets containing what was needed for a new life, and a little more.

I'd heard about the truck before from Father. That morning

he'd been sent on an errand, and when he returned he saw it in front of the courtyard fence. He ran after it until his legs gave way, sat down on a bench and cried, and then continued on down to Kačićeva Street. Men in uniforms were carrying out the merchandise and furniture. One of the apprentices spotted him, took him aside, and then out to his home village. His family let Father stay in the hayloft above the stable. He slept there until the war's end, taking care of the cattle in return. For fear, he only went out at night. He returned to Zagreb at almost at the same time as the liberating Partisans. But he didn't find anyone he knew. The shop was buried in rubbish since the building was missing all its windows and doors, and the Medveščak house had been occupied by a man with a moustache, lots of little stars and a resolute tone of voice. He arranged that Grandfather be taken in at a refuge for war orphans. After his three years of holidays, he went back to school. The curriculum was modest and the tests could be sat in advance. He soon caught up with his age group and, as an especially gifted pupil, earned a scholarship to study architecture. Towards the end of Father's studies, Grandfather returned. He was another person altogether as if he'd been taken apart, limb by limb, and reassembled clumsily.

The notebook went into who and what had been in the truck, although the description was rather impressionistic. It was certain that the family was separated at the detention camp – a cluster of barracks somewhere on the outskirts of town, windowless and without beds, surrounded by barbed wire and guarded by thoroughbred German shepherds. When the accommodation was jam-packed, pure-bred Croatian selectors went through and sifted the human refuse, under the supervision of German delegates. They talked politely with every piece of refuse, and all the information was neatly recorded. Those fit for work were rewarded with a trip to Germany. Despite his germanophilia and assurances that he was still strong and healthy, my great-grandfather was rejected and sent to a holiday home somewhere in Croatia with my great-grandmother and their small daughter. Years later, Grandfather met a man who swore that all three had escaped during a mass breakout: they weren't among the corpses piled up as a didactic installation to intimidate the local population. But another fellow maintained that he'd seen them along with about twenty others lined up on the bank of the River Sava that day; one after another, obediently, they stepped up to an Ustashi sledgehammer and then floated away lifeless down the river.

German technology was far more refined. Straight after their journey in a cattle wagon, Grandmother and Father's brother were designated for the special showers and ovens. When the cattle were unloaded, they were divided once more. Like Grandfather, Grandmother was pointed to the right; but she didn't allow her child to be torn from her arms, and so after several lashes of his whip the officer said *Na gut,* and gave her a towel and bar of soap; Grandfather was sent off with a group to have their heads shaved. This side or that, it all looked the same to him at the time – merely a question of sequence in the schedule of arrivals.

He must have been exceptionally resilient and resourceful. Step by step, he ascended the camp-inmates' hierarchy. After a series of jobs *outside* in the rain and snow, with coal, cement and iron pipes, he advanced to a section of the barracks known as *Canada* after the fur coats which were sometimes found among the surplus possessions temporarily stored there. The punishment for theft was death by hanging, but the odd bauble, gold hairpin or tooth still made its way out of *Canada* in secret inner pockets to be exchanged for food or tobacco. He didn't smoke before the concentration camp; he came out a hardened addict. If things had gone on for much longer, he probably would have set up an import-export firm with branches beyond the wire.

Riveted to his bunk with typhus and meningitis, he was among the few who didn't wander off into the unknown before the Russians arrived, and the only one in his block who was still slightly alive. He wasn't able to tell them his name or where he was from, so they took him along for a time as they advanced westward. As soon as he was able to walk again, they left him by the roadside. He roamed hungry from village to village, begging for food and sometimes stealing. Until one day he called on the widow of a German soldier and was able to stay on as a farm labourer, later as her husband.

You could make a living in the country in those days. Grandfather even went back to his trading alchemy, turning flour and lard into gold in the nearest city. In many respects, life began anew for him. Everything from before the concentration camp remained in darkness. He would quite definitely have started a new family and a new chain of family businesses if his wife hadn't hung herself two years after their marriage. What for? They'd found more than comfort and hope in one another; their happiness had been almost tangible; besides, that wasn't a time for suicide but rather for picking up the pieces of broken lives. But it's a mistake to always expect people to act logically.

That event gave Grandfather his memory back. Straight after the funeral, he packed all he could into two suitcases and travelled to Zagreb. He searched in vain for his father, mother and sister, or at least some trace of them. But he was able to find his son, with the help of the moustachioed fellow, who in the meantime had earned more little stars and consequently a more fitting house – a donation from well-to-do Jews. Now, as a sign of gratitude, our street was named after the Jewish Communist Moše Pijade. Moreover, thanks again to Comrade Mustachio, Grandfather managed to get permission to move into the vacated house. The building in Kačićeva Street wasn't available, however, because the fire brigade had set up station there. He was allowed to use two attic rooms of the house; the rest was shared by two families who had fled from the Kozara hills in Bosnia.

Although written in this time of cohabitation, the notebook didn't say a word more about conditions there. But Father filled in the gaps for me. The main problem, among many, was the bathroom, and in particular the toilet. There were a large number of residents already, and to make matters worse they arranged an informal roster to keep the toilet constantly engaged. This was just one part of their pact against my father and grandfather, whom they openly despised for being tainted with capitalism and urban decadence. They tormented them with loud songs from their home region and heavy smells from the kitchen. This olfactory and acoustic barrage was discharged up the stairs by opening their doors wide, and every now and again a stink bomb was thrown in through the attic window. They egged on their children to imitate Grandfather's gait, which was contorted from his time in the concentration camp, or to fart loudly, which made them all laugh hilariously. Particularly because Grandfather was easy prey. They knew he would make a little scene as soon as they provoked him: he would roll his eyes, gnash his teeth like an animal and flail his fists in the air, though he wasn't at all dangerous. Any little thing could irritate him. Then he would pace up and down in the attic for a long time, unable to restrain himself, shouting profanities and biting his arm in frustration.

A part-invalid with a very shady past, *the German*, as he was dubbed, was unable to find a job. But the gold from his suitcase helped him launch back into business, and into gambling and boozing as well. This bore strange fruit. He would acquire a rare, expensive piece of equipment with the intention of reselling it, which usually didn't work. He sought long and hard for someone to buy a pre-war British radio, for example, only to exchange it for three telephones. These, in turn, went to pay off a gambling debt. The culmination was the machine for producing ice-cream cones, which he'd bought off a bankrupt pastry-cook *for a very favourable price*. Of course, he didn't know how to assemble the thing, let alone get it going. It outlived him, still dismantled, up in the attic.

Luck did smile at him from time to time, though. He would immediately invest any gains in opulent meals and unlimited quantities of wine. This regularly resulted in cycles of drunkenness, lamenting, lifeless staring at the ceiling, and promises that it wouldn't happen again. No one knows why – whether perhaps it was the return of repressed horrors from the concentration camp, but he came up with the idea of spending some of his earnings on hunting gear. The only photograph I have of him, the only one he left for posterity, shows him in that uniform with a green velvet hat, brilliantly polished knee-high boots, a bulging cartridge belt and a rifle over his shoulder. He'd actually never been hunting before buying the stuff, nor did he for several years afterwards. He showed off in the gear in vain, dreaming of a mountain of feathered and furry delicacies. One day he finally joined a hunting party and went out for some kill. When he took aim at a flock of wild pigeons, the cartridge exploded in the barrel and blew his face off.

Thanks to his connections, Father managed to have one family evicted and then the other. Finally he bought the house from the government. But now it was too big for the two of us alone, and too rich in ghosts.

* * *

Sorrow began to accumulate in me at a very early stage. I didn't call it that straight away, and even later I only used that word as a blanket term for things whose exact reason and origin I couldn't discern. When there was pressure from the outside I found the strength to resist; but in periods of peace, when the latest breaches had been stopped, I was plunged into an unjustified mood of dejection and listlessness, which revealed the extent of my weakness.

Money, together with the absence of my father, was the central theme in our house for as long as I can remember. Both issues lay at the root of every conversation although we were at pains not to mention them; perhaps for that reason they guided our every step like a hidden magnetic pole. Mother would never borrow money even when there was someone she could have borrowed from. She was a staunch proponent of belt-tightening and making-do. We repaired cracked glass with adhesive tape and pretended that the loss of the picture on the TV screen didn't bother us. The TV was reduced to a radio, but so what? Mother did the laundry by hand for months until we'd saved up enough for the repair man to come. I learnt to deal with the plumbing and electric wiring without any instruction, which I definitely should have been proud of. Yet I came to hate that house with which we lived in symbiosis. We were vitally addicted to it, and it mirrored our inner states and limitations, never hesitating to show its disdain for all our efforts to retard its ageing. As restless as it was thankless, it added fresh cracks to the collection on the walls, rescrawled its mouldy graffiti in corners only just repainted, left rust on metal, and heralded each spring with clogged drains, peeling woodwork and a leaking roof. Selfish and ungrateful like a pre-pubescent child, it demanded constant attention to restrain even just the outward signs of decay and made us pay dearly for any neglect. And outside there was always something crying out to be pruned, cut, dug, heaped up or incinerated, and at the very least there was sweeping. Together with the everyday martyrdom of dishes and laundry, shopping and garbage, that cycle of Tantalian torment, neatly tailored to human size, demanded to be borne until it had consumed every last ounce of *joie de vivre*.

As more and more tasks fell into my responsibility, my desire for revenge also grew: to leave the house to the mercy of the elements, weeds and pests. I rejoiced at the thought of camping amid the ruins. And the more sickly Mother became and the less she was able to look after things herself, the harder she took their imperfection. Her illness, combined with life's tragic twists and turns, seemed to mellow her and she lost her imperious ways; I tried all the more to gratify her and anticipate her remarks, aware of how much it pained her to be losing control of things. In her bedridden last months I also read a mournful rebuke in her eyes for things she couldn't see from her bed, like the matted cobwebs up on the first floor and all that happened in my life outside the house.

Not that I grew up in great poverty. True, of all the literature I devoured I was most inspired by descriptions of fantastic feasts and the names of exotic dishes I could only imagine, but I had almost everything the other kids my age had. The only difference was that I didn't have them at the same time, and that delay often hurt, but I learnt to live with it. My clothes, although seldom new, were always neat, and every year there was just enough to spare for me to go on summer holiday.

Mother didn't consider renouncing hers to be a sacrifice at all; she'd seen more than enough of the world.

My first proper sexual experience was at the seaside during my studies. There had been inconclusive attempts prior to that, more because it was something others had long boasted about, than due to any true desire on my part. Nor is it really correct to call them attempts because the initiative came exclusively from the other side; but the girls whose curiosity I evidently aroused gave up on me one after another as soon as they saw beneath the surface. Later, too, I never got anywhere near flirting, although I was strongly attracted to women. One could say painfully attracted: I craved for their feminine curves, their softness and warmth; but I never made any moves.

I'd known *her* since childhood, in a remote sort of way. We lived close to each other, but our two years' age difference was an unbridgeable void for the hope that welled up in me each time we passed: that she might find something at least vaguely interesting in me. She would wander past, not looking at anything in the visible world, and wearing the clumsiness of a big, force-landed bird. She always walked along the outer edge of the street, stumbling into walls and stopping from time to time as if at a source of danger which only she could discern or perhaps was intended for her alone. I only found myself next to her on a few rare occasions; and discovered she had a soft voice and seldom spoke. From time to time, she let out strange sighs without any reason at all; and if she smiled it was with visible effort. Only with a lot of goodwill could you find anything beautiful about her face, or even anything resembling individuality; still, that face often came to me when I was feeling lonely because of the closeness I felt between us. But this became rarer and rarer until I forgot her entirely.

Nevertheless, that summer holiday in a town by the sea, she not only recognised me but was glad to see me. It was at an improvised disco in the cellar of a family house, the only recreational facility of any kind to spite the wartime slump in tourism in that hole of a place, wisely omitted from all tourist brochures. The largest part of the improvised dance floor was occupied by a puddle of unknown origin; two or three guys were hanging around there and trying to shake it down to painfully deafening music – the DJ must have been a bricklayer's assistant; and from the depths of the place, so dark that I could hardly see, someone waved to me enthusiastically with a broad smile.

She wasn't only glad to see me, but after a brief and futile attempt at conversation she took me by the hand – hers was surprisingly cold and clammy – and walked me down to the nearest beach. There I realised, without verbal procrastination, that her breath was heavy with alcohol and that the joy in her eyes had little to do with me. But the clarity of her intentions and the nimbleness of her hands weren't impaired; with just a few movements there on the sand as romantic as emery paper, beneath the utterly disinterested stars, she freed me of the burden of virginity.

I wasn't her first, that's for sure, but I was probably the last. Two weeks later her obituary notice went up on lamp-posts in our neighbourhood; she'd swallowed everything she could find in the medicine chest. My inquiries comforted me to an extent: it hadn't had anything to do with me but had probably been the culmination of a process which had been brewing in her since childhood. Those who were better informed spoke about a recently lost love, but they tended towards the assessment that it could only have been the straw that broke the camel's back. Still, it had been my first time, and when reflecting on that it was hard to completely avoid egocentrism and not to think of the unpleasant connotations.

There was only one more time during my study years, but it was to take on the trappings of permanence and develop into what they call a *relationship*. I had enough other chances, but my chronic lack of talent for seductive small-talk, plus my tendency to stay glued to the wall between lectures, ensured that I was soon put into the same category as the faculty inventory along with the eggheads, four-eyes and pimple-faced nerds: those who are only ever spoken to for some practical reason. Borrowing my lecture notes was really worthwhile because I noted down everything like a model clerk. That doesn't mean they were processed into something spectacular in my head; I mean, I would have loved to have shrewd and heretical things to say about books and other issues, but it became increasingly obvious that my mental potential was reserved for information collection and friendly genuflection. I learnt to live with this, too, which was all the easier because no one seemed to be bothered by it.

Mother had frowned on Phonetics. She was somewhat more positive about German despite her own German episode: knowing the language could still be of real benefit. But when she saw she couldn't change my choice she embraced it as her own, as the only correct decision, and went all the way back to my childhood for arguments to convince us both that I was predestined to study German and Phonetics. At exam time, she would exempt me from all household chores, go about on tiptoes and make me coffee for late-night study sessions. All her concern was driven by her strong and equally mistaken premonition that I was going to lose my motivation and drop out before the end of my degree. That would confirm and seal our common fate – inevitable however much we struggled – because the omniscient hand wouldn't release us from the enigmatic guilt which had been dogging our family for generations. The symbolic value of a degree was far greater than its practical significance; it became my mother's horizon and her life's project, crucial in tilting the balance in the grand equation of sense and senselessness. If, after my degree, I fell into vice or dropped out of everything and became an absolute zero, that would have been less of a tragedy; the main thing was to get that degree.

I was among the first of my generation to do so and immediately enrolled in postgraduate studies. On the wings of a degree done purely to satisfy the external world, I chose Literature – I had the courage to reach out for what my heart desired. But once I'd attended all the lectures I had no aspiration to sit the exams. Day after day I opened my notes, stared at them, and then closed them and returned them to the shelf, where they gradually petrified. Although Mother had supported my scholarly ambitions, she didn't protest when I gave them up; after all, she'd already got 'her' degree.

My first *relationship* tapped me on the shoulder at one of those lectures. It was being held by a professor famous for his knitted woollen bag and the very long hairs sticking out of his nose. I don't remember the title of the particular course – it might have been "Living Milestones in Theory" – because that living relic of our Critical School, which is mentioned in every good textbook, lectured by simply reading out one of his numerous articles. His writings were broad in scope and inscrutably interrelated. He would take the photocopies out of his bag, lay them neatly on the table and read from them in a monotonous voice, calm and solemn. He eliminated page after page in this way, without lifting his eyes towards the audience, who blithely chattered or read newspapers.

I had noticed her before. She came to lectures with another girl, and the two were inseparable. The other girl would undoubtedly have been judged the *more attractive* by anyone who approached them with any intentions. Since I didn't have any intentions, I probably wouldn't have made the acquaintance of either if the pretty girlfriend hadn't been sick that time, and I certainly wouldn't have received a note over my shoulder about the lecture being sooo exciting. This was just an invitation to move on to other topics, which we did, and another twenty or so notes were passed to and fro, but it came to nothing more than smiles. Then we each went our separate ways, and that's definitely how it would have stayed, had we not come to the next lecture and found out that the professor had passed away.

Without this unexpected boon we definitely wouldn't have gone for coffee. The following coffee, two days later, inaugurated our relationship *de jure*. Nothing more or less happened at that second coffee: we chatted like people who strike up an acquaintanceship while waiting for their trains at the station or sitting in the waiting room at the dentist's, in a casual mode unburdened by any thought of joint projects. Our second coffee, however, wasn't coincidental but *premeditated*, with a follow-up in the form of a third, and that eliminated all doubt: we were in a relationship.

She was pretty knowledgeable about legal matters and put great store by them. It ran in her genes, no doubt – inherited from her lawyer father. She'd actually wanted to study Law, and then at the last moment, who knows why, she veered off into Literature. I'm sure she would have made an excellent judge or expert in insolvency law; but, as things turned out, they took her on as an assistant after her Master's, and to this day she pedantically performs her duties at one of the country's Literature departments.

The development of our relationship, slow but steady, led us to the verge of intimacy. Her virginity posed a threshold here, in a formal sense, although it wasn't an emotional issue, nor did she contemplate the loss of her hymen in ethical terms.

The problems fell into the domain of substantive family law: she worried what would happen if she got pregnant and she was only partly placated by my pledge that, in such a case, I would act in the most honourable of ways. It clearly would have meant more to her if we signed a pre-coital contract. Her father's field of specialisation, Author's Rights, would undoubtedly have been valuable here. But even if we reached an agreement that a particular act was to take place, there still remained the question of *how*. One of her parents and siblings (two brothers and a sister) was always at home; and we could forget about my place. So for two or three months, until the first experimental occasion, we merely theorised about sex.

In the meantime, I gained the right to be introduced to her parents. They received me cordially and inquired, smiling, about my family, and I smiled as I tweaked my replies. She said I left an impeccable impression of *decency*. Every visit, she played something for me on the piano, a Beethoven or Mozart sonata, pieces created so as to be reanimated by affable young ladies for as long as humanity endures, with tea served in art-déco porcelain brought in to us, sometimes with pastries and always with a kindly smile, by her exceptionally attractive mother with her barely perceptible limp.

Those were moments of unimaginable aesthetic bliss for me; occasions which the concealed connoisseur in me – my inner aesthete shackled in existential chains – had long awaited. She would place the stool at a precise distance, sit upright like a goddess, throw her hair back over her shoulders, exhale deeply as if freeing herself of everything which kept her earthbound, and inhale equally deeply, but no longer the air breathed by ordinary mortals. Wings would unfold above the keys, ready to carry her innocent soul heavenwards. Apart from the pleasing visual aspects of her throwing back her hair (her ear must have been crafted in a famous workshop because its like was not to be found in nature, and her alabaster neck was poorly chosen: how could one caress it without leaving greasy fingermarks?), it also brought fragrant waves of lavender, chamomile, mint and cinnamon. And then her two butterflies began a courting dance above the keys, fluttering and flirting around them, now bashfully, now full of the fervour of that magic dance, dizzyingly intricate and yet structured down to the very last movement.

Her mother always visited herself upon us at least once, but she never came in without knocking, so we were able to bridle our embraces on the couch. More than by inquisitorial motives, she was guided by boredom, wrapped in genuine sympathy for our relationship. There wasn't a tad of housework for her to do because a cleaning lady came twice a week; her husband considered the flat nothing more than a bedroom; she'd completed her career as university lecturer, and after thirty years of theological research she'd clearly run out of undiscovered realms. She would come and sit with us and drift into evocations of her younger years, and a youthful glow would blossom on her already remarkably well-preserved face. Only when contemplating her face – that powerful defence argument of the most insidious of all mass murderers: time – did I recognise the full beauty of her daughter. She was one of those who don't sparkle at first glance but reward your patience, and, what's more, turn the years to their advantage. Before my eyes was revealed the resplendent beauty which maturity would sculpt and perfect in her features, and I sensed already that it would sweeten my old age. There were moments when that almost seemed possible – entirely possible.

I could see myself start up as a court interpreter for German in the annexe of her father's law firm, and over time I would build up a translation agency for all fields and all major languages. Our wedding present would be a thirty-seven square-metre city apartment; we would exchange it for one twice the size and pay off the difference in sixty-eight monthly instalments. My tasks would be unpacking the dishwasher, picking up our daughters from kindergarten and doing the fortnightly household shopping at one of the malls. When our elder daughter enrolled in Design we would buy her a one-room flat from our savings, although a good part had been spent in vain on operations in Switzerland when the younger inexplicably lost her sight. We would enjoy inviting friends over for dinner; I would take over the cooking on those occasions, reproducing the creations of master chefs from the luxurious volumes assembled on a separate bookshelf. My dear wife would depart when I was seventy-four, but we would be reunited forever, three springs later, in a silent, ivy-clad vault at the Mirogoj Cemetery.

Realistically speaking, it was about as possible as Gregor Samsa *truly* turning into a giant beetle.

But it was all present back then, albeit embryonically. It seemed quaint and optional, a safe distance away; it felt like a film which, however moving, monumental and timeless, ultimately comes to the credits. And the scenario grew and developed, fitting itself to my body with terrifying speed and feeling ever more at home there, until it finally took over and merged with everything around; the scene became ever more exotic, bathed in a different light.

Once it reached full maturity it never left me again. It only changed faces, adding new countenances as variations of ones already seen, yet mainly just duplicating old ones with manic repetitiveness.

I imagined myself standing naked to the waist in front of the wardrobe where I'd already been hovering for fifteen minutes. I'd got my trousers on somehow but then just stood staring at all the other clothing, unable to make a decision, powerless to even move, let alone go out into the street. I was disgusted by my increasingly hideous and stubbly face, my socks which had started to stink on my feet and the snotty handkerchief lying on the floor for days, but changing any of those things demanded too much effort. I couldn't focus on a single word when a colleague at work announced that his father had died, I camouflaged myself with a pained face and shocked silence and put my hand on his shoulder. And another one, this time over the phone, explained why his wife had needed a hysterectomy, while I leafed through the magazine which Peugeot Croatia used to send me as an owner of one of their products. I replaced the receiver and immersed myself in the editorial by Jean-Claude Fontas, the general director, who was happy to greet us again and glad that our numbers had swollen; he hoped the summer had been fruitful for us all. The article was headed by a photograph, and Jean-Claude Fontas evidently knew what happiness was: his cheeks were clean-shaven, his teeth very white and his watch of solid gold. I remembered feeling something like happiness or, to tone it down a bit, excitement, at the smell of the new car purchased on credit, when I opened the door and carefully sat on the plastic-wrapped seats. I'd never seriously thought about suicide because it presupposed a degree of bravery and, ultimately, initiative. But there I was, in the middle of the night on the top-floor balcony, begging that God existed so he could at least crush me to smithereens on the spot or whisk me away to another world. And now I am faced with yet another spring, another winter, another load of washing to be hung on the line. Which sight is less unbearable: crows on the winter skeletons of trees, or the vernal euphoria of budding? Why does blooming magnolia just remind me of vomiting?

And so you're not 23 any more, but 28, and you can hardly tell the difference between the numbers; or maybe you're thirty-eight, you can't remember; there's nothing worth remembering in those fifteen years, but at the same time they're sadistically full, and you're sinking and suffocating in those memories, all stale, dead and foreign; you shovel away at that muck day after day, digging to exhaustion, hoping in vain to catch sight of something new, something different, something of your own; you watch to see songbirds migrating from the south, but more and more crows arrive instead like morbid Christmas decorations which hang from the branches like faeces, like corpses thrown up by the sea after an eschatological earthquake in Southern Asia; ah, that would be the only relief – if everything was flattened, but there are no earthquakes here, only minor faults and breakdowns of the TV set, kettle or boiler; you don't know how to fix those things and yet you don't call the repair man but simply try to live with the situation; you don't go out onto the balcony because a thrush decided to die there, with its little legs erect as if in prayer; you take this as a sign from heaven, a message addressed to you personally; you take everything personally as if everything has been arranged precisely so as to increase your suffering; your self-pity has walled you in with ramparts, beyond which nothing exists, and what's really sickening is that you've become fond of them, you won't do anything to breach those walls even though the whole world hurts wherever you touch it; you're sick of your own egocentrism but you've learnt to live with it; your only fear is that people might see through the charade, so you look them in the eyes to see if they've noticed and if you can glimpse a message; you feel like going up to strangers in the street and asking them how they manage to get where they're going and how they're able to take another step; you even want to ask a tree how on earth it manages to stand tall for so many years; you're afraid to open your mouth at the post office or the butcher's in case something monstrous slips out, or you burst into tears because anything can make you cry or throw up: the massacre which time has inflicted on a face you haven't seen since primary school, the smile a child in a passing stroller throws your way, the leaf which has dropped from a branch to lie silently beside its fallen brothers, the fatigue of thinking about all those leaves which grow on the branches only ultimately to fall, the dust relentlessly accumulating, the books perfidiously pressing down from their shelves in mute sarcasm; it's too hard to even try and remember anything written in those books, and a colossal weariness weighs down on your shoulders; there's more writing here on the desk, five hundred pages which need proof-reading so that the next five hundred can be done, and so that five hundred books later you can take over the editing desk and send hundreds of equally futile texts to the proof-reader; the author was born in 1963, or 1955, and you want to call him and congratulate him on his perseverance, on the fact that he still puts lines down on paper; you'd like to go and see him at that very moment and ask him how he manages to stay alive; and here we are now in a traffic jam, almost alive, squeezed from one set of traffic lights to the next in the pouring rain, autumn and spring; now we're not moving at all but each sitting here to the swish-wish of our windscreen wipers, it feels good like this, and miracles do happen sometimes, so maybe the rain will decide never to stop and we'll stay sitting in our cars until they rust and rot, and our bodies along with them.

Yet our relationship lasted almost two years. That is so phenomenal that I have to write it again: almost two years. That's more than six hundred days and dozens of visits to the cinema. Her favourite genre was romantic comedy, with sweet music and a happy end, if possible with a peroxide-blonded Edward Norton (the very notion!) in the role of a priest who after perilous introspection only just manages to tear himself away from the temptation of infatuation. It also meant a hundred sittings in cafés and a hundred teas with her mother. However much she tried to look elsewhere, her gaze landed sooner or later on my dark complexion, hair and eyes, and her overall sympathy couldn't conceal her anxiety at my possible marital intentions towards her daughter.

Moreover, there were flashes of a corresponding message, elaborate but articulated with the precision of a cut diamond and tuned to the frequency of my most intimate receptors: firstly, that the cosmetic allures with which I held her daughter spellbound in no way altered my *untouchability*, my belonging to those who are only likeable up to the doorstep; secondly, that I was only seeing her daughter thanks to her heroic maternal magnanimity; thirdly, that I should be under no illusion that my success at enchantment, coupled with her magnanimity, could be anything other than temporary; and fourthly, that I was expected to make amends for transgression and theft by making myself scarce pronto.

What a fitting word, *temporary*, so quintessential. Early on, I developed a sensitivity for that aspect of existence, temporariness, to such a degree that everything constituting it started to appear exclusively in the light of temporariness. I had ever greater difficulty seeing myself as anything imbued with power of duration. That doesn't mean that I had apocalyptic visions or that I was at all worried about the future of humanity or the local community. It just became unlikely that it would also encompass *me* or that anything more long-term than tomorrow could affect me. I know how that sounds, but that's how I felt.

And yet after every afternoon tea there was always another, and another. Sooner or later, as if by coincidence, the conversation intersected the ellipse of my father, and there it foundered; it was becoming ever harder to keep him *indefinitely* dead. So I had to come out with it.

'Bone cancer has the nasty reputation of being one of the most painful ways to die. My father needed exceptionally long. He was penniless and had a strong will to live, so he refused morphine and fought to the last moment, with unimaginable screams. I'd just started school,' I explained.

That certainly got rid of him as far as further questions were concerned, but at some stage I had to bring Mother into it too. Luckily, this was after Mother had given up smoking once and for all – so radically that she missed no occasion to rail against tobacco – and this certainly fell on grateful ears. Unfortunately, more or less simultaneously with the last cigarette, the Holy Ghost fizzled out for her, and in this respect, too, she swung to the opposite extreme.

I must say, my prospective mother-in-law held out well until the very end of afternoon tea, nibbling her lip when necessary. And as they were seeing me out, after she'd evoked God's will and God's help in health and life in general for the umpteenth time, my mother spoke through me in a gentle voice.

'You know, God our Creator only helped himself by having himself crucified, and He'd admit it if he had a smidgen of self-criticism. But that was long, long ago,' she said *in absentia*.

And with that my mother waxed lyrical, although no one had asked for it; the faces of the two listeners showed the damage inflicted by every word like a taximeter as Mother, through me as a medium, presented her vision of longevity together with her programmed bonus track:

'Of course nothing comes after death, there's no doubt

about that. But perhaps at least the young will live to see fairer times –' my virtual mother nodded to me and my girlfriend, and a ray of optimism lit up her face, 'an age where the organisation of life will be taken over by science and everyone be given an equal allotment of years; fifty or a hundred, that can be laid down later. Everyone will know in advance how long they have and will be able to plan their life and arrange things nicely, and when their time comes they can go in peace, not like us who spend our lives in fear and trepidation of being taken away while still in our prime, or of lingering on as a burden to others when we've turned into a caricature of ourselves, an insult to what we once were.'

Undoubtedly there was noble-mindedness in that thought, but it was too ambitious for the audience. In that way the topic of Mother was ticked off.

And so, in spite of everything, it lasted two years. That also meant two summer holidays in the family's beach house. Right by the sea, secluded, surrounded by luxuriant Mediterranean vegetation. Everything seemed to have been made and aesthetically maintained just for the two of us, down to the fireplace clad with ornamental stone and the intimate little beach by the house, triangular and fashioned with dry stone walls to the shape of a pubis. Here we were like the first people on Earth, or the only ones left after the justified annihilation of the species, and now responsible for begetting another.

Here we finally devoted ourselves to discovering physical love. Although we'd often spoken about the occasion, you couldn't say we were all revved up and ready to go. My sole previous experience had not whetted my appetite, and she considered self-restraint a virtue. But that only brought us closer: we both saw sexuality as a part of us which doubtlessly existed but was located somewhere on the periphery, in an indefinite dimension, like the overseas relatives with whom you maintain purely epistolary contact; the discovery was all the more delectable.

The first time, she got undressed and waited for me to grope her in the dark. She didn't hold back her surprise at what my hands discovered in her body; an *Oh, how lovely* escaped from her when I penetrated her forest of sighs and the spurt of pent-up juices. Liberated, her body rushed to make up for all the years of inattention, giving itself blindly, faster than craving demanded. There were amazing smells in her: bottled up to ripeness and fermentation, they now gushed and flooded, lifting us up on a foaming tide and roaring past, too fast to be given a name. We collected ourselves and then started riding that wave once more, and then over and over again, tirelessly, diving ever deeper, exploring fibre after fibre of flesh.

We spent the rest of the time on the beach, each with their own book, reading each other significant passages and finding identical feelings in them, which in those three weeks of utmost devotion constantly revolved around our communicating vessels. Our mutual devotion didn't abate, nor did it permit anything or anyone else in that environment. Once we were disturbed by a few foreigners, whose discretion didn't mitigate the affront caused by their presence on the beach. I cast them a caustic glance to show what we thought, and it proved effective.

Our lovestruckness deepened by the day and was reflected all around: in the astral blue of her eyes, in the silvered sea, in the cricket chorus in the cypresses. We loved the same hues of dusk and dawn, the same shapes of pebbles, the same fruit, the same herbs and spices, the same sorts of fish, be they roasted or salted. We were equally insatiable of one another. We only gave in to sleep when we were completely exhausted, impatient to feast our eyes on each other again.

My gaze constantly sought her and she rewarded it abundantly. Everything in us and around us was a joy for the senses, unimpaired by the slightest squabble – unless it be the rivalry of who would do the washing up or surprise the other with something tasty from the bakery. All was serenity and grace: her talent for marvelling at the moon, or a melon, *Oh how marvellous, oh how cute*; her voice, falsetto like a girl's, and old classroom anecdotes and stories of school excursions, retold time after time, with comments equally rooted in her childhood; her passion for euphemisms and diminutives; her multiple extended phone calls to her mother every day to thoroughly discuss the weather, our food and her dreams, and all this in limitless mutual joy, full of *My mouse* and *my darling*, full of sympathy for others' colds and gastric distress, *Oh you poor dears, oh the poor thing*, and with a complex farewell ritual at the end of each call, *Cheerio then, speak to you again soon, I'll tell you how it all goes, bye-bye, ciao ciao, kiss kiss, night-night darling, and take care, thanks, you too, I love you, and say hello to him for me*, which after extending the conversation to two or three forgotten topics was usually all repeated.

The manifestations of her conservatism, Christomania and xenophobia, which she inherited but also furthered with her own gratuitous inspiration, could be seen with a little effort as folksy, witty adornments. The same applied, I guess, to her strong feelings against the Serbs: she still wholeheartedly defended our Croatian Fatherland from them years after they'd ceased to endanger it, with arms at least, even though her family had lost neither personnel nor matériel in the war of the nineties. I related with some sympathy to her improvisations on themes borrowed from her mother's repertoire, such as the sanctity of the Family and the Fatherland, or the diabolicalness of divorce, abortion and atheism, which she elevated to expressions of outright loathing for other religions, nations and skin colours. But mine wasn't all that dark, no no, and she had lucidity enough to pass over my Gypsy nickname and my dubious degree of religious and patriotic ardour.

But the next summer holiday, our relationship was as dead as the pebbles we turned over on the beach as if searching for something to add to our used-up words.

What they once meant had evidently evaporated. Both of us clearly felt it, though we tried hard to convince each other of the opposite through smiles and little gestures of endearment. Her beauty shone at me no less splendidly than before, but I found it ever harder to perceive. She hadn't hurt, disappointed or betrayed me in any way, nor had she done anything wrong. It simply became inconceivable to repeat the same movements: the very thought of them wearied me. I didn't want it to be like that, but I didn't know how to prevent it.

Some inner resource was expended; it had dried up and flaked away with frightening speed. I had matured to an extent, no doubt, but I felt as if I hadn't *lived* that maturity but only skidded through it into what lay beyond. Whatever others enjoy in sensible doses for decades, I'm just allowed to sample. Something always draws me straight to the toxic sludge of things.

Still, we kept seeing each other after the summer: going to the pictures, sitting in cafés and having tea with her mother. For months, without the courage to state the obvious. Until one day she met me with furrowed brow, her face awash with guilt, her insecure hands picking and fussing around at her clothes and things on the table in search of support; and gathering resolve like for a statement in the Church's monthly magazine *New World* to obliterate the old, she announced that she'd *met someone*. However modest, that expression brought on an immense silence. The regret in her eyes was unbearable; I looked away to the clock which, full of self-assurance and with precisely measured steps, ticked towards the zenith of its secessionist circle. The final euphemism, the culmination of secession, the end of the session.

At the door, as she was feverishly searching me with a gaze to gauge the destructive effect of her admission, and certainly also fixing my countenance in her mind for brief reminiscences in her old age, her eyes briefly brimmed over. *Don't be too sad*, she just said, and I promised I would try, grateful that she was releasing me without the torment of comforting words about fate and inevitability, without apologetics for all the effort we'd invested and our good comportment, for the unforgettable moments we'd shared, the even more unforgettable ones still ahead of me, etc.

That *someone* she'd met, I found out, was just a passing acquaintance, probably interested purely in carnal knowledge. After that I didn't hear of her for years – not until a virus played around with her email address book and I, together with who knows how many others, received an extensive letter beginning with *Dear Mustafa*, which revealed details of her divorce proceedings and its pivotal content: the guardianship of fourteen-month-old Alija, whom Mustafa was evidently in no hurry to send back from Abu Dhabi.

Sorrow. That word was like an incantation. Spoken aloud, it invoked all my idle demons, and I opened the door wide for them and was an ideal host. For some time, the romantic tragedy functioned as a justification. I devotedly erected a monument to my grief, which in return shielded me from the world, like a cocoon of mist. But the vapours dissipated and I discovered that the melancholy came from its own source, indeterminably far away and much older than my individual existence. My rare receptive capabilities and my (to put it mildly!) below-average power of resistance made me vulnerable and I wished I'd been able to raise a dike before its long, patient waves which come rolling in, crash, and carry away all volition.

I was forced to discover the irrefutable fact that I scarcely had enough spark in me to maintain the prerogatives of a functional individual. On rare occasions, paradoxically, I would find a drop of true vigilance in myself – the comprehension that I was alive here and now in this particular body. But what use was this realisation? I spent the rest of my time trying out all the ways I had of obliterating time.

In the dimensions accessible to the eye, that didn't significantly set me apart from the majority of people around me. But they were better at giving it other names.

The people around me, apart from Mother, were reduced to those I saw at the office. Each of them cultivated their own identity, trying as best they could to wrench themselves away from indistinguishability through mannerisms, political stances, and their choice of perfume, cigarette brand and radio station. A few even had extravagant hats to crown their swollen heads. Some ate lunch in the café across the street, others brought sandwiches from home. Some had children, others had a pet, and there were those who had both. The majority burn out at work, endeavouring with their whole being to rise another rung in the social perception of their libidino-economic achievements; then there are the others, frankly speaking more numerous, who constantly groan with their eyes set on the next public holiday – the moment when they'll slump down in front of the TV and switch off, finally free of the scrutiny of others and able to spend a little while alone with their genitals.

Being among them didn't traumatise me too much, nor did I feel substantially better or worse at home; but the trip in one direction or the other demanded ever more effort.

Sometimes, carried away by a moment of inspiration on

the way back from work, I would turn left instead of right, or continue straight on, until the petrol or the road ran out, and then keep going on foot across fields and wastelands, through forests and tall-grass prairies, across tundras and moors, all the way to the mountain crags; there on high I would brood and discharge the toxins in me. With my soul purged by the panoramic views, I would then go back down under the wing of humanity, maybe even with a message which I myself would only realise much later. Sometimes I would get out of the car at the traffic lights, start snapping the wipers off other cars and hurling them like javelins at the faces of the drivers, calling them all sorts of names and mounting heroic resistance, kicking, biting off ears, until the butcher came running up to finish me off with his axe. Sometimes I would sit blissfully smiling in front of my soup instead of eating it, and when Mother asked anxiously and then hysterically what was wrong I would reply with a verse of Goethe's, or with psalms. Some evenings I would go to the neighbour's for a game of chess, or to strangle his dog. Others I would spend writing Christmas cards and Easter greetings, wisely preparing them before the fever of the respective holidays, and joyful letters to friends expecting children. Or correspondence to government officials, present and future, banning them from making any decisions in my name. To Jesus Christ, requesting that he get down off the cross and stop dying for my sake. To my father, so he would cease to exist in theory as well, and to future generations so they would abolish the concept of fatherhood. Or I would decide to call someone, and the only acceptable person in my whole address book would be a girl I hadn't seen or heard anything of since primary school.

She would be really happy that I'd rung and suggest we meet that same evening, although I seem to remember that we hardly exchanged more than a sentence in those years long past, and my memory, far from recording her face, was obviously deceiving me with a hastily slapped-together facial composite. I wondered if she was who I thought she was, but did it matter? A few hours would suffice for us to stir up the love which had been smouldering in us since our pre-school days. Me and my old-new flame would leave the café holding hands and get married on the way home. Three months later the first of our six children was born. She produced them at regular intervals; number five became an accomplished bassoonist and UNICEF Goodwill Ambassador.

Unless the voice in the receiver happened to be masculine, and still heavy after being roused from sleep, and slurred from booze; he would recognise my name, and after exchanging all our news about classmates – who was killed in the war in the nineties, who became minister of foreign affairs and European integration, and who had a stand selling Thai jewellery in Rovinj – he would agree that we meet the next week or in one of the coming months, or that we should definitely call each other from time to time, and when we were saying goodbye he said I only just moved here recently. How did you find me? and it would turn out that we'd gone to school in totally different cities.

* * *

Yesterday I went to visit Ines. It was her eldest daughter's birthday, and I couldn't put off seeing Josip, her number three, any longer. A nasty business, all in all, starting with buying presents for the children: there were dolls which blink and sing, cyborg warriors with monstrous claws, board games to do with conquering territory and amassing riches, teddy bears in all colours and sizes with little bow ties, aprons, rattles and kitchen utensils. All right, if nothing else there are always books. But which should you choose ahead of others, and how can you subdue your apprehension when browsing through them? Stories of olden days full of malice, robbery, fratricide and rich with long-faded morals. Or contemporary ones by our own local authors. Take the story about the wizard who could do everything and perform any miracle, except get the others to let him join the wizards' guild. And all because he wore funny pyjamas. That made him so sad that he left his castle and wandered the forests. One day he came across a little girl wearing exactly the same pyjamas; she was crying because her parents had been eaten by a dragon. Actually they hadn't, as we learn at the end – the wizard had found the dragon just as it was about to roast them and, with a wave of his wand, turned it into a cell phone. They were all overjoyed about their new friendship and were constantly calling and texting each other on an attractive domestic price plan. And why not, after all? *Buy Croatian!* as the campaign says.

And then there was chocolate. It's a safe investment. Lots of chocolate. If you just bring a book they'll look at you with hungry eyes. For Josip, I got a mobile with little stars and moons which dangle around at head height just waiting to poke you in the eye. All parents love them.

On the way home, I stopped by Dolac open market. Hatred of the unmarried filled the air and it was like running the gauntlet. I tried in vain to buy two hundred grams of French beans for my lunch. She, a hard-working mother, had got up at five to feed the livestock, her husband and their small child before rushing to market laden with the fruits of her labours, in the hope of earning a few kunas for the family.

'Two hundred grams?! That's an insult to my work-worn hands.'

'Here's the money for a kilo then, but just give me two hundred grams.'

'I can't weigh such a tiny amount,' she snapped, and a lust for revenge glinted in her eyes.

'Never mind then, thank you. May your beans yield a bumper crop, envelop your house and sprout from your nose and ears.'

Luckily there are such things as surimi – crab-flavoured fish fingers. It's a shame they're not made in other flavours too, like watermelon, *Sachertorte* and stuffed toy. They're bound to be riddled with carcinogens, but what's that compared to the fact that they're ready to be consumed without cooking? But no, this time I turned to a culinary friend true to me since childhood: the local dish of curd cheese with sour cream. That's all I need for a meal.

A Gypsy boy was sitting at the bottom of the stairs holding out his hand with that grovelling look and his shirt open to bare his chest, as if to spite the cold.

'A few coins for a pastry, lady? Mother sick, brothers and sisters also hungry...' I took him by the hand and led him to the nearest bakery.

'Here, choose what you like.'

'Get fucked!' he snorted.

The guy on the placards near the market soured my cheese

with his dire prophecy that local produce would be gone from our markets if we didn't stand up to the imperialist despoilers of our culture and values. Now that I've bought Croatian, every plate of curd cheese with sour cream I eat will involuntarily be seasoned with the endorsement of that cretin. You can sleep in peace when people like that are hounding you, but you've got a nasty problem if they're suddenly on your side!

When my mood had recovered a little, I walked past the shops and watched people buying clothes: the fifty-year-old secretary, with a round body and a dying perm, in search of a blouse to match her eyes; the belle whose face reflects the martyrdom she'll suffer if she denies herself that pair of shoes; the management virtuoso who's already signing a new contract thanks to the brand name on that suit; the immeasurably patient father who has slumped into the armchair with his one hundred and fifty kilos and, smiling, winds a finger-thick gold chain around his finger while his daughter tries dozens of pairs of sunglasses on her bulldoggish face, not daring to say out loud that she actually wants the most expensive; each pair suits her better than the last, the shop-owner avidly emphasises, yelping with enthusiasm and kowtowing before his profit margin.

That child-centred event was on my nerves all day. No, I exaggerate; the thought flashed through my mind from time to time, and the next instant I sank back into my painting. It stares at me from the easel like the others, and I have that same feeling of not knowing how I did it. I just remember lighting and crushing out one cigarette after another, although the buzzing in my head intensified; and getting the curd cheese out of the fridge and pushing it aside after a few spoonfuls because it wouldn't go down; and the bell ringing some time before that – it can only have been my mushroom lady – sorry, I'm not here.

A male body spread across the entire canvas. Naked, with disjointed limbs, caught up in a whirlpool which is already pulling them away, although his torso resists, every muscle is strained to bursting-point. But it has to yield, be torn away from its invisible hold somewhere in the air, which is stabbed by the wind, a gale-force gust right in the middle of his belly, his bowels explode and a polychromatic brightness bursts forth, and several objects shoot out like comets. But nothing falls, all the movement is horizontal and breaks the border of the painting, and the sucking, rending airstream seems to emanate from an all-mighty magnet hidden beyond the canvas. The body is, or rather was, that of a man of mature years, but the face has delicate, unblemished features, soft like a child's; except for his eyes, which gape in anticipation of disaster. It draws me in too, and I almost don't mind. I sit in front of it and ebb away; a soothing white comes from the inside, washing over me in waves, tenderly spreading a soft, muffling satisfaction, like being gently rocked to sleep.

The phone tore me away.

'Is everything OK? We said around seven!'

'Sorry, I...'

'What time did you think it was? You could have called the Speaking Clock or something!'

Slip on something decent. The presents aren't wrapped yet, blast! Why exactly do people wrap presents for children? No doubt, so the mother can encourage her child to admire the paper for a second before it gets torn to pieces.

The staircase up to their landing was densely populated with pot plants, some reaching boldly to the ceiling, others in the first fling of youth and visibly sustained with a lot of love. A smiling baby elephant on the doormat. Two surnames on the door in a calligraphic font, slanting and linked in an embrace over the peephole.

They'd wanted me to come and see out the Old Year with them. Oh, nothing pretentious, just two other couples, three at most. *Hmm, couples.* We'd have something to eat and then watch a film after the children had gone to bed. I lied that I'd love to but had already promised others. Around eleven on that maddest evening of the year, I stuck in wax earplugs and finished off the vodka; it worked pretty well. When the fireworks intensified, I liked to imagine good citizens gunning each other down in the streets and fighting to the last man.

She rang on the morning of the twenty-ninth of December. All these years, she's never failed to call and wish me a happy birthday. Nor do I fail to reciprocate. That exchange of birthday wishes is like a tribute to a long-faded friendship, a tax incurred twice a year. Regardless of whether it's time to give or take, we both approach the task with due respect: we wrap our words in a festive tone and do our hearty best to gloss over how hollow they are.

Fortunately, her children's birthdays have long since done away with all attempts to embellish our own in any particular way. The final such episode, before her wedding to Marko, ended in a bar in trendy Tkalčićeva Street; it wasn't our first that night. Already blotto, we went and sat with the last guests, some boys who were humming to a guitar together with the waiter. When it was time for last orders, the lights went out and cheek-to-cheekers were put on. I danced and was soon smooching around with the guitarist, whose inquisitive hands didn't waste a second. Several dances later, equally bold, he switched to Ines. On the way home, to my consternation, she raved on drunkenly with detail after detail. It felt like she was nipping the bud of a unique romance. But I was in no state to remember things and the next day I had no idea what the guy looked like.

Later that day, I called Father and told him I was coming for lunch. Like so often before, lunchtime was spent listening to the news and current affairs on the radio. A funereal voice informed us in great detail about the premier's latest meetings, price rises for petroleum derivatives and turmoil in the trade-union leadership. Afterwards, with coffee in the living room, I summarised my recent achievements in a few sentences. He added his unshakeable *Yes* to each of them, which means whatever you want it to – usually that he'd heard it all before. The subsequent silence, punctuated by the tick-tocking up on the wall, inspired me for a masochistic moment to ask him how he was. He lifted a watery gaze, gave a deep sigh and pronounced his usual *To be honest, I'm not all that well.* The tick-tocking took over again. We each stirred in our coffee dregs until I said I had to go, and he sealed the matter with another *Yes*.

He saw me out to the courtyard door. After a few steps I looked back. His propped-up head hung over the fence. Words started to come but fortunately got stuck in my mouth. Instead of saying *It's my birthday today, you know,* I just waved.

It had been a good six months since I'd seen Ines, and again I was taken aback when she opened the door. She'd put on even more weight. Her daughters flung themselves at me, embraced me and immediately withdrew with the booty, moderately satisfied. I found Marko in the kitchen making salad. That smooth, intelligent face, those soft eyes and hands which make you want to take him home on the spot. Damn his eyes, some people get more than they deserve.

It was amazing how much fitted into their kitchen, thanks to the ingenious layout. If just one thing was moved, something would have to be thrown out. The mosaic of cups and crockery hanging from nails on the wall was complemented by decorative ceramics and artistic photos of food. Herbs greened the windowsill. And a family of terracotta pots arranged pedantically from large to small had made its home above the kitchen cupboards together with a collection of style-conscious glass jars filled with dried fruit, pasta, pulses and packets of various organic, do-gooder junk.

Marko brought in Josip, the baby, holding him under its arms.

The little thing waved its tiny legs and flapped its arms, uncertainty in its beady eyes, not sure whether to smile at me or start cooing like a bird. Without taking its eyes off me, it slowly reached its hand towards the finger I proffered; its amazingly long, already perfect fingers looked fake on the body which had only just outgrown the larval stage. One by one, they wrapped themselves softly around mine and stayed there, without lifting it mouthwards or exploring further, as if they'd found what they were seeking and now clung to it.

I felt something crack and shatter inside me. One part of me fled in panic, vanished in the dark and covered its ears. At the same time, a warmth spread through my other part and made everything flaccid; all my will melted and drained away through my finger imprisoned in that downy palm. Laid in a bassinet in the middle of the room, the little creature now gradually lost interest in me and was quiet apart from the occasional gargle. But it went on silently pulling me apart, dismantling me bit by bit.

They wanted me to tell them everything about the exhibition at the gallery, they said. They didn't mention the invitation I'd sent. They were excited to hear about the prize one of my paintings won in Ireland, and about the invitation to the biennale in Korea. Marko put on a video they took last summer in Istria. Well-informed and enthusiastic, he talked about the towns they'd visited with an abundance of amazing details. Then he withdrew into the kitchen to finish the cake. Ines told me about her new antidepressant.

The daughters came back together from their rooms. After blowing out her eight candles, the eldest was sent off to get her violin; that's right, I was sure her name was Dora. The violin was a recent therapeutic measure, her parents whispered, an attempt to counterbalance her sociopathy and loathing of school. We listened to the two scales she'd more or less mastered to date, and then clapped. She put the violin down on the floor and entrenched herself at the edge of the couch, her lips squeezed tightly shut and with dark circles around her eyes. Every now and then, her mother routinely pulled her fingers out of her mouth. Sweat stains spread under her arms. The younger daughter, Sara, took over the stage. An endless source of energy, she chattered and hummed incessantly and brought out doll after doll; she animated each of them with different voices and performed gymnastic pirouettes, until these were interrupted by her landing in the remains of the cake. Marko changed her in the blink of an eye. Now she brought out drawings and explained each one in great detail while fidgeting on my lap, playing with my hair and giving me little kisses on the cheek.

That sweet, bouncy little thing on my knee – so much loveliness in her, so much fresh, zestful life, hungry for love. That hurt. My whole body hurt.

All the more so because Sara's face was reflected in a spiteful, derisive mirror on the other side of the table. Dora took after her father a bit, but the little one here was a spitting image of her mother. Or rather, Ines was a poor copy of her: spent, sucked dry and spat out.

As I looked from one face to the other, the living chasm between them brought forth memories. Year 11 Applied Art at a school for those who have no scholastic ambition and envision their future differently, or not at all. Ines and I found each other in our 'touristic approach' to classes. One meaningful look sufficed, and we'd skive off to get our kicks around town. In the evenings we'd often end up at the Mirogoj Cemetery, jump over the fence and loiter among the graves. When we came across a newly masoned tomb, she'd get into it and lie down to *try it out*. For Ines back then, that was really quite banal, a drop in the ocean of similar things. She loved experiments, especially if they ended in destruction. When *Fight Club* came out years later, there was every indication that the character of Tyler Durden was modelled on her.

She lived with her grandfather, although her parents were alive and kicking, and normal, or maybe exactly for that reason. As well-to-do intellectuals of liberal convictions, they let her do what she wanted, even when it was as clear as daylight that things had gone amiss. It was important for them that she realise that herself. They almost cheered when she told them she wanted to move to live with her grandfather. That way she would mature more quickly and learn responsibility for herself. Her grandfather was a wonderful old man and always happy to see me. He would bring us fruit or hot chocolate in Ines's room and empty our ashtrays on the way, nodding reproachfully but without insistence. He didn't recognise the stubs of joints among all the others. His working life had been devoted to producing souvenirs like gingerbread hearts, peasant moccasins and kitschy umbrellas. He endured his wife's death bravely, although the flat was then turned into her reliquary. But he didn't allow age to crush him: he was an avid hiker and was always reading something or doing crosswords. *So the cogs don't get rusty*, he said. He borrowed books from us because he was interested to find out *what young people read today*. Ines would give him *Ulysses*, or Carver on her darkest days, or de Sade. He would sometimes join us to watch Wim Wenders's films from the seventies, or Tarkovsky. His head would soon droop. Ines would prod him with her elbow at particularly interesting moments, like the sequence in *The Goalie's Anxiety at the Penalty Kick* where the protagonist picks up a girl, they make love in a hotel room, and he proceeds to strangle her.

Once she spiked his soup. It was something very special, the dealer had said with an enigmatic smile. It was called *The Witch*, and there was a drawing of a broomstick rider on the wafer. At first we were going to share it but got cold feet and gave up the idea. The trip spent several weeks between the pages of *Madame Bovary* until Ines turned up at school one day with a giggle on her lips. We dashed off after the first lesson. Her grandfather wasn't at home. We rang at every neighbour's and turned the area upside down. We called several hospitals as well as the police, and left our contact details. Finally, after dark, the doorbell rang. The police had brought him home, his hair wildly dishevelled, with only one shoe and not a trace of reason in his eyes; he'd been subdued while attempting to hijack a tram.

Unease reigned for days, but we all acted as if nothing had happened and gradually things returned to normal. Later Ines came up with another ingenious idea: she started sending him anonymous letters. She pretended to be a lady who had yearned for him since her youth, when they experienced a moment of tenderness together, as unique as it was calamitous, before life had separated them, and only now at the close of day, when all joy and tears were spent, did she come to the painful realisation that they'd been spent on the wrong people, that it had all been a surrogate, a lie to herself and to others, and she was obsessed with the endless promise of what the two of them could still enjoy together. She didn't dare to contact him in any other way because he probably didn't remember her. When Ines's grandfather opened the first letter, he stood thunderstruck in the middle of the kitchen, blushing and on edge. He read it over and over again, unaware that the two of us were watching from behind the half-opened door and rocking with laughter; in the end, he tore up the letter and threw it in the bin. But when the next one came, he slipped it into his pocket as soon as he recognised the handwriting, went off to his room without a word and quietly closed the door. They kept coming, and now he mostly sat gazing away somewhere, frowning, his lips moving without a sound. Ines brought him one letter and said: *Look, it's for you. Can I open it?* He snatched it from her like a pouncing tiger, and panic flashed in his eyes. With every letter the lady became bolder and freer. She no longer abstained from explicit fantasies. Finally she mustered the courage to propose him a rendezvous, in the coffee house on the main square. Grandfather went there all spruced up, with a tremble of anticipation and looking twenty years younger; he returned grey and wizened. There were no more letters because Ines decided she'd had enough of that sort of fun.

She went to bed or to the pictures with boys when she couldn't think of anything better to do. Not that she collected them; she simply took whatever was on offer. Some were kept in circulation for a few weeks, others were ditched the very next day. The only thing you could be sure of, was that she would break off the relationship as soon as a guy started showing any signs of attachment, declared his love, or the like. If he got clingy and claimed there was something meaningful between them, something he couldn't live without, she was happy to recommend him a psychiatrist or meditation techniques.

In the middle of her degree she started getting into drugs in a big way. I only saw her sporadically, enough to follow her decline as she lost teeth, took on a greyish complexion and developed that glassy look. She borrowed money from me when she wasn't able to steal from her parents or her grandfather. Several times I thought she'd reached the bottom, but it always went a bit deeper. And that went on and on until, by a curious turn of events, she got hooked on some really hard stuff: she was torn from one of her deliriums by the realisation that she was in a church, alone, sitting in one of the empty pews. She was staring at the figure of Jesus depicted up on the dome, and tears ran down her face. She fled the church in disgust at herself or in fear. But a few days later she decided to devote herself to Jesus. And to do that she needed my help.

You're out of your mind, I said when she dropped in and

demanded that I accompany her to a spiritual renewal seminar. It was actually meant as a sarcastic practical joke at her own expense, with me in the role of the audience. But at the same time, aware that she was just a step away from the point of no return, she didn't completely reject the possibility that this might be a straw for her to grasp; my hand would give her a push, or stop her, when she went into withdrawal. How could I not agree to help?

Cunningly, she didn't tell me until the last minute that the whole shebang lasted three days and we had to spend day and night in a kind of quarantine. That Friday morning, the bus took us to a Franciscan monastery out of town. A hundred or so souls were already milling here, in ardent anticipation of Renewal. It all began quite unpretentiously: we just had to write our name in the list of participants and pin a name badge to our clothes. Then they let us go into a hall painted with multiple Jesuses, of both the crucified and the hovering variety, as well as the odd Mary and St Francis with his animals. They'd all been painted by a naive hand, actually in keeping with the concept of humility. The pictures were ablaze with bright colours, which filled the hall with optimism. An athletically built young man in an Adidas tracksuit entered, took a guitar and spoke a number into the microphone. That was the page of the songbook *Servant of the Infant Jesus* which was waiting for us on our chairs, but almost none of the others opened it. They all knew the songs off by heart and sang gutturally, in the exalted joy which overwhelmed us. We sang to the Shepherd and Teacher about his gifts and love, and also about meekness, purity and liberation. Every now and again we had to kneel and fold our hands, or stand up and sway like grain in the wind. And all this was harmonious and perfectly orchestrated although without a conductor, despite the diversity of the multitude. The majority were high-school girls with glowing, angelic faces, but I also saw colourfully painted ones and others with many piercings. And a lot of gold, and the words *Made of Stone* on one enviably taut T-shirt. And a handful of ladies with rosaries, who heartened each other, hugged and held hands. There were three or four broken-looking men with bloodshot eyes as well as several maimed, dwarfish and disfigured folk on crutches or in wheelchairs. Plus a boy who didn't open his mouth for the whole three days; he just stuck to the wall, trembling like a jelly and puffing intermittently, while his eyes flashed wildly. The priests went up to him countless times to ask if he was all right and if he really wanted to stay, as if it was touch-and-go whether he would collapse in a twitching heap or commit an obscenity or massacre.

I was just waiting for them to expose us, for all eyes to suddenly turn towards us and the whole thing to end in debacle and scandal. Because apart from us moving our lips very unconvincingly, Ines had put off getting clean until after her conversion. Every little while she went off to the toilet, and she sneered between verses and hissed brazen comments in my ear.

The songs, prayers, Masses and lectures went on and on. And the more Ines got on my nerves with her scantly concealed subversion, the more stubbornly I concentrated on the message, finding hardly anything to protest about. It was about renouncing Evil and its servants (I needed no persuasion), having courage for the truth, because it would free us (who wouldn't wish for that), and letting the certainty of Divine Love clothe and lead us (that really would be wonderful). I learnt that the world was our enemy because it forced temptation upon us as well as rules contrary to God's law, and once again I could only agree; as well as with Jesus' advice that we *be in the world but not part of the world*. Oh, I'd already got to know the world, and I hated all the works of Darkness almost as much as the priest who enumerated them did: addictions such as alcohol, drugs and gambling; the craving for money and all material evils; violence in the family and society; pornography, although he seemed to equate it one-to-one with the internet; prostitution, sodomy, swearing, envy, lies, and TV programmes which enslaved us to sex and the all-encompassing, insatiable urge for Pleasure. All these things kept the nation in a condition of perpetual adolescence and turned adolescents into morons.

That's not exactly how he phrased it, but I clearly read his thoughts and felt greater and greater closeness between us.

The rostrum was periodically taken over by fresh converts who testified to the perils of the wrong choice and the felicity of the right, based on their own experience. A particularly long talk was given by a fellow who introduced himself as having an MA in Sociology. Middle-aged, with mouselike eyes and a goatee he liked to stroke, he described his calvary, emphasising in particular the imperceptible ease of declining from a fine, upstanding young student to a follower of Satan. Every step seemed innocuous because the forces of darkness always disguise themselves as something attractive. Sex, marijuana, occultism, the internet, crime: he descended the whole ladder. And at the bottom, in his case, was yoga. Yes, it had to be clearly said: it was a *sect*, one of a growing number. They easily found victims, unfortunately, even among sincere Catholics, because this world smothered us in information and caused stress. We were ever more tired, ever more in search of a way out. So we clutched at the so-called *relaxation techniques* which they used to lure us, concealing their true goal: the destruction of our soul. He only realised this when they gave him the mantra *Hong-so* to repeat while meditating, which in translation meant *I am God*. This meant renouncing not only God, in whom we believed, who made us in his likeness and watched over us from above, but ultimately ourselves too. Because alleged meditation emptied people of their thoughts and feelings, of everything human, so they could unite with some abstract energy. In other words: give their soul to Satan.

He said all this much more intricately, with a host of dramatic effects. But the outcome for him had been intriguingly reminiscent of Ines's experience in the church with the picture of Jesus: he'd fallen to his knees and the tears had come all by themselves.

Different speakers focussed on different manifestations of the enemy: New Age, abortion, magic, clairvoyance, cloning, the combination of drug addiction and heavy metal, and in all that they saw one and the same source of Evil, that other pole of supernatural power. Everyone agreed that there existed only two possibilities, with a clear line in between: either you were on God's path, with a cross on your shoulder but truth in your eyes; or, in all other cases, you were a minion of Evil.

God loves us, we sang for three days, *God heals our wounds. God is calling us, God needs us, and we don't need anything except God's love.*

His love was a gift to us, but we still paid for it: the leading priest in charge of the seminar underscored this aspect in a Mass which formed the culmination of the seminar. God was watching us, he explained, and he required that we please him; not just with good behaviour – He also demanded sacrifices of us. To sacrifice didn't mean to give what was in surplus but to deprive oneself of what was most precious, to renounce precisely that. At this point I became concerned. What an enormous demand! Is that how God shows how much he loves us? What can I relinquish on his behalf? What do I have which is precious? What do I care about other than painting? Would it please him if I gave it up? Would he then take me to his bosom?

The leading priest illustrated the thesis with Jesus' praise for the woman who put a few paltry copper coins in the collection box at church after the others had poured in golden ones. Because the poor woman sacrificed far more for the Church than the rich did: her last coins. So there do exist protocols and scales of sacrifice? It's quantifiable, and the Church is here to keep accounts?

That was just the beginning of his argumentation. Next came the story of Abraham, which he personally considered one of the most beautiful in the Bible, he had to admit. He paused and showed us his angelic teeth. Joy blinked in his eyes behind his metal-rimmed glasses, and he suddenly looked like a rag doll or an amiable cartoon character in his brown hooded habit with the cord dangling at his side.

Because what could be greater than the sacrifice Abraham was prepared to make without a second's hesitation? To return to the Creator his only child, for whom he'd prayed for so long. His son! That devotion was an eternal model and source of inspiration for us all. We had good reason to consider Abraham the forefather of faith.

God, in his goodness, therefore demands that we be prepared to kill our own children for Him if he so requires. No one asks them what they think about it: their sacrifice is of no interest, only their father's. But the Pater, knitting his brows again, was quick to attack those who doubted God's intention and asked how he could demand such a terrible act, even if they knew God would stay Abraham's hand at the last. That doubt was the Serpent, he said, which had been among people ever since Adam's day. It incited them to pass judgement on God and reach out for powers which would put them on par with Him. Our serpentine tongue always said there was a knowledge higher than His. We had to resist the temptation of knowledge with all the strength we possessed.

I still couldn't withstand the temptation to think about the millions of poisonous snakes which crawl the earth, or all of God's other creations whose life depends on killing and devouring. Just what ecumenical mission did He entrust to His crocodiles and scorpions, or to the leeches, ticks and hookworms? And what of the bipeds, who started out as their epigones, only to rapidly surpass them and become the only species which kills not only for food but will also do it for the love of the editors at CNN?

Their advocate wasn't to be rattled. Leaning forward over the pulpit, his gaze fixed and transfixed every pair of eyes. He called on us to look deep inside and ask ourselves if we'd allowed ourselves to be led astray. Where were we heading? Who were we following?

I found no answer in the ensuing silence, nor would I today. If I really am heading anywhere, I can't imagine where or why. My thoughts slipped to the Abraham waiting for me at home, who, I could rest assured, wouldn't take me away anywhere on an ass. Nor show in any way that he cared I was alive, nor make an effort, at least during lunch, *not to groan* with every mouthful as if he'd been stabbed, and try not to chew whatever I cooked for him as if it were glass, leaning silently on his elbows and hypnotised by his suffering. It's all he has left, and he'll share it with me whole-heartedly until his dying day.

But, at the conclusion of Mass, the child burst through to the fore. After God's wrath had scorched Sodom and annihilated all those who had spoiled the earth, a sign was seen in the heavens, a woman clothed in the sun, with the moon beneath her feet, and on her head a crown of twelve stars. Being pregnant, she cried in the pains of birth; but another sign appeared, a fiery Dragon with seven heads and ten horns, the heavenly master of the Serpent, the seducer: Satan himself. Although his tail swept away the stars, he was unable to devour the son the woman bore because God had embraced the child, assigning him to bring life back to earth and to rule all peoples. The forces of Good cast out the Dragon because life always prevails. The woman also saved herself by fleeing into the wilderness.

All that wheeled around in my head while the little lamb Sara gambolled around on my lap, and a wilderness gaped on the other side of the table on the face of her mother.

Not even the Bible could elucidate for me exactly how the Dragon was vanquished. The angels overcame him by the blood of the sacrificed Lamb and the word of their testimony, and they scorned their own lives. I tried in vain to visualise the Dragon fleeing this in mortal fear.

After Mass, each of us received and swallowed a small piece of the Lamb's body from the hand of the Shepherd. I only wish I hadn't passed him just beforehand at the entrance to the toilets and noticed that he'd come out without washing his hands.

What made the seminar such a crowd-puller was saved up for the end. (Its popularity endures today, especially since its attracted pop singers and TV compères and the papers declared the Pater the best preacher in this part of the world. No stigmata appear on his forehead and it's hard to charge people for taking photos, but believers still come from far and wide to hear him.)

Everyone had to write a wish to Jesus on a little piece of paper and give it to one of the priests, who would include it in his prayer. Ines wrote: *Dear Jesus, please spare me all the blah about love. Just give me sex.* I sighed and gave her another piece of paper; then I read what she'd written: *Jesus, give me the strength to march on towards the Kingdom of Heaven like you've helped me get up out of the mud. Only You could have done that. Bravo, maestro!* I tore off the ending and gave it back to her, then I wrote something similar, though less ambitious, on my own piece of paper. The priests stood in line, the supplicants stepped up to them, and a body-builder in a T-shirt with the seminar's logo and the words *Teacher, let me see the light* stood behind each of them with arms outstretched. We immediately found out why: the priests placed their palms on the top of people's heads, prayed for them, and every single one of them fell unconscious; the colossi caught them and laid them on the floor like bundled sheaves of wheat. All this was done with speed and skill, with mechanical precision: as each new person knelt down, about to be laid tenderly on the ground, the person before them was already picking themselves up and moving aside, blissfully smiling.

Ines insisted I go first. The priest stood long immersed in my wish, although it was stunningly simple. Then he prayed, staring intently into my eyes, and scowling ever more because I didn't swoon like I was supposed to. He was the youngest of them and probably hadn't yet fully mastered the technique, but still I didn't feel like falling flat just to please him. In the end, he drew a cross in the air, released me and moved on to Ines. No sooner than he'd raised his hand and begun to murmur the prayer, she sagged. That wasn't just another performance. From the moment she got to her feet, and then unceasingly all the way home, she spoke of a burning heat which she still felt on the top of her head, together with an indescribable bliss.

She devoted the next few months to her transformation. She enrolled in catechism classes and was thoroughly infused with the Holy Ghost. It was picture perfect. For a while she even flirted with the idea of becoming a nun. At the same time she returned to uni, finished her degree, and in the end even got a job in a public-relations agency. She never touched synthetic opiates again.

She met Marko during one of the visits to the Pope, organised by the parish. What flared up between them in those few days was enough for him to leave the seminary and his vocation as priest. The marriage was a hurried affair, as was the embryo of family expansion, although not without resistance, especially from his large, poor and barely literate family. Marko was their pride and hope, and she'd ruined him; they never failed to remind her of that, and there was many an occasion because Marko stayed true to them and was always there to help, both emotionally and financially. On her side, things were not dissimilar: although it would be an exaggeration to say that her parents preferred her in her previous phase, they didn't conceal their contempt for her holy roller of a husband. But they didn't try to influence her choice and the lack of independence it revealed. They made it clear that she shouldn't reckon with their financial reserves, which they put into travelling and a comfortable retirement.

Ines counted on her grandfather's flat when he died, and for the time being they moved into a rented one. Deep down, and then ever more outwardly, she hoped that her parents might have pity on her after all, given her increasingly cramped circumstances. Each new child was meant to add to the pressure. Meanwhile, they enthusiastically consulted architects, bought interior-design magazines and accumulated furniture and designer objects. But her parents proved completely resistant and her grandfather exceptionally longevous. Even today, at over ninety, he'll hear nothing of an old people's home.

At the same time, her depression grew. That doesn't mean she broke with the Holy Ghost. On the contrary, crucifixes still cling to the walls and around her neck. But they don't work like before.

An attentive eye would have picked up the worrying signals she sent out even at the peak of religious exaltation. Maybe Marko needed precisely that – a soul he could lift up and drag out of despair day after day. He says he's never regretted giving up the vocation of priesthood. That sounds convincing, because in addition to his job at primary school he does most of the work at home. Ines worked until the intervals between her bouts of depression became ever shorter. It began after the birth of their first daughter: she developed a delicateness and hysterical attentiveness such as a daughter can only wish for. But whenever there was a lull in the demands on her, as soon the eyes of others were gone, she fell into a black hole. Food provided partial consolation, and gaining weight was an excuse for depression. But psychotherapy aided by medication achieved a realistic goal: it made her self-hatred easier to bear.

The whole family waved goodbye to me from the window, including Josip's little hand, held up in Marko's. So much *humanity* condensed in that illuminated rectangle. A fine drizzle wept down on my head through the mist, and puddles sloshed underfoot. The cold immediately crept under my coat, which I pressed in vain against my body.

At home, I sat down in front of the blank paper on the easel with the sole intention of smoking three or four cigarettes. But I was still sitting there when the first sounds of morning roused me, and all at once a mighty weariness descended on my shoulders. Without undressing, I just wrapped myself in my quilt. I was woken around midday by a presence in the room. A painting was watching me, intrusively and akimbo, in the middle of the space which it absolutely dominated; it was doubtlessly finished and complete, although I can't remember a single stroke. A winged dragon in black Indian ink inhabited the upper left-hand corner on a blank background. It had come from afar, and in its gruesome fangs it bore a baby, naked and freshly born but obviously already dead, its limbs pitifully limp. The whole right side of the painting was taken up by the figure of a woman. She too was naked, with sturdy legs, broad hips and bulging breasts, her elbows upraised as if in defence, but with absent, vacant eyes. Through the top of her head and her nest-shaped hair there showed another head with gaping jaws quite like a dragon's, but only smaller: the head of its hungry young which dwelt inside the woman's head.

*   *   *

I found work straight after uni. I would have contributed to the household budget earlier by getting a casual job on the side, but Mother wouldn't hear of it: nothing was allowed to distract me or slow me down on the path towards my degree, that crucial threshold in her life and mine, that achievement which would enable us to face Saint Peter without fear. My study years coincided with the war and Mother was unemployed; the piano lessons she gave in a few houses turned into cleaning jobs in others. We lacked money at that time even for the indispensible minimum of dignity, but dignity is one of those things you learn to do without when it's unattainable. After the war, when house owners began to compete with showy roof tiles, aluminium-framed windows and garages for more and more cars, our house ignored the upbeat trend of nouveaux-riches society, as if spiting it with the haughtiness of a bankrupt aristocrat. If our needs had moved beyond the most basic we would have been in a nasty dilemma, not knowing which repairs, replacements or emergency work to prioritise. But since everything was equally impossible to improve, we dug into the comfort of resignation, which deflated every problem and made it unreal. How we survived from day to day was incomprehensible, and that led us to think about the future flippantly, almost humoristically. That was incredibly liberating and took us a telescopic distance away from worldly things.

    I escaped having anything much to do with the war thanks to Mother. The idea of avoiding compulsory service in the Yugoslav People's Army evolved in my head half way through high school. I wasn't aware back then that military service was considered a patriotic act, nor did the Army know (or at least publicly state) that it would become Croatia's enemy within a year. I wasn't overly preoccupied with the plan and assumed that a bit of dramatic play-acting would suffice for the truth about me to shine through: that I was a faulty human product unfit to be stored in a confined space with the healthy ones. But the recruitment commission – one guy in uniform, one in a white coat, and a lady with hair permed like a fur hat – weren't convinced of the dangerousness of my symptoms and sent me for 'observation'. Instead of being able to go home with some certificate or other, this meant that I was immediately imprisoned in a room with six beds in the company of five characters whose state of mind was... well, I won't go into that. What distinguished them from me was that they belonged voluntarily to a military machine which had put them in hospital for therapy because of various acts of violence in barracks and public houses. They were united in the delight with which they awaited me – a new toy to help them while away the day, and particularly the night. My arrival put a new lease of life into this clique of junior officers and excited a waggish sadism in them which most people grow out of in puberty. Men like this were undoubtedly in their element several months later, howitzering besieged towns and cities.

I don't know how long they planned to 'observe' me for, but Mother found me the next day. They only condescended to hear her out after much shouting in the corridors. Whatever she told them about me behind closed doors, or they concluded about her, the result was that the guy in the white coat came in with a look of concern and announced that I could go. That had a twofold advantage: not only did I elude the army of occupation when it was stocking up on young cannon fodder for its criminal assault, but the army of liberation didn't take an interest in me either.

The war lasted for some time, the front pages of the papers left no doubt about that. It was constantly vigilant on the radio; as soon as Mother turned it on, it would start to count shells, maimed children and knocked-out enemy tanks, and she would nod with a smile of pity like an anthropologist whose dark hypotheses were coming true before her eyes. Now and then it also left its marks on the lamp-posts in our neighbourhood in the form of black-framed obituary notices, and with some of them I had to go to the grave, throw in a handful of earth and drink a glass of *rakija* while squeezed between family and relatives at a table with a candle burning. I had to listen to stories about me and the now-dead Tomo coming back all muddy from gathering chestnuts when we were boys, ho-ho-ho, and keep quiet about the fact that I'd never gathered chestnuts, and endure the looks that said *Why are you not at the front too?* and *Why is he dead and you alive*?

But such things could only ever touch me superficially, devoted student that I was, immersed in deep structure, allophones, enclitics and catalysts, with a diligence just waiting to be rewarded. And my lucky number came up: I was invited to a job interview, with a reference from a lecturer under my belt.

The lecturer was a relative of the employer, who had returned from the diaspora several years before to support the progress of his native country with his capital and business acumen. He'd acquired both abroad, trying his hand in a whole range of fields, from catering to purchasing tamburitzas for his emigrant clientele. Then he became a sales representative of a Korean car-parts producer for all of Eastern Europe. Once he'd built up a commercial empire for himself with a glitzy headquarters in Stuttgart, he was able to devote himself to noble deeds for the good of Croatia. But what exactly? It wasn't yet modern at that time to do what is seemly for a man of his calibre: to run for president. Besides, he revered and loved the president too much to want to threaten his rule – you revere and love the hand which has fed you since it found you lost and alone in the wilds. The first thing I saw, which was the first thing everyone had to see when they entered his office, was the portrait on the wall right above his armchair (with jacaranda armrests and the leather of some sophisticated animal) and his desk: the president expressing his famous, cheesy charm through the gap formed by his drooping lip. And whenever and for whatever reason you entered the Boss's office – we only ever called him *Boss*, although he never explicitly requested it – you had to think twice what to say because you were actually addressing the two of them; the top boss refrained from commenting but proctored every conversation with his strict eyebrows, and when our Boss signalled for you to go he would gently and proudly lower his hand for you to kiss.

In short, someone prompted him that it would be noble and wise to invest his capital and know-how in publishing. That was a God-given time for publishers, especially of school textbooks, because so much material needed to be redevised – history, language and our centuries-old spiritual heritage, and particularly for those publishers who fought their way up to the altar of New Knowledge and came together with important catechists. The Boss was very sociable and loquacious, with a broad smile and hands. Nor were books foreign to him: there were always one or two on his desk in case he had a free moment between his innumerable appointments and phone calls. He even tried his hand at poetry back in his student days (though he never once mentioned the name of the institution which earned him this attribute) and, persuaded by our chief editor (about whom I'll gladly say something later), he dug up those works of romantic and patriotic inspiration and published them in a volume which formed the basis of our *Poesis rediviva* series, although it was not followed by any other titles. The book was beautifully illustrated by a well-known Croatian artist and given an inspired presentation by a member of the Academy of Sciences and Arts at the launch held at The Croatian Centre. National TV news reported on the event, and the daily paper *Večernji list* dedicated a whole page to it with a brilliant review by a prominent critic, which today hangs framed on the wall of the Boss's office together with the legendary presidential lip.

But let us return to our first conversation, to the time when all I knew about him was that he was the manager of an ascendant publishing house famous above all for its textbooks, which had swept away the competitors, undoubtedly owing to their superior quality. All he knew about me was that I had a degree in German and Phonetics, had demonstrated talent in postgraduate study of literature, and had undoubtedly asked myself how I could turn that talent to gold. Theoretically, he could have left the interviewing to someone else, but it turned out that he didn't even let others design Christmas cards or order paper clips, be it due to the confidence he had in his own aesthetic criteria or because he feared others could do deals to line their own pockets. After all, there was no one at the firm in charge of human resources or any kind of planning, and the only rung of the hierarchy between him and the ever more numerous staff was a persona he called the Chief Editor. But the fellow suffered from a strange communication disorder: he never looked at the person he was speaking with, took every rebuttal as an attack on his integrity, and then backed away and thought feverishly about what you *could have meant*. If you entered his office he would make a pained face, immediately start compulsively looking at his watch, reach for the mouse and read mails with one eye, reply purely with *yes, yes*, successfully turning you into a piece of furniture miraculously endowed with a mouth, which you opened for a moment longer like a fish out of water, and then withdrew, finally aware of your own nullity.

Regardless of their different titles, everyone employed at the firm ended up doing everything, except for the Boss's wife in the office with the plaque *Technical Director*, who didn't do anything. Although she could have done that equally well at home, let's not underestimate the need of the human being, that social animal, to be surrounded by other animals of the same species. The Boss's daughter was also 'employed' at the firm, so to speak; she turned up periodically when she had nothing more entertaining to do, once as Finance Manager, another time as the editor of a children's book; what she did best was jetting around to visit book fairs throughout Europe. Everyone else blundered around in others' work, improved it according to their momentary inspiration or redid it; usually they were unable to complete their own and left it to be discovered weeks later by whoever took a fancy, or to be embraced by oblivion.

A foreign publisher once sought the rights for a book we'd published and brilliantly marketed two years earlier. The cover image of a different book was shown in our web shop by mistake, and the assiduous buyer tried in vain to organise things over the phone; two months later the books turned up in our stockroom – a thousand copies, still packed. At one launch two catering firms turned up. At another, the author didn't appear because no one had informed him of the change of date. A third was attended only by the author and the presenters because the promotional material had been sent by van to Rijeka instead of Osijek. We had many and varied series, but since the editor of medical dictionaries also loved literature, the occasional novel which touched on medical matters in some oblique way also slipped in among them. Most of our titles were translated from foreign languages which the editors, intriguingly, usually didn't speak; most often the translations were checked by their wives, sisters, mothers or – even better – by a relative with a different surname, a family friend or neighbour. Some manuscripts *were* edited properly: twice in parallel, on two different printouts, in two adjacent offices. The colleagues might have told each other if they hadn't had a complete falling-out long before due to some tactless comment. The graphic designers were keen to improve linguistic style and throw out sentences they found redundant. The artwork for the jacket was discussed from the accounting section to the stockroom and everyone's opinion was equally relevant, all the more because no one in their right mind would engage the services of a professional designer, so arrogantly overpriced; finally, two or three delegations presented their separately perfected visions to the Boss, and he compiled the most successful elements and regularly arbitrated in favour of his own version because design was his secret passion – to the joy of all the city's art critics and those who consider themselves such.

The amorphous organism of the firm pulsed to the rhythm of the Boss's capricious, boundless appetites, which saw that ever more picturesque landscapes of human wisdom were annexed, from gardening to chess, from statesmen's biographies to entomology. Magazines were started up, printing companies, binderies and trade-fair stalls purchased, and new bookshops were opened up to take over the country foot by foot. New recruits were deployed, though not as a response to demands and occasional cries for help from the rank and file but rather when the Boss had inspiration for an injection of fresh blood – just as he felt from time to time that a particular staff member was no longer needed, for example because of their inappropriate clothing habits. The employees always struggled to keep up with the burgeoning volume of work; newcomers were strung out between several sections, and depending on the urgency of the tasks at hand they packed book orders, negotiated with agents, made coffee or wrote blurbs.

But let us try and go back to the conversation which preceded all this knowledge about the firm. It wasn't an easy interview because talk of allophones and enclitics wouldn't help us much; the Boss had heard of catalysts but only in an automotive context; in short, it was best not to mention phonetics at all. Instead, he picked on German, which isn't a particularly fertile topic, so he transformed it into a means: he asked me *wann ich geboren bin, und wo, und was ich im Krieg getan habe, und was ich sonst so gemacht habe, und ob ich katholisch bin*. He was satisfied with all my replies and cheerfully noted them in his memo book with a golden fountain pen. He didn't stop grinning even when a pause ensued, which he filled by puffing on his cigar. At the same time he deep-scanned me with crafty eyes – he had remarkable extrasensory perception – and just one further question sufficed. What were my expectations in terms of salary? And when I told him I hadn't thought about that, the big boss up on the wall said *Gut, gut, nimm ihn*. We sealed the mutual rapport with a handshake, but I almost spoiled the grand occasion by knocking the cigar out of his hand with a clumsy movement. He quickly picked it up and looked at it apprehensively for a moment, but he overcame his disgust – the cigar was expensive and he'd just started it. Neither did he toss me out, and I stayed at the firm for almost nine years.

The decision to take me on, which I vindicated with absolute submissiveness and an impeccable performance in everything required of me, was most correct, like almost all his decisions. Such business instinct can't be learnt at management school – you're either born with it or you're wasting your time. In the space of just a few years he built up one of the most respectable publishing houses in the country from almost nothing. What I call 'almost nothing' was a body which had grown on the humus of Yugoslav self-managed socialism; it printed the doctorates of labour-movement theoreticians, monographs of prizewinning artists, ballot papers and the like. One day the employees were informed of a change of ownership, and several days later they were out of a job. Only the manager stayed on; though soon he too 'retired'. However, he made sure to drop in once a month for many years to come and invoice for obscure services which helped the firm to flourish. There were rumours that he was close to the Government Commission for Textbooks, but without any firm evidence.

Textbooks were needed, of course: the Boss bought up the rights for those the Commission had rejected and then accepted after all. Money was also needed to print them: the Boss had some great contacts at a newly-founded bank, which vanished into thin air soon after opening generous credit lines. Above all, one needed hard-working staff: he creamed off the best from rival firms, masterfully arguing that it was better in his, if necessary emphasizing that it was worse elsewhere, and he could also go off on the tack of *If you don't want to, there's a crowd of others who do*. His best achievements were in the related field of forcing down the price of labour; he was able to intricately gauge how little he dared to pay for someone's service and still have them agree to do it. Only because justice is rare in this world did he miss out on receiving an honorary doctorate from the Employers' Association.

I've never met another person who could lie so naturally and ardently, with all their heart. With the average and even the advanced liar, what's concealed or fabricated always shows through in the flicker of an eyelid, a minute dilation of the pupils or a twitch of the lips faster than a hummingbird's wings; but the Boss was able to pronounce the most transparent untruth and remain plastically smiling from ear to ear, like Jack Nicholson in the role of the Joker. In that way, he would win people's favour, or at very least leave them speechless. But with him it wasn't a conscious perversion of the truth; rather, his consciousness spontaneously produced whatever suited the demands of the moment, and his ingenuity and eloquence truly came to the fore when presenting reasons why he couldn't pay a penny more for something.

From time to time, a pretentious editor would have the cheek to claim that his self-sacrificing commitment had been exploited. A puerile author would come up with the idea of asking exactly how many copies of his book had been sold. A grotesque translator would suddenly find the rate of pay an insult to his intelligence, that he ought to be paid for the spaces between words too, or that six months waiting for payment was too long, or that he was entitled to royalties on subsequent editions. But even after the troublemaker had surrendered, the Boss continued to pound away with arguments and explain in endless detail how heinous his demand was, and what a threat to the integrity of the firm, the dignity of the publishing profession and all the efforts to advance the community as a whole. Did this ungrateful employee's egoism prevent him from seeing that yielding to one individual's unreasonableness would be the first stone of an avalanche which would to come down and crush the tender young plant of his publishing business? That others similar to him would then throng in, not caring if their avarice meant that a kid went without a picture book, a single mother without her child allowance or a Croatian war veteran without antidepressants? The grumbler would then of course repent, forego the outstanding money, and ask if he could help the publishing house with a loan.

Be it because of this talent or other qualities, he was appointed assistant to the Minister of Culture, specifically for the Publishing and Literary Heritage strand. This didn't significantly change the routine of his work since he carried out the ministerial mission mainly from his office. What did change, however, was the image of the firm: our editions became more splendid, our launches as well. They soon grew into first-class cultural events, epicentres of glamour which flooded the country. Not to attend them would have been suicidal for anyone who cared about their literary stature – for every aspirant to the intellectual elite it would have meant marginalisation, exile and annihilation. The only thing that could temporarily save you from sinking into oblivion, into the distant past, was the lens of a big-name photographer brushing you just when you were toasting with the mayor, an art historian or a plastic surgeon at the launch of the *Encyclopaedia of Mushrooms* or *What Is My Dog Thinking?*

After conquering the textbook market, the Boss's restless spirit turned to the literature most precious to the nation in those post-war years: books on esoterics, astrology, psychological self-help, and handbooks for gaining one's first million and immigration visas for overseas countries. It was a real heyday, with people buying our books even if they could scarcely afford bread. And each edition, on the second-last page, thanked the Ministry of Culture for its generous support.

But still the Boss renounced a political career and channelled his surplus creative energy into working with the Government Commission for Supporting the Book Sector. That brought yet another gust of wind to our already straining sails; the number of series multiplied and the catalogues blossomed. The costs of printing – in our own printing company – reached dizzying heights, but that didn't bother the Commission or the libraries which placed the orders.

At the same time, our publishing house devoted itself more to fine literature, above all that of Croatian authors. This was for patriotic motives, needless to say, but also because their works didn't need to be translated or the rights bought from foreign publishers. Many didn't even need to be paid because it was the peak of their aspiration to see their name on the cover, ideally with a colour photograph. Moreover, many were prepared to pay for this themselves, or they found a sponsor in their spouse, a successful Croatian firm or their local parish. But government providence radically altered the situation; soon it was no longer a problem to print a book but to find enough authors in whom to invest all the subsidies which the Commission showered on the publishers.

Even if there had been space further up in the firm's hierarchy, I personally wouldn't have got far in my nine years there; I lacked the crucial assets of idealism and enthusiasm. For the first few years I sincerely strove to justify the trust which had been placed in me: that mainly meant correcting the texts on my desk as best I could, within the narrow bounds of the permissible. I didn't feel a need to produce any writing of my own, either then or beforehand. Every day, across all meridians, parallels and diagonals, more and more new texts accumulate on top of the billions already written since humanity has been around. That thought alone is terribly taxing; why should one add anything, and to what end? But whatever arrived on my desk didn't need to be plucked from the void or rescued from the brink of the chambers of superfluity. Here evidently was an author who had gathered sufficient self-love for the feat, and the result strutted before me, magnificently real and blatantly irrefutable. I would grab hold of it like a cherished anchorage, perhaps the last relic of terra firma in the great flood of indefiniteness, revelation and dissolution – that orgy of despair which longed to lift its disguise and would soon need no more pretexts to show itself in its full glory.

It was a mute and gratuitous despair, inexplicable even

when you consider everything people come up with, and all the more destructive. It arose as soon as I'd assured myself a place in the community of diligent citizens, as soon as my immersion in that terribly real world was complete.

For a time, the bulwarks of manuscripts kept the despair at bay. I lived beneath them like in a greenhouse, hibernating under paper membranes. Through them, I watched the universe above me; it stretched into unknown expanses far away, exhilarating and infinite, whereas my role was to keep the pieces together down here – the delicate spots in complex sentences like conjunctions, word order, spelling, commas... To tighten the strings where they were loose and to do the fine tuning of their tick-tocking. I loved my vocation of text mechanics and the focussing of my gaze on ever tinier parcels of the world, its written relics. In an age of universal expansion, where continents were busy colliding and distant galaxies called us to boldly go where no one had gone before, I picked around at paper fossils, examining their texture with magnifying glass and microscope. I would gladly have disassembled every single letter into atoms and meditated endlessly on all its molecular bonds. I was untouchable and myself on the path to disintegration into subatomic oblivion behind the sign *Work in progress. Do not disturb.*

But the atmosphere at the firm more resembled a beehive besieged by wasps; everything was always behind schedule, literally everything, and the blame for this state of affairs forever hung in the air like a guillotine ready to fall, inflaming hysteria and chaos, reciprocal accusations and threats. We were constantly seeking a lost diskette or envelope, at the very least a cigarette lighter, and this sometimes led to the mobilisation of the entire staff; new manuscripts came in by the hour, hot on each other's heels. In brief, the circumstances weren't favourable to meditation; I was expected to deliver results in my proof-reading. On the other hand, it didn't take me long to realise that the objective could be achieved by declaring the text ready to print. Not only did no one check how much work was behind this announcement, and not only was there no authority capable of gauging the value of that work: it was damaging and even dangerous to correct others' work, even in the case of glaring mistakes or plagiarism, because sooner or later it would come out. Everyone prefers their own mistake to being corrected by others. It just provoked fury and made enemies who thirsted for revenge. The writer, for whom you puttied up gaping holes in his pieces for primary-school textbooks, became an enemy (they were actually stylistic flourishes, he said). As did the translator who gave free rein to his fantasy whenever he encountered something he didn't understand, hoping no one else would either. Or the translation editor who happily sacrificed meaning and common sense on the altar of grammatical correctness, and as a sworn follower of orthographical orthodoxy, barricaded behind rows of dictionaries, would defend any madness as if they were his own children.

Therefore I devoted all my efforts to furthering mutual respect and friendship. Whatever the hand of the translation editor touched I considered flawless. I saw no need to denounce the translator who forgot he wasn't the author of the original. There was one who freely added ideas of his own whenever he thought something was missing. Another used footnotes to record his associations, or particularly interesting everyday events. A third attached an apology to his translations for omitting whole sentences in some places because of the chronic headaches which crippled his concentration. Another translator was working on several projects at once and sometimes got them mixed up; the encyclopaedia of contemporary architecture contained some passages of theological debate. And why not, when everything is interrelated? With or without them, I was pretty sure the world out there wouldn't perceive any difference; I just checked to make sure no commas were missing. And every instance like that confirmed what I expected: not one single reader complained.

But the domestic Literati certainly did: we'd ruined their book, and our shameful indolence was to blame for only seventeen copies having been sold; the critics had picked on it to vent their frustrations; an evidently illiterate idiot had snatched the prize from beneath their noses; they hadn't been invited to take part in the talk-show although they'd won it, and because the whole literary scene behaved as if it was none of their business and irrelevant; the book's key statement unmasking all that hypocrisy and falsehood once and for all had been edited out; the apparatchiks had prevented them from being internationally successful; their collected works had still not been issued, in a leather binding impregnated against ageing; a monument still hadn't been erected to them here in their home country; they had a creative block of many years' duration and were calling the editors for no particular reason to kill time until the next tide of inspiration came; we'd treated their manuscript with criminal negligence, and why, oh why was there no room for a quality book like theirs, given all the shit we'd published?

Our country may be small, but it can pride itself on having so many Literati. In terms of membership, their associations need not fear comparison with telephone books. Moreover, some of them have produced several books each. Not that anyone reads those books, but one likes to talk about them, especially if they're exemplary in demonstrating the author's feeblemindedness, vulgarity, betrayal of national interests, or even more far-reaching evils.

It turned out that my greatest talent, my most valuable

contribution to the firm, lay precisely in the domain of communication with the Literati and other collaborators. Something about me encourages even complete strangers to confide in me and tell me their innermost feelings, and our staff recognised that. Regardless of whether they had outstanding claims against us or owed us money, people clearly preferred to discuss the situation with me, often as a package deal involving an exhaustive case history and explanation of the side effects, which took up most of my working time.

At the firm they were dubbed *patients*. Once a colleague, just to be witty, put one through to me unannounced in the middle of a long discussion I was having on the other phone about a translation, late but almost finished, which burglars had made off with together with the translator's computer. Soon all such calls were routinely transferred to me as soon as the patients had introduced themselves.

My docility and pliancy could turn into servility if required; I wasn't proud of it, but nor did I interrupt what they considered necessary to tell me. Some preferred to come in and see us rather than talking on the phone, to sit down in an armchair and explain, sometimes for hours, the multifarious ordeals they went through to feed the family plus the children from their previous marriage and to afford their mistress a liposuction in the hope that it would cure their insomnia. I learnt the patterns which made up the mosaic of their depression and the odds for their liver, which charlatans had already written off twice. Some kept a bottle in the filing cabinet, and in it dwelt their decades-old animosity due to an article which ruined their career right at the very beginning, before it had properly started. Then there was the unhappy romance with a Russian beauty which had lasted only as long as the post-modernism symposium by Lake Baikal or Lake Balaton, or was it in Bratislava? The magnificent live-poetry episode in Brazil, where their verses drew rousing ovations from capacity grandstands at the Maracanã...

Some patients opened newspapers and, with a satyric smile, admiring their own lucidity and wit, gave themselves over to the passion for dissecting and glossing the world. With others, the mask of politeness unsuccessfully concealed that they'd actually come to glean information about their rivals and enemies, to search for a trace of a conspiracy, the behind-the-scenes dealings which caused them so much torment. Some, when no one took note of them any more, stayed sitting like wax figures, their arms crossed and mouth pouting like abortive decorations angry at their maker.

I must admit that, despite the stress, occasional friction and hostility, it was an agreeable and stimulating environment to work in; people liked to spend time there. There was always something going down: a scandal from the life of another publisher, a freshly unearthed scam, a public debacle, or at least someone getting dirty in a mudslinging match. My colleagues never lacked hidden illnesses, domestic tragedies or symptoms which prompted us to elaborate diagnoses. A family spirit of mutual care prevailed. Problems to do with keeping pets and children were resolved in working groups. If a female colleague had her period, or the onset of her period was delayed, everyone knew by morning coffee. Whatever delicate matters someone mentioned on the phone were retold almost simultaneously in the other wing of the building.

Everyone contributed to this vivacity in their own way. Some ladies developed a peculiar sort of humour among themselves which consisted in imitating children's speech: talking with squeaky voices, mispronouncing things, saying *l* instead of *r*, calling out to each other from one end of the corridor to the other, usually for no reason, and all the more if someone had asked them to stop or blew their top at them.

The colleague at the desk next to mine listened to the same cassette of his favourite soft-rock artist at least once a day; it disappeared, of course, but the next morning he came in with a new one; then of course the cassette player was sabotaged, so from then on he carried it around with him. Another guy had the secret passion for breaking wind as soon as others left the room. But it happened that someone came back in soon after the crime. This would be embarrassing for both of them and he would turn bright red. But it didn't prevent relapses.

Although tight-fisted in his business dealings, the Boss was never miserly when it came to the satisfaction of his extended family. At the very least, he endeavoured to stimulate our work ethic in ways he considered appropriate. That didn't include frills such as air-conditioning, hot water for washing hands or paid overtime, but instead he used every opportunity to turn work into a party. We celebrated each step in the development of the firm and would come together in the meeting room at the end of the day to mark the occasion with a little feast. The Boss would order wine by the canister, a roast suckling pig, and sometimes a lamb as well. Music was put on, and often there was singing. This merrymaking was tacitly considered a work commitment, and to excuse oneself, even on the pretext of an illness in the family, was risky.

One of these occasions dragged on until late evening. People needed to be driven home; I took two. One was a lady from Accounts shortly before retirement, who was rumoured to be a lesbian, but maybe that was just because she lived alone. The other had been in Marketing for two or three years, and that's also how much older than me she was; that was all I knew about her. She'd glanced at me several times with eyes that could have meant something, but that didn't mean she had her sights set on me – she looked at others that way too.

Bashful snowflakes had appeared that afternoon, and now the snow was falling in thick clumps. The lady from Accounts lived close by; now we were heading slowly for the suburb where the other lived, at the opposite end of the city to me.

The wipers were working flat out, but tons of the white stuff descended as if it intended to stop all movement. No one could be seen in the streets, just the occasional stray headlights like will-o'-the-wisps. The radio played American lullabies from the fifties, one after another, with velvet voices and violins.

As we got closer, I reflected on the possibility. I didn't find her particularly attractive in any way. She wore clothes which were probably those recommended in women's magazines, but they regularly looked wrong on her. Her mouth was always brightly lipsticked and looked like a warning sign. She spoke too loud and her laugh was somehow artificial, coming at peculiar moments like a hiccup and showing the gap between her two top front teeth, which some were sure to find charming. As we drove she was constantly fussing around with her tresses, plucking at them in search of hairs which had fallen out. With each hair she found she would first straighten it out, meticulous and frowning, then roll it between thumb and forefinger into a neat little ball, put it down on the floor and start all over again. The instinct to beg her not to do it any more became ever more urgent.

Still, when she asked me in front of the building if I'd like to pop up for a coffee, I said *Sure*. Instead of looking for her keys, she rang. A boy of roughly ten opened the door. She said she would just put him to bed. I asked if I could use the phone.

I should actually have been thinking about the possibility of a polite withdrawal. The flat was tidy, even disturbingly so:

pedantically neat, without a single thing where it didn't belong, without crockery left in the sink to drip dry, without a speck of dust. That brought back unpleasant memories and claustrophobia. I went to the window; the snow had become one of those winter wonders you wish will never stop once they've set in so well. It looked far too strenuous to go out.

When I declared to Mother that I didn't know when I'd be getting back and that she shouldn't wait up for me, she gave a snort of disdain and hung up without seeking an explanation. *Go and get snowbound if you're too dumb to come home on time*, she thought, and washed her hands of it.

Except for at work, we saw each other exclusively at her flat. Six months? A year? That time is lost beneath the snow. I only know that we never once went out together; out relationship wasn't of that kind.

I did go out with her son, though. I took him to the pictures and ice-skating – I even tried myself for the first time – and once to his recital at music school. He played the bassoon most brilliantly, his teacher said; she was really glad to have met me because she'd heard a lot about me. In fact, he and I really became close friends. He was exceptionally well-behaved, quiet and a little timid, and outside he held my hand.

I saw a photo of his father. He'd never seen his son but only heard his voice over the phone on some of his birthdays. His mother saw him for the first time at a party, they'd had a lot to drink, and he later claimed not to remember anything. She was booked in for an abortion, but in the waiting room she suddenly got up and went home. After the boy was born, the father showed a few signs of good will and then refrained from any further efforts because he didn't have strength enough even for his own life. He was studying film direction, punctuated by periods of intensive drug-taking. I recognised him on television a few years later as the co-author of a prizewinning omnibus film; and a few years later still, in a discarded news-paper while waiting to board the plane which took me out of the country: the photo showed him being taken into custody after robbing a foreign exchange office.

No one at work knew we were seeing each other. Perhaps she was ashamed of it, perhaps she wasn't; we pretended by tacit agreement that nothing was going on. Why exactly did she choose me? Because I didn't show any outward signs of interest? Possibly she was seeing others at the same time; I didn't ask. I went to her place when she called me, two or three evenings a week, sometimes with intervals of ten days or so. Gradually the relationship turned into a kind of friendship. On some evenings she preferred to chat on the phone; in the end, we just watched television together at her place. She kept calling from time to time, without saying why, but you could hear the solitude washing over her in those moments and her going under. She carried quite a bag of blackness along with her, whatever was inside; we didn't touch on those things.

Some conversations were difficult, punctuated by inter-mittent sighs and long silences; in others, she talked about her admirers. About one of our colleagues from the firm who didn't know the meaning of *no*, although the police had twice prevented him from spending the night at her door. About the man she'd met over the internet who sent her a one-way ticket to Cape Town. About the one who'd sent her a bunch of tulips every birthday since high school. About the university lecturer who would drop his wife and three children at her single word. About the high official in the Ministry of Defence who was gay and offered her marriage for appearances' sake. About a chair of a board of directors, voted Manager of the Year, his villa with five-metre banana trees and his insistence that she sexually abuse him. About the crime-column editor of a daily paper and the weekend spent with him in Vancouver.

About the extreme-sport enthusiast who introduced her to hot-air balloons and paragliding. I'm sure that at least part of it all was true.

Our relationship ended for good when she resigned from the firm without warning or explanation. She didn't call me, but then again I didn't call her.

That's how much I knew about love when I met you.

* * *

My first love. That's what went through my mind when I saw him this morning on the way to Father's. His eyes met mine as soon as I got out of the tram. There was an unrecognisable ambience in them but they hadn't aged a day. They were still that same watery blue and had the same boyish simple-mindedness in them. An immunity to any complicated thoughts. He'd been the hero of several volumes of women's diaries and the main demon in the nightmares on his male counterparts. Or a role model unattainable because of his cool conceitedness undergirded with tragedy. This was based mainly on the reputation of his elder brother, with his police file and time in various correctional institutions. He himself hadn't collided with the law, but he had an irresistible talent for reflecting outlawishness in his eyes and showing the romantic suffering it brought him. He wore it so photogenically.

As a girl, I was long dazzled by that look. And when finally he met me in the dark one time and told me he just happened to be going the same way, how special I felt! I trembled with excitement as if I was the chosen one. As we walked towards home, I felt that something terribly exciting was happening which would mark me for the rest of my life. There was ample opportunity for that because he only occasionally muttered a few words. That increasingly became a problem over our next few encounters because the only topic which interested him were his brother's exploits and the paper-tiger imitations of his own. The rest of the time was consumed by awkwardness and a nascent boredom. But these were drowned out by the chorus of my exalted peers. And so I finally asked him if he'd like to kiss me. But of course!

That was the goal of the operation – remuneration in gold for one who had endured so much hassle!

I was thirteen, he fourteen. Both of us invested great effort in our first kiss to make up for not yet knowing how. We didn't relent even when the saliva was running down our faces and our jaws cramped up. We may not have been having sex but we certainly showed no lack of passion. He fumbled around to unbutton my shirt and slipped his hand inside but quickly pulled it out again, probably to spare me the shame of such futile groping. When we were worn out we stopped for a breather and then repeated the exercise. That's how the next two or three dates turned out too, and we realised it was hopeless. Even with the best will in the world, there was nothing with which to fill the gaps between our exchanges of spit.

All that I'd heard about him until this morning was that he got married straight after high school. I saw him as he was carrying crates of empty beer bottles out of the shop. He still sported the remains of poetically flowing locks, despite his now bear-like frame. His blue overalls nicely accentuated his eyes. They rested on me for an instant as if a memory had come alive, and he put down the crates he'd been carrying, clapped the dust off his hands and came across the street... straight to one of those tin kiosks where *joie de vivre* babbles and morning self-confidence is downed by the half-pint. Who knows how far his brother made it – to Lepoglava prison or to a high position in government.

I was met by the smell of burned milk. Grime crackled underfoot like fine glass. The kitchen was chilled and the windows wide open, but bitter smoke still filled the air. Father lay sprawled on the couch, his eyes riveted to the ceiling and his face covered in tears.

'There's nothing more for me,' he moaned, his whole body lifeless, 'they can come and take me away now.'

His jumper was covered with grease spots and the bottoms of his trouser legs were encrusted with dried mud.

'Come on now,' I said, wiping the milk up off the floor and then scrubbing the stove with a sponge. 'It doesn't work like that. You don't get taken away when you want to be.'

How many little old ladies with rosaries in their hands send prayers to heaven day after day and still end up waiting for years. Theoretically, instead of lying on the couch I could have found him hanging from a rope, but he's not like that. Every morning he carefully counts out his daily serving of tablets and replenishes supplies as soon as they start running low. He hangs onto that butt-end of life if only to show how much he despises it. He hates doctors because they don't listen to him – understandably so, because whoever sees him a few times knows off by heart what he's going to say. They also remind him of the unlikely truth that he suffers most of all from old age and knowing he'll never be a day younger.

I did the mountain of washing up. I asked why Vera hadn't come, the woman who occasionally did the cleaning. He'd forgotten to call her. It was the same with flushing the toilet, he forgets that too, and he forgets to change his underwear before it goes mouldy. He *hadn't* forgotten to turn off the radiators. Every visit, I turn them on, but in vain: the next time I find the house as cold as a cave again. In the cold it's easier for him to revel in how rotten he feels.

I changed the bedlinen. He'd managed to soil it too, with patches of different colours, and there were crumbs of food as well. Here he trains hard for the final, and that makes him famished. As soon as he forgets it, he loses his appetite and remembers to start groaning again. When his last moment comes, bringing ultimate relief and salvation, he'll want to put it off for a minute so he can groan just a little more. Best of all to spectators, because otherwise it's not worth it. I must admit I'm a poor audience – I neither clap nor cry. But talk about faithful! I've watched the same performance year in, year out without protest.

Then again, what medical or legal authority can certify the legitimacy of suffering and the line beyond which its reality ceases? What person can undo what they see as the only reality: that everything is dead, along with them? How naive it was of me to hope that he would at least occasionally look up and be different, that he could snap out of it for a moment just to satisfy me, out of possible love for his child.

I asked him how his eyes were. I could tell he was having trouble with them. The cataracts were advancing like a blitzkrieg. But he wouldn't hear of an operation. How enthusiastic he'd once been about medicine – the human body had interested him as much as humans' buildings. His vocation had been to plan the uprightness of concrete structures, but his amateur passion was now learning how to demolish the architecture of the body. He liked to demonstrate his knowledge of the diseases of every organ with the zeal of an unrealised lecturer. If you inform yourself well about the enemy, they'll withdraw in fear. As far as the brain was concerned, he believed there were no areas inaccessible to another brain – that you could see it like a ground plan and redesign it with a skilful pencil.

I remember the photograph he procured for me of lungs eaten away by cancer: lifesize and in colour. That was after the educational episode with the fisticuff lesson in sexual medicine for under-age girls. The result was perhaps a little disappointing for him: I didn't beg for absolution but lit up a cigarette in front of him the next day. Although that was a clear opportunity for him to teach me another lesson by the same method, instead he decided to get terribly offended at me razing his didactic edifice to the ground. He didn't speak to me for three days, but then he found a way of converting me – with that photograph. Lovely! I had it framed and hung it over my bed. There's nothing like certitude. How practical it is to know what you're going to die of rather than to live in fear of everything that can endanger your life. Until then I'd only smoked a few cigarettes and had to force myself. But now smoking took on a higher purpose and I decided to overcome my aversion. Before the end of year eight I was on a packet a day, and soon I was fuming a lot more.

Father took my upbringing rather personally. He considered me one of his projects, just as important, in fact, as those which he submitted for national awards and sometimes won. He had his certificates framed and hung them by the glass showcase in the living room. When the educational moment arrived, he would sit me on his knee; later I sat beside him almost as his equal. He would clear his throat and proceed to lecture me, in a solemn voice, about making use of one's life, not forgetting to cite himself as an example. The vocabulary evolved together with my ability to assimilate it, but was based on the same essential truths unchanged since my pre-school days: life passes tragically fast and you need to seize it by the reins, he told me. You have to be able to appreciate that gift and fill it with meaning through your own work. You have to give your utmost because only the diligent survive. You need to have a clear goal in front of you, go straight into its embrace, and you have to do this and have to do that. These guiding thoughts were supposed to settle and form firm foundations in me. He wanted them to continually fascinate me, so he periodically refreshed them, even in the days when my schoolfriends and I would air our heads with glue in plastic bags after class, or on the eve of the holidays.

That one time he replaced his lecture with a beating, the result was indeed enormous. I made a firm decision that it wouldn't happen again. And more broadly, that I wasn't going to take shit from anyone any more.

He never mentioned my sexual rights again. Of course, I kept seeing the boy I lost my virginity with. How quaint that sounds. I lost it, and in return I gained lifelong guilt, having betrayed paternal love with my genitals. Your virginity is gone and now for the rest of your life you bear the brand of that moral fall and the obligation to redeem yourself in the eyes of your father and all their surrogates. Every love takes you a step further away from your father's. All your loves will be but a surrogate for the one you kill first, so they say. The only attainable ones are those painfully reminiscent of the unquenchable yearning for love, paler and ever paler copies of the original no one has ever seen. There's no love comparable with what we owe our Creator. That debt is carried on from generation to generation, with interest. Since its original creation, the principal has grown at a bewildering rate. It's immeasurable. Invisible to the simpleton's eye! It can't see the tree of love, on which it is only a bud, for the wood of vulgarity all around. It doesn't perceive the vertical of the tree, which extends to the very heart of love, to the heavenly superfather who created us all in the image of His own narcissism so long ago that He's long since forgotten it.

My first proper boyfriend and I saw each other for months before we first had sex, and who knows how long it would have been if I hadn't insisted. He had some problem with it, as if the Inquisition was looming over him. As if he would maim and mutilate me by picking my flower. His considerateness was as noble as it was quixotic, incongruous with the rest of his personality, and I loved him all the more for it. But it disappeared once we'd crossed the Rubicon: we'd tear off our clothes as soon as we got to his place.

I was fourteen, he twenty-six. The day we met, I was dancing and he hung around the bar smiling ironically, his eyes glued to me. He seemed to have found something interesting enough for him in the desolation and now didn't feel like looking at anything else, but without being intrusive, as if that sight was all he needed. If I'd left, he probably would have just stayed there smiling and observing the space I'd occupied. That's what he was like. I went up to him and asked what exactly he wanted. An absolutely banal question, and he choked on the smoke and just said *yeah, it's great*. All the words we exchanged were like that: fateful in their format, more dramatic than life, but devoid of sense from the very beginning. The world consisted exclusively of deep dilemmas and reasons for crying, but we scoffed at them all.

Ever since childhood he'd reaped the rewards of his parents' divorce. His mother went abroad on the wings of her artistic career, while his father was tied down by managerial responsibilities and his new family. They atoned for this in the most sincere way possible – with money. They trounced their guilty conscience with combined forces when he finished school: he was given a flat and a comfortable student's allowance. He enrolled at the Academy, majoring in graphics, and for the first few years he really did study. But over time he stayed away ever more assiduously. He didn't have anything against the place, nor was he disappointed or embittered. He'd simply lost the reason to gain a degree, build a career and show his pictures. When I met him he'd stopped trying to uphold the illusion of studying in the eyes of his sponsors. He waited patiently for them to cap the resources, without the slightest concern for the consequences.

That doesn't mean he gave up painting. On the contrary, he just shifted entirely to his inner reaches. He had a smile like a Cheshire cat for the outer world, as good-natured as it was empty. Countless times, I had to repeat the words I addressed to him so they would sink in, and he needed a long time to build up an answer; you could see in his eyes that he was coming from afar. He could be very gentle and always spoke with a smile or a little laugh, but in his moments of silence he left me and disengaged completely. Several hours could pass and he would never be the first to speak. He would just sit next to me, clumsy and too big for his clothes: he was so tall that he jutted out of every garment he tried to fit into. And although I felt how much my presence meant to him, he was never able to focus on it for long.

I loved to watch him paint, especially his arms and hands. They were whiter than a sheet, his fingers long beyond measure and bent at the ends, and his veins stood out so much that they looked like they'd been stuck onto his skin from the outside. His hands belonged to the rest of the body only in theory. It remained numb, as if deflated, and he hardly seemed to breathe. But his agile hands, in the grip of their own fever, would raise a new world from the void, one uncharted, unpredictable to the very end, boundless and dizzyingly intricate. He most liked sitting on the floor with his splotchy legs, in just his underpants. Stuck in the corner of his mouth and immediately forgotten, his cigarettes burned away one after another and the ash fell in clumps onto the canvas. He would nonchalantly brush it to the floor with the back of his hand or just paint over it if he was working with oils.

There were always remnants of food on the floor: fruit, chocolate, cheese, things that didn't require more than unwrapping. He kept almost all his belongings on the floor, too. The only furniture he owned were two foam-rubber cubes, which his piles of clothes prevented from functioning as chairs. He washed his clothes by hand, in the washbasin, and not particularly often. He always bought only the cheapest of clothes and sometimes threw them out when they got dirty. Fleecy balls of dust lay in every corner. He never cleaned the flat but from time to time did a big tidy-up, at intervals of a few weeks or months.

All small objects then ended up in the rubbish container, including his current favourite cassettes which he played from morning till night while painting. And books, whether he'd read them or not: sometimes he browsed in bookshops, and if books made a positive impression he'd steal them, although usually he didn't even touch them again afterwards. And his pictures too, whether he'd finished them or not. He painted very fast, without hesitation or correction, as if following the moves an invisible hand made to guide his, as if they were already traced on the canvas and he just needed to bring them to life. But sometimes he broke off in the middle of it – they weren't going anywhere, he said. He put them aside with the others, standing stacked against the wall, and only took them out to the container when he decided they were taking up too much space.

Each painting evolved over several days. He kept going back and adding to it, even when it seemed not to need a single brush stroke more. Whatever technique he'd started with, he would always apply something different as if to attack it, flooding a drawing with watercolour or cutting sharp lines into an oil painting with a knife. Lines and colours built up crazily, fighting a struggle for superiority to the point of complete saturation and the worrying impression that the picture was about to explode. Everything pulsated, vibrated, trembled, rotated around its axis or reached into the distance. A devastating, centrifugal force gathered strength in that seething mass of details, capable of breaking through the frame and setting off an avalanche of destruction. But instead of that, an inexplicable equilibrium would arise – a symmetry woven by hidden threads. Through this incomprehensible reversal, the whole composition would suddenly evoke a feeling of stability which was precious because of being so hard-won and dependent on the enormous number of intricately interlocking components. This inner stability would emanate peace and happiness despite the intense heat of its genesis.

Each of the pictures, in its own way, showed living labyrinths: scenes of teeming action, dense and compact, full of interlaced movements, collisions, rifts and transformations. They were covered from edge to edge in intricate patterns, calligraphic tendrils and arabesques which intersected and merged, plunging into one another, vanishing into depths and forming bizarre figures here and there, amalgams of the recognisable and the incomprehensible, the earthly and the galactic: animals with monstrous extensions in the process of metamorphosing into another animal, a plant, an angel, or an anthropoid being, themselves half mutated into mysterious machines performing some function for other, larger mechanisms. Everything was being productive, but the end result couldn't be seen, only a chaotic, spasmodic state of confusion; the whole always looked to be wavering between transmutation into a higher stage of existence and falling into degradation, degeneration and ruin. They included both morbid and pathos-ridden scenes, and naivety as much as cynicism. Their leitmotifs, in many variations, were the human staircase, the human fountain and the human whirlpool, and each of them at the same time rose up and ran back into itself. There were eyes shared by two beings, one good-natured and the other sanguinary. And window-eyes, through which you could peer into a house or an underwater seascape populated by sexual organs instead of seashells. And planets consisting of a confusion of disfigured limbs, with a hole in the middle, through which another such planet could be glimpsed, and so on. Trees grew atop canopies of human arms, winged balconies detached themselves from buildings, and broken skulls gave birth to little skulls. I remember a swan coming down to land in the nest with its prey in its beak, a dead cygnet, while snake hatchlings grabbed for it from the nest with greedy mouths.

Your eyes would search his nightmare visions for an island

of stability, for something steady, but in vain: mirages and optical illusions sucked everything into a realm of dizzy disorientation where it spun off centripetally. Any yet, if you took a few steps back, especially with your eyes half-closed, you could feel a peace radiating from inside like warmth. It was reflected on his face as well, when the picture was finished, but not for long. Within a few hours, it would be extinguished.

All that he had left after covering the most basic necessities he would invest in his illicit mental superstructure. It didn't develop into classic addiction: if the money ran out, he could wait for days. But when he had it, he pedantically maintained the level of narcotics in his body as if he was on antibiotics. He approached it just like a therapy, like his life's project, curing himself of his worldly side with genuine conviction.

Of all that was available on the market, he most liked peyote, which his seaman friend periodically supplied him with. But a particular plant which mountaineers brought him from the Velebit range worked equally well. We would get into a tram and let ourselves be carted from one end of the city to the other for hours, and it was better than the cinema and more technicolour than the Amazon jungle. The streets teemed with clowns, caricatures and animals unconvincingly disguised as people. There were also ugly scenes when people we stared and laughed at took it personally. But most of the time we stayed isolated in ourselves, washed up on separate beaches, and when his eyes met mine they showed astonishment that I was there. Most of the time I felt out of place at his side, redundant, and I found myself less and less interested in the relationship. It had been makeshift from the very start, just a sum of moments wrested from coincidence. Any day could be the last.

And that's how it ended, too. First he used up all the credit of his student status. When his investors, again in agreement, decided that the hour had come for him to tread an independent path, he didn't twitch a whisker. Both sides dug into their positions and the crisis intensified. But he avoided dying of hunger through a compromise: he agreed to move temporarily into a down-to-earthing centre. This was conceived as a transitional phase of his full inclusion into the world of sanity and expediency. Weeks passed, and he didn't show any signs of the intended improvement or any desire to leave his new residence. The chemicals were altered a little, but he said that people were kind to him there, the food was OK, and they brought him whatever material he needed for his painting. I visited him every day and he would always be glad to see me. In a very similar way, however, he was also happy when they announced it was time for dinner, and when I said I'd go he'd just say OK and didn't ask if I'd be coming again. And one day I really didn't go back. My heart was breaking, but I purged it of all that bound us. I never saw him or heard anything of him again.

I ironed Father's singlets, a stupid thing he doesn't even expect me to do, at least not explicitly, but I just got on with it. It's enough for me to know what a tragedy he considers it to wear unironed singlets, although he'll then keep them on until they're crusty. I was at the door when the phone rang. It was his friend, with news of the death of another friend. *I'll pass that on, I'll tell him. Thank you ever so much,* I said.

His few former associates who still introduce themselves as his friends, although all these years he hasn't had anything else to say to them than *To be honest,* etc., are departing at fairly regular intervals. As if they're trying to maintain the temperature of death in him, everyone's death in general, and drive him even deeper into his own. I returned to the room, sat on the couch where he'd already dropped anchor for the rest of the day, and slowly, circuitously, prepared him for the nasty news. But this time there was no folksy pathos when he found out, he just fell silent for a few moments, and then sighed, *Oh well*.

The ease with which he wrote off yet another companion was a positive shift, and in his case any shift was a big event. I didn't disturb his circles any more on my way out. He remained on the couch as if petrified in that ease, with his arms crossed and his eyes fixed on the vase which had long forgotten why it stood on the living room table.

Yet how attentive he used to be. When I was about five, I began to have what several specialists long and unsuccessfully treated as insomnia. Finally it became clear that I simply need less sleep than normal people and can even stay awake for nights on end without adverse consequences. Before that, he left no stone unturned in search of the reason and made up for the subsequent failure with an indeterminate feeling of guilt with genetic or perhaps mythical roots. He seized that guilt with both hands and repented, and in nights like that he'd come in countless times to assure himself that I still wasn't sleeping. Or he'd stay and play ludo with me all night until dawn and then trudge off to work, all worried and worn, although I assured him that I wasn't afraid of the dark and would rather be doing things by myself. Parental love seems not to know the borders of reason. It only seems to come in forms you don't need.

In the tram on the way home (it was nice to use the word 'home' even though I didn't feel I had one of my own) something happened which I needed like I needed a hole in the head: I ran into the professor I'd graduated under. She was sitting exactly opposite the door and our gazes locked; there was no escape. A twitch of unease flitted across her face but was instantly replaced by an almost maternal benevolence.

'How beautiful you've become,' she exclaimed. 'The years have done you good! How long has it been since we first...'

'Thirteen years.'

'Thirteen? Goodness me, and I remember that girl as if it was yesterday: clumsy and scatty, but with such big eyes, avid for everything...'

Err, yes. And then *she* had beamed forth and nourished those eyes with light. There was I, pure as mountain dew; and she with her tutor's cap and shepherd's crosier led the way, guarding and guiding me around the precipice.

'How are things?' I asked.

'Oh, you know, doctor's appointments and diagnoses by the bagful. They find much more than they're looking for! You go in with a minor complaint and they end up putting a whole cohort of colleagues to work on you and turn your body into a building site. You come out sicker than you went in! The diagnoses let you lay a mosaic of your manifold, fatal deformations. Things you didn't even feel before now become unforgettable once you know what they're called. It drives out all your other thoughts. Oh, this is my stop... It was really great seeing you. You really should call some time and drop in so we can have a good chat! You haven't told me your news.'

And with that she was gone. Not a word about the invitations I'd sent her for the exhibitions or everything that had been written about them. As if she herself hadn't talked about me to whoever wanted to listen for years already, though in a different tone, because someone had pronounced one of my paintings to be better than all of hers. Quite an insignificant someone, but cause enough for her to blast my first portfolio after recognising it as a blatant, outrageously impudent betrayal of all she'd taught me; at the same time it revealed my mediocrity. She didn't stop at being offended but went to lengths to help curators and grant-giving commissions to bypass my work.

In first year she had really welcomed me and treated me in a motherly way. But rather than that encouraging me, it aroused the envy of others and put me in an awkward position. She made no attempt to conceal that she treated me differently and that I meant more to her than the others in class. She praised my paintings with shouts of enthusiasm; she also showed them to later years as an example of how to apply the paint, how patiently layer after layer had to be done, and above all as proof that effort and perseverance counted for much more than talent.

No doubt she saw in me, or wanted to see in me, a reflection of herself at the start of her career – of what she should or would have become if her cards had been laid a little differently. Fortune smiled on her and she was able to go abroad at an early stage. She had notable exhibitions, received several flattering offers and was awarded a few prizes, and then she got pregnant in the middle of it all. She returned and accepted a job offer at the Academy shortly after the birth of her son. She dedicated herself to him when he was small, to the detriment of her painting. And today they say that she's transformed the degree course with organisational skill as well as human warmth and the rare inclination to devote herself to her students. When her son was ten, he was hit and killed by a truck on his way home from school.

That probably also attached her to me. There were five or six of us in the class, and we all knew each other's family situation. She must have sensed my lack of a mother. On her initiative, I used to visit her at home, and we even went out together. She asked me about everything, and like an elder sister she really wanted to be part of my future, as well as my current pursuits and relationships. She acted as if our twenty years' age difference was irrelevant and showed understanding without being judgemental, even for things I was ashamed of myself. I found that increasingly suffocating as time went by. The portfolio I prepared in secret to surprise and perhaps even amaze her was above all a gasp for air, a way of showing myself that I could breathe without a respirator.

I really didn't expect her feelings to shift to the opposite extreme.

Or that she would cease to be important to me so soon. I even found certain enjoyment in the obstacles she set in my path. It also made me sad, of course. But when something in me dies I can lament as much as I like – there's no reanimating it.

She'd also returned to painting. And very successfully too, judging by the critiques. She was no longer invited abroad, but television crews came to every exhibition. Her third monograph had been published, and each of them added a little more to the specific weight and universal human depth of her opus, its historical breadth and span. She displayed exceptional sensitivity to relations with the state apparatus and institutional art: parties of both the right and the left commissioned her to produce works on patriotic Croatian themes and crowned her with laurels. She'd already earned herself a posthumous bronze bust in the Academy foyer, beyond any doubt, and could now settle down and occupy herself with her various medical conditions.

According to the study guide, at least, you could enrol in tertiary studies without having finished high-school, so I tried the first time after finishing year eleven. Although the next year I was just under the cut-off, like everyone who applied to enter those hallowed halls I felt that no genius could make the grade without aid from an insider. Father tried hard to persuade me to give up my attempts. When he saw he was unsuccessful, he asked one of the senior staff at the Academy, an acquaintance from his youth, to take me on for what amounted to private lessons. So I went to his studio for months and painted while he was busy with various other things, drank at the pub across the street or, much more rarely, produced art of his own.

There are intrinsic necessities in the choice of media. The material itself likes to choose the artist and incarnate their soul. My mentor was chosen by polyester at an early age. He fused with it and scorned all other sculptural media. Everything else, even clay, has its firmness, stability and character, but polyester is amorphous – a gooey mass. I personally find it hard to restrain my revulsion when I touch it. Besides, it's toxic: the fumes had avidly penetrated his brain and eaten away at him, and the end result was spectacular. But that's how my teacher built his international reputation. When the polyester trend came along, he not only introduced it here but distinguished himself among its proponents around the world. And it didn't bother him or those who made him chair of the sculpture department that, in spirit, he hadn't left his native village. Like the majority of Croatian sculptors, he came from rugged limestone country. The natural forms of those landscapes are inspirational: they create an instinct for relief, volume, and shaping things with one's hands. They sculpt stone patterns in their own image in the artist's mind. His whole mental world was like a mountain range: immobile and eternal. Albeit cast in polyester resin. Nothing else interested him – neither contemporary developments nor art history.

To what extent that qualified him for ushering me into the world of art was less important than him agreeing to take me under his wing. At the first of our lessons he tore up the pictures I brought along: how conceited I was, did I think I'd drunk my fill of genius with my mother's milk? Later I found out that wasn't particularly original; the greatest shortcoming at the Academy was to know too much beforehand, and only 'material' willing to be shaped would be admitted. I fulfilled the desires of my shaper: I said goodbye to my own fantasies for a while and drew still lifes of assembled objects from the studio or copied reproductions of famous portraits. This became wearing and seemed to have little to do with the fame I aspired to. But before moving on, I had to satisfy some of his other desires when he got up the courage to declare them. So it was that I also found myself quite literally under my teacher's pinions.

By tearing up my pubescent experiments he achieved the status of an unquestioned authority. From that moment of initiation, his knowledge was transmitted spontaneously, mainly in the form of sharp glances cast in passing at whatever I was drawing. Over time he began to make the occasional comment, stand behind me stroking his beard, ever closer, and then lay his hand on mine, only then to return it from its roving. If he'd caused revulsion in me, I would have rejected him. But I felt nothing, except perhaps pity for him as an old man with a corroded brain – what the polyester hadn't destroyed was washed away by alcohol. It was quite understandable that he salivated over me. I didn't take it personally.

I went there once a week. The lessons continued into Pygmalionesque extra time whenever he hadn't had enough to drink. Afterwards, in the mood, he'd recline into his smelly old armchair. First he had to dethrone his blind dog, which whined and later growled when he was aggravated by our sweat and other smells. Not at all ashamed of his geriatric nudity, he would get out his cigarette case and holder and calmly contemplate me getting dressed. He really had a kingly stature, with square shoulders, a grey beard and hair tied back in a plait. The hairs on his broad, inflamed chest were long and grey, and they stood out against his dark red skin. His eyes revealed how satisfied he was with his act and all he'd taught me.

As I gathered together my things, he would sometimes be visited by the muse of inspiration. I had to listen to his meditations on the meaning of art. He considered that art sucked the life out of people instead of giving it to them. In devoting their creative urges to art, people were transformed into something like sand, which briefly came alive and created the illusion of a surrogate life – a much better life where everything was possible and reachable; but it was all made of sand. By stirring it up and wallowing in it, we came ever closer to turning to sand ourselves.

In short, I made it over the cut-off mark at my third attempt thanks to him.

Of all the subjects at the Academy, my favourite was nude drawing. I was fascinated by the people who sat for us. They made a living from it. Some of them had been doing it for years, for who knows how many generations of students. They sacrificed their bodies for art, and in return it gave them the means of subsistence. You could see on their faces that they found it terribly boring. There's nothing money can't do; it can even stir up hatred of sitting nude if that's how you earn it. A lack of choice clearly doesn't make compulsion any more bearable.

They were mostly homeless people and retired prostitutes. Their services didn't overly burden the Academy's budget. Only on exception were we served a fresh, desirable body. All the others displayed human filth, decay and wretchedness. They all gave empty or scornful glances, had black under their fingernails and flaccid folds of skin. Deflated old breasts, withered mouths with rotten teeth, bloodshot eyes, flab and scabs. Some of the men got erections from gaping at one of us girls. Others shook in feverish anticipation of the moment they would be able to rush to their dealer with the money. One peed on the floor when his bladder packed in. In front of the professor we pretended not to notice such things, but whenever she went out, we'd start a dialogue about them. We exchanged fire over the barricades of art and ignited artificial tension between us. The nudes turned their subordinate, naked position to their advantage, with complete freedom of speech. They called out obscenities to us as they sat or lay spread out before our collective gaze – victims now expertly commenting on their ritual torture. Male models shamelessly offered themselves to the girls. Women provoked the boys, belittling their virility and dimensions. The braver boys went on the attack: one time they ganged up like a pack of hungry dogs to embarrass and offend a humpbacked woman who'd given them absolutely no cause and didn't even defend herself.

One of the models was actually good-looking, although past his prime. A fellow student of mine even got a crush on him. Perhaps she was taking her inspiration a bit far, or perhaps she did it just to spite her fine upbringing and cultured background because he was a welfare case by vocation and a small-time thief. The affair resulted in a child, and the father disappeared without a trace. With motherhood, her inspiration for her studies vanished. Maybe in the next generation. Art exacts sacrifices but is also mindful of regeneration.

A strange atmosphere reigned at the Academy – a closeness which was often claustrophobic. Something ominous hung in the air, a mutual envy and fear of others' tongues. A rebuke would sometimes crush a thin-skinned student. The more poisonous a remark was, the faster and louder it spread down the corridors, the better it adhered to its target, and with a little luck even liquidated it. Still, we went out a lot together. There were venues which belonged to us Academy students. Intruders instinctively felt their inferiority. We helped the less sensitive of them with meaningful glances. And with posturing, whose remuneration was better than money: the elevation of our artistic egos. We had to demonstrate our apartness from the rest of the world and our contempt for it at all costs. We stylised every public outing into a performance with provocative slogans, unique mannerisms and filmstarish ways of holding our cigarettes. Or at least with a subversive hairstyle, cynical beardlet or ripped clothes. One or two of us had a serviceable trait in our genetic baggage such as a tradition of epilepsy or schizophrenia. The less privileged compensated for their lack with creativity: they publicly fell into mystical trances, had spectacular nervous breakdowns or plunged into nihilism.

We sustained this elevation with different stimulants depending on our personal preferences. Some were already familiar with uppers and speeders, others did the works to make up for their lack of prior experience. It's a notorious truth that works of art created without opiates are boring to look at too.

Every Saturday, and sometimes even in the middle of the week, our outings ended at someone's flat or weekend place out in the country. There was usually an unlimited supply of home-grown grass in jars on the table, and really good hosts used it in pizzas or cakes. More exclusive things took place in the toilet. Stripteases and hallucinations were regular events. One guest took a liking to a bearskin rug and left with it on, having deposited his clothes in exchange. Another managed to convince the whole group that they were sitting on a railway track in front of an oncoming train, and every single one of them jumped off the balcony. Once they fed a cat Ecstasy, and in the end it climbed up onto the china closet and vomited down. When all the bedrooms were occupied people didn't seclude themselves to have sex. In benign cases, the boys would rustle up an open-minded high-school girl with a love of visual art, and after she'd had a bit of pizza each of them would have a turn with her.

One of them was keen on me, but I just couldn't give in to passion with him. I suppose I would have been able to handle his ugliness, of the sort which no extravagance could camouflage, if he hadn't smelt so bad. But he persisted, my refusal evidently spurred him on, and his declarations of love became ever more romantic. At the peak of elation he went yelling down the hallways of the Academy, threw plaster busts down the staircase, and then himself, ending up with both his arms in plaster.

Only one episode of sexual distraction became worthy of description. In the middle of the night, Romeo came up to my window and I let him in without demanding a poem or serenade, only to discover that he was so drunk he could hardly stand. That was his one constant – the way he watered down the rage in himself. He would then discharge it onto his canvases, and it was their central and almost sole content. Painting complete abstractions with just a few bold strokes, he managed to express so much concentrated negative energy that everyone had to feel it: some were in awe, while for most others it made their stomachs turn. He'd been allowed to enrol at the Academy because his exceptional talent could not be overlooked. They kept him at an arm's length like a possibly brilliant but definitely dangerous mental case and made no attempt to shape him. His fury would surge beyond his canvases again and again. It unfailingly recharged and controlled him like a puppet on strings.

He made a certain degree of effort to control himself. He mixed with people and tried to participate and communicate, but soon the muscles on his face would start to tremble, he would glare and bite his lips, and he proceeded to down glass after glass of booze with visible distress, sweating profusely, and didn't give in until it made him drop.

Externally, he was the exact opposite of what raged inside him: his body was boyishly weak, smooth like a woman's, everywhere soft and fragile. He was also under the sway of various allergies which broke out especially in the springtime. Pollen in the air sent him to bed with fever and bouts of choking. He was tirelessly assailed by new and different agents of eczema, scabies and swollen eyes. There were few foods he tolerated, and after a while his allergy extended even to them. In return, it receded from some others, though of course without informing him, so every meal was an experiment. The only thing he could rely on not being allergic to was alcohol, but it bowled him over, knocked him out and put him in dangerous situations. Once he drank himself into a stupor like this and fell asleep on an anthill. At the casualty ward his body swelled up to twice its size and he learnt that nothing gave him a worse allergic reaction than formic acid.

For some reason I provoked neither his allergy nor his rage, and who wouldn't feel a sense of privilege and an inherent compliment in that. We discovered it by coincidence. He virtually had to force himself to go to bed with me as if he wanted to prove to himself that it wouldn't work and there was no point trying. But all at once there was an almost audible twang as barrier after barrier burst asunder and he opened up to me inaccessible regions of himself. There was nothing particularly pleasant there, only a ragged, furrowed wasteland. And endless banks of bitter dregs. A bit like quickmud, which he skilfully accumulated. It acquainted me with the sickening inclination to immerse myself in others which lurked in me, just waiting for fertile soil. And he revealed the tick in himself – his hitherto underutilised talent for getting under my skin. When we found each other, our threads instantly intertwined. As if a substance had glued us together. He presented me his intolerance of the world and his sprees of drunkenness as if they were prize exhibits, and I demanded more of the same, although pretending to resist. In turn, that prompted him to pour out all his vitriol and to build up even more through self-abnegation, forming it out of thin air if required. Thanks to me, he even learnt to enjoy it. And worst of all: I embraced a sense of guilt for not being able to help him. I immersed myself in misery, took it to heart ever more, and pitied both him and myself. He didn't need any help but rather a mirror so as to better marvel at his own misfortune.

Who knows how long that idyllic symbiosis would have lasted if they hadn't mobilised him at the start of Operation Storm. They didn't consider any other male student from the Academy sufficiently reliable, but he was indispensable to them, multiallergic and alcohol-sodden though he was. They couldn't have done him a greater favour. Several hours after getting the call-up notice he was in a train for the front. Today he lives in New York, esteemed, rich, and married to a beautiful Chinese lady who owns a chain of galleries.

During the war years, artists who weren't able to take refuge abroad had to either keep their head down or become involved in the defence of the Fatherland, if only through art. Some works of art even went like hot cakes: larger-than-life paintings involving Golgotha, the Croatian chequerboard coat of arms, red-hot shackles, and tanks. When things calmed down, four years later, I too began to earn a living from my work. Again, this was thanks to one of my lecturers from the Academy: he had entrepreneurial talent more than anything else. He hand-picked several of us for his master class, where we produced Mediterranean land-scapes for days on end – manifold compositions with ready-made motifs of stone houses, boats and olive trees. The treetops were completely individual creations: we stamped them on the canvas with a little sponge dipped in green paint. He would just crown the pictures with his artistic pseudonym, and then they travelled in consignments by the hundred to his Adriatic homeland, ready for the tourist renaissance.

At the same time, my more intimate, less market-sensitive work began to make a mark. Without plan or conscious intention, each painting revolved around a female body which either contained something else inside, changed into that thing, or lived with it in bizarre duality. Take the woman turning into an elephant: her body, depicted from behind, is still graceful, and her arms are even melancholically elongated, but she's already grown elephant ears. Or the one who's half butterfly but at the same time is sinking into the ground, and her limbs have changed into roots. And a line of bodies whose skin is creasing or tensing up in places: whatever lives inside is preparing to burst out, and sometimes you can discern an eye or a claw of the creature. And countless clay figurines which are melding two beings into one body, as well as heads with a second face at the back. But the most frequent motif in the pictures is that of a young woman whose bones can be seen through her body. One such woman watches children playing in the sand and hovers over them on a swing without supports. Another daydreams up in a tree and gazes into the sky, across which a flight of skeletons are streaking like comets. A third reaches out her arm towards a bird fluttering above her, black with a fiery crest, as if she's holding up some seeds to it in her hand, but one of her bony fingers is actually in the bird's beak. Another woman sits on the brink of a chasm and stares into it sadly, with a ladder jutting out of her back as an awkward extension of her spine. Yet another is wearing a mantle like a wedding dress, but it could also be bees' wings, and she's holding two children with bare skulls in place of their heads. One woman is surrounded by little animals – lambs, squirrels and mice – with their skeletons showing too. Another woman is performing in a circus, which by the lighting could just as well be a brothel: she dismantles her skeleton piece by piece, and the audience is also made up of skeletons in different stages of disassemblement; some of them are holding their skull under their arm, others take off and put aside their lower legs like boots which have given them blisters. In one painting the skeleton people are queuing at a counter like a butcher's table, except that the transactions are in the opposite direction: the thickset, ruddy proprietor, in smock with the sleeves rolled up but from the belt down himself a skeleton, weighs the pieces his customers give him – their ribs, pelvises or collarbones, while his assistant pays them at the cash register.

Although my paintings garnered some praise here and there, they were generally not taken seriously. People thought of them when they needed to emphasise a point or illustrate a lucid theory they'd developed, but they wouldn't actually support my work. Let alone buy it. They'd come and look and devote them a second or two of great lyrical tenderness... and promise themselves they'd return when they plucked up the courage.

In the meantime, I needed the wherewithal to live on. So I turned my hand to art for those of middling courage. I painted the city's sights, suitable for hanging over dining tables where veal escalope, Zagreb-style, was served. The hunger for art became almost insatiable after the war, but stomachs were still sensitive. They needed bland, pleasant scenes. The fast-growing market demanded that aesthetic excellence be supported by the patriotic vertical. The compositional axis of my collages of the capital were the steeples of Zagreb's cathedral, and hussar generals on their steeds floated beside them as if full of helium. But my best-seller was the evergreen motif of the Stone Gate and its shrine, with an old woman kneeling at the threshold of her promised Home.

And then I put together *that* portfolio. It was based on an erotically provocative inspiration – a bold step into the backstage of the soul, to put it mildly. Put less mildly, the pictures were full of nudity and as challenging as they were outrageous: young female bodies offered all they had to give, fucked cripples, geriatrics, billy goats and demons, and wrapped themselves around crosses. In one picture, three little girls rode in elation on a penis the size of a Zeppelin.

Not that they sold. But they gained me a certain renown. They prompted the editor of *Nacional* weekly to do an interview with me, which came out as a centrefold with nude photos of me and the title *I dream of sex with a cardinal or at least a bishop.* I didn't actually say that, but never mind.

Gallery owners and art agents now also discovered an interest in me. It would regularly come to light, straight after the preliminary negotiations, that their interest had little to do with my paintings. All of them wielded the cardinal's sceptre and took offence if I didn't get down on my knees in front of them.

It was still mainly those panoramas of the city which financed me. I sought love, even if I didn't call it that, in everyone who promised anything of the kind, though over time I consented to less and less.

And then, in the spring of 2004, your editor offered for me to illustrate that Chinese cookbook and decorate the recipes with the animals of the zodiac. Who could refuse such a challenge? That promised a whole menagerie of illumination, an osmosis of the senses and mind.

* * *

I'd seen my share of times when one nasty thing brought on another – when it rains AND pours, with the Murphy factor on top of that – but 2004 exceeded its own worst ambitions.

It began with the Vila Marija episode at the firm, when the Boss's wife was caught on the graphic editor's desk. More dramatic still, the discovery was made by the Boss's daughter, whose reaction revealed that she'd established similar working relations with the editor. This made the atmosphere unbearable for a time, but then the famous smile returned to the Boss's face. He was made of German stuff, after all.

Then there was the business with that writer. The Chief Editor had discovered him among the best-sellers in Finland, celebrated abroad as well – the voice of a new Finnish generation. The translation of his book of short stories was arranged, and he agreed to enhance the launch by attending in person.

But consternation prevailed among the editors when the translation arrived, because the stories were preoccupied with one single topic: the author's depression. He wrote about it most frankly and in the first person rather than hiding behind ficticious names. Depression manifested itself in everything his eyes touched and was nourished by marital tragedy, the harsh climate, physical decline, the polar night and chronic insomnia. It had long run in the family: his father, grandfather and great-grandfather had all suffered from depression. When he felt he wasn't living up to their standards, he fuelled it with alcohol, as did almost all the other protagonists in the book, or they used drink as a way of coping with depression in general. And everything in his stories was credible and consistent, from the first page to the last, without a single ray of light, without any stylistic embellishments or a shred of interest in the rest of the world.

In the final story, however, depression was allegorically disguised as a wolf. In the hope of escaping the ill fortune brought by his various urban debacles, the narrator moved with his wife and two small children to live in the tundras of the north: to be with nature and raise sheep. The summer months were salutary, almost idyllic. But in the winter a wolf came down from the mountains and started to kill the sheep. It would enter their pen at night and carry them off one at a time. So the narrator wrapped himself up in furs, took the rifle, and spent two nights in the pen watching and waiting; the wolf didn't come. On the third night, weariness overcame him. He woke up just before dawn. The sheep were all there. He went back to the house, and there a scene awaited him: his wife and children lay in pools of blood with their throats ripped out. Game, set, end of career.

No one mentioned the translation for a while. But the translator had to be paid, and the rights had already been bought, and an airline ticket had been sent to the author. So the book was published.

One of the secretaries was delegated as an escort to meet him at the airport and provide any help he needed. The next morning she came in, furious: in the taxi he'd asked her to buy him some cocaine, and then, seeing as no other entertainment was scheduled, he'd taken it for granted that she would spend the evening in his room.

So the task of accompanying the launch fell to me. It was scheduled for midday at the Finnish Cultural Centre, which was financing the event. This was to be the first in a series of mutually beneficial joint projects that year, intended to present Finnish culture to the Croatian public.

At eleven thirty I called him from the front desk. There was no reply. The receptionist hadn't seen him go out. I went up to his room and knocked, without result. The door was slightly ajar. He was sitting on the bed in his underwear and with one sock on, staring at the carpet. I needed to make a major effort for him to focus on my presence, and it kept slipping away from him. I helped him into his clothes, which demanded quite some heroism, given his alcoholic breath. The bellboy helped me bundle him into a taxi.

I began to seriously doubt the prudence of the venture as soon as we set off. He swung at every bend and corner as if he was made of rubber, and once he tipped over onto my lap. Still, when we arrived at the Cultural Centre he partially revived and even made it up the stairs to the second floor without assistance. We were late; the cameras were waiting, the auditorium was full and the staff of the Centre were on tenterhooks. He zombied past them all, ignoring the ambassador who was left holding out his hand. Without taking off his coat, unshaven, with a crimson face and a tuft of hair which stuck up abruptly on the left as if it was reaching for the sun, he slumped into the seat he was directed to in the middle of table, flanked by the Boss and the Chief Editor on one side and the translator and ambassador on the other. The diplomat spoke first, or rather read, from many sheets of paper, showing himself to be a great friend of our country, in which he found similarities with his own as well as stimulating differences, almost boundless riches, etc. His face still revealed a certain unease and offendedness. But bliss played on the Boss's face; his part was spoken quickly. The Chief Editor needed much longer, not due to the abundance of his words but because they came with great effort. The audience started to get involved, giving him prompts whenever he got stuck, and this turned into an interactive game which continued up until his closing, enthusiastic statement that it was a pleasure and a privilege to meet one of the undoubtedly greatest European writers.

When the author was asked to read, he didn't move for a good ten seconds. Finally he reached for the book, started leafing through it and weighing every page as if it was a tremendously touchy decision, cleared his throat, and then time really stood still. He read in a terribly tired voice with enormous gaps between words, and every one of them caused him tangible pain. Silence and apprehension reigned in the auditorium, with no one knowing if he was going to collapse on the spot or vomit over the book and its promoters.

But he didn't. He made it to the end of the story, the audience timidly clapped, an actor read out the Croatian translation, and there was general relief when no one felt the need to ask the author any questions. Likewise, when he responded to the invitation to join us for dinner with the single-word utterance: *Hotel*.

In the taxi, his head drooped and came to rest against the window. When we arrived I shook him: *Mr Uusitalo?* And again, harder. To no avail – he was dead.

A cardiac, the doctor said. After years of struggling with coronary insufficiency he chose to capitulate here. The embassy took care of the transport of the body, but first they had to sort things out with the police. And with the journalists, who the story greatly appealed to. They were all immediately put through to me, of course. They called from different countries. Three Finnish film crews descended on the office, and even the most obscure of Croatian papers had questions. They wanted something anecdotal to do with the event, a perversion from the author's opus, public life or childhood. The weeklies vied in giving exhaustive descriptions of his final hours. The Boss took over negotiations and at one stage sold exclusive rights to my statement, with a photo reconstruction. But my story didn't prove graphic enough; it came out in a weekly with flourishes penned by our most noteworthy writer under the title *He Came Here to Die*. This was later expanded into a novel, published by us, of course. In the bookshops, Uusitalo's prose outsold even Beckham's autobiography.

On the fifteenth of March, Mother had a stroke. It happened at night. For the first time I can remember, I didn't find her up and about in the morning. She slept very little. In the winter months she would get up before dawn and sit in the kitchen for hours with a cup of coffee.

That winter was exceptionally long. The crust of snow didn't melt and the birds were at the end of their strength. They attacked each other, shrieking and trying to grab the last scrap of wrinkled apple or morsel fished out of the rubbish. Goldfinches, hawfinches and species I'd never seen before came down from the forest, very close to the houses, and peered inside.

In the second week of March it finally started to warm up. Within just a few days everything came alive, emerged from the ground and budded. The sky went a mighty blue. Aeroplanes hummed optimistically overhead. And then I found Mother in bed, her face strangely contorted, her lips twisted and her eyes cheerless. She didn't answer me. I tried to sit her up straight but her body remained limp.

It wasn't actually that much of a surprise. Her health had been going downhill rapidly for several months. She moved around with difficulty, ever more bent at the waist, holding on to the furniture and reaching out for it ever more slowly with her trembling hand. She stopped going out. Whatever existed beyond the house became uninteresting for her and deserved only contempt. She withdrew into herself and waited for the end.

She wasn't even particularly alarmed by the government's campaign against illegal houses. The threat of the bulldozers turning up became increasingly real; they could be seen every day, not just on television, reckoning with structures raised without the government's blessing, while ministers stood beside the ruins congratulating each other on the rule of law. Our house fulfilled the conditions for being flattened, but we only spoke about that once, beating about the bush and reaching no conclusion. Mother was already elsewhere.

Confirmation in writing that we belonged to the priority targets, in other words notification of demolition without a date, arrived one week after her stroke. It had evidently been decided that our courtyard urgently needed turning into a national park, or Disneyland. Although still immobile, Mother began to speak a few syllables in the days that followed. Her speech gradually returned. It wasn't quite comprehensible, and her face remained skewed, but soon she was able to get up again and take a step or two, at least as far as the toilet. Although the impending victor was within sight, she'd wrested one game from him.

I didn't tell her, of course, that the municipal council had us in its sights. But the threat was actually less immediate than the paperwork suggested. Before the German adventure, Mother had started the registration procedure for the house. That had meant months of wrangling with surveyors and architects, as well as the ingratiation of court officials and land-registry staff, and when all the requisite documents had been obtained there was no money left over for greasing a cog in the machinery which was stuck. A top cadastral official made it perfectly clear to her that he could have the matter resolved instantly – or she could wait an indefinite number years. And she would have gone and somehow obtained the amount he demanded if the romance with Steinhammer hadn't catapulted the house out of focus at that crucial juncture. The state she was in when she returned dispelled all thought of legalising our existence. I could have taken over the project, but I was already up to my eyeballs in work every day just to prevent the house from collapsing. Besides, part of me actually longed for that to happen – so I'd be rid of it forever.

At the municipal council, the day after I'd received notification, they sent me to the staff member responsible. This wasn't the gentleman who could resolve the matter instantly but a lady who painstakingly gnawed down an apple almost with disgust, while listening to me, and chewed on for a moment when I'd finished; then she made a brief phone call, got up and walked away, calling out over her shoulder that cases from that year weren't in her office but in Archives. In order for the staff there to look for it, they needed a form with a duty stamp and registration number. I didn't have the number; in the registry, the information I gave was insufficient to find it. At the archives they accepted the form nevertheless, only to return it to me an hour later and declare that they'd never received such a file.

'How could it have gone astray?' I asked. Braced against her desk, the woman searched me with her gaze over the rim of her glasses, smacked her lips in disinterest and shook her head.

I went back to the lady with the apple; she was now eating yoghurt, rhythmically scooping it with a teaspoon.

'Look, is it my problem if it's not in Archives?' she huffed. 'What do you want of me now? Where else am I supposed to look? Here, see for yourself!'

She put aside her yoghurt, opened the cupboard behind her which was crammed full of files, and immediately slammed it shut again.

'Nothing older than ninety-seven! That's when I was transferred here, and these here are all my cases!'

'What about your predecessor?'

'He doesn't work at the council any more!' she snorted.

'But where are his cases then?'

'In Archives, of course! How long are you going to keep harassing me with this business? Would you be so kind as to let me get on with my mountain of work?'

Mother was a vegetable at this stage. We had no copies of the building plans and whatever other documents had got held up. The land register showed an open space where our house stood, a vacant block, and it was looking ever more likely that that would be its status in future, too. Our existence increasingly resembled the transparent paper stored in the archives. Little squares were drawn on it in places; human habitation sometimes merited that. Some folk left at least that much trace – small squares on the ground plan – but there was nothing of us to be seen.

Suddenly I felt trapped in that office. The rest of my life had foundered like the frigate Medusa, and this was her raft. Taking a chair, I slowly pulled it up to the table, straddled it and laid my chin on the backrest.

'I'm sorry, madam, but neither you nor I are leaving this place unless you find me the documents,' I pronounced calmly, wondering at my own eloquence.

Unless was a crucial flash of genius. *Until* you find me the documents wouldn't have made the same impression and would have led us towards some nebulous postponement, but *unless* revealed the sharp edge of an abyss. I should mention that it was becoming increasingly popular at that time to resolve matters in courts and local councils by resorting to weapons. Although I was sitting quite calmly, without any idea what scenarios could flow from my little ultimatum, I saw in her eyes that I had an explosive belt strapped beneath my T-shirt ready to detonate if she said another wrong word.

Not letting me out of her sight, she ordered me to wait and escaped through the door on the opposite side of the office. In the ensuing silence, interrupted only by the flushing of a toilet somewhere nearby, I speculated what exactly was going to happen to me: would she call Security or perhaps even send in riot-control police with German shepherds? How long would she be away for? Long enough for me to start thinking that she'd simply leave me there to die of hunger. But finally she appeared and thumped a bundle of papers down on the table; I couldn't tell if she was furious because she'd found what she was looking for or because I was still there. She leafed through the documents, eyeing them one by one, and then went back through the pile again.

'Will you tell me what's missing?' I asked timidly.

'Everything's here –,' she said, holding the pile out to me, 'but it's all old.'

Rejuvenating the paperwork took several weeks and cost an amazing amount of money. But now, with the registration number, I could stand tall in front of the bulldozer drivers.

Things at home began returning to normal: to the state of permanent inundation and the painstaking struggle to at least keep our heads above water. Although it was impossible to stop the leaks, it looked as if we'd at least evaded the torrent for the time being. But on the twelfth of April, when I returned from work, I found Mother lying on the floor. That blow was the hardest.

The coroner came and did his job, followed by the woman from the neighbourhood who helped in cases like this out of pure humanity, refusing any remuneration, but with a strange gleam in her eyes. They say she'd been doing it ever since her only son died in a traffic accident. When she left, the house was enveloped in silence. A thick, pulsating silence gushed from the walls, filling the whole space and burning my throat. I went to bed around midnight; Mother lay directly below, down on the ground floor. Needles stabbed from the depths of the night. At around four, the birds began to call with their inexhaustible joy at the breaking of a new day.

In the morning they drove her away, wrapped in a sheet. I rang work. After quite some hesitation I also called my mother's brother. I really didn't want to, but I sort of felt it had to be done. I'd only seen him once, when my grandmother died and I was about twenty. My grandfather had died long before and Mother didn't remember him. Her brother had a daughter roughly my age in Zagreb but I don't think he'd seen her since he moved to Slovenia, where he had two or three more children. One of them answered the phone and put down the receiver without a word when I attempted to introduce myself. The conversation with my uncle was very brief, but I stayed sitting by the phone for a long time afterwards, trying to recall what his *Oh!* at the news reminded me of. I finally remembered that the pensioners I used to watch playing chess in the park near my school when I was a boy used to react like that to an unexpected move by their opponent.

No other member of his families came to the funeral. When it was over he asked if I needed any help. A rather unusual question, when everything is added up; I saw on his face for an instant that he was aware of that. We shook hands and he left.

I'd had to make a decision for or against Mass. If only her last few years counted, it wouldn't have been an issue; but accounts are kept for one's life as a whole. There were only a handful of us at church, mostly old ladies from the neighbourhood who go to every funeral and never miss Mass. The priest spoke briefly about the good deeds of 'our sister

Mira', her gentle soul and also her occasional weaknesses. Mira hadn't been perfect, but even when she sinned it was without the slightest ill intention; she did her job on earth and all her failings were forgiven, just as she forgave others. He was young and had just taken over the parish, so he'd definitely never met Mother; but the statistics underlined the absolute appropriateness of his words. Then he waffled on, wishing that our sacrifice and his be pleasing to our Heavenly Father – it's nice to know that He too follows the pleasure principle. In the end we wished each other peace, I paid and we all went home.

Mother and I had never talked much, or about anything important. Everything else wore down to the bone over the years, too, albeit painlessly. But now an ominous, icy silence blew through the house. After work, the effort to dissipate its deafening onslaught consumed all my strength. The TV was on all the time, in neutral. All the lights were on, but darkness rose from the floor and lapped around the furniture and fittings, clinging to them and weighing them down. Torn free of gravity, they were like a leaden weight in my hands. A teapot or watering can could bowl me over onto the couch, and sometimes it would be a whole hour before I came to.

Returning home from the office was like a journey to the isle of the dead. The house awaited me, gruesomely shrouded in darkness, gaping between its neighbours like an extracted tooth. The door closed behind me, tombstonish.

On 8th May, notification came from the municipal office that I could pick up the building permit. Victory! But at that moment the concept of building couldn't have contained an ounce more sarcasm.

Everything in me came to a standstill. A thick wall of glass sundered me from the world. From inside, I observed my own movements as foreign, in slow motion. Every morning I had to remind myself all over again why I was alive, how I differed from the boards I lay on, what a toothbrush was for. In the outside world a contest of colour, mobility and haste was culminating: Croatian idols and local government bodies were being chosen on television as the wheels of Euro-Atlantic integration gathered pace. Invoices and advertising leaflets with even more favourable offers of detergents and smoked pancetta diligently arrived in the letter box. But they were only cellulose illusions, flotsam from a sunken world. In the house, everything was running out: to use up the last little sliver of chocolate or the leftover packet of soup was like to forever abrogate their existence. The things around me vanished one by one or became hollow from the inside, leaving just an empty shell. When I met people on the street it felt like I was seeing them for the last time, and whatever we said felt like a farewell. Every set of traffic lights involved the possibility of me just stopping and sitting there like a mummy until the emergency team arrived. At best, I lived two or three hours a day – that's how much life, for want of a better word, I managed to scrape together.

The plant kingdom, on the contrary, was experiencing its renaissance at that time. Grasses burst from every crack and fissure to rise up skywards. The ivy wove brows above the windows, while climbing roses crossed their thorny halberds over the little path to the house. The courtyard at the back was choked in bindweed and nettles. The only way up to the back, lost in an impenetrable thicket of blackberry bushes, acacias, ferns and creeping mutants, would have been with napalm. Yes, even I became a grim reaper on occasion: a bearer of ill tidings for butterflies and hummingmoths, a feller of tall poppies. But a scythe wasn't enough, our yard called for a lawnmower like those that were heard elsewhere in the neighbourhood and grated on my nerves from early morning till after dark; without it there was no hope of prevailing against the green pestilence. But now I kept putting it off until the next day. That didn't make the problem any smaller: I dreamed of nettles with stems thicker than my arm sawing the walls with their serrated leaves, and a nest of green mambas beneath my bed. But I was still unable to overcome my loathing of gardening and any other conceivable intervention.

And ants! They're part and parcel of human habitation, especially in the summer months. In most dwellings people treat them as intruders and pest-control them out of existence. I no longer had the strength to combat them in any way, I just hid food from them, but they found and plundered every hiding place. Ultimately I gave up and got used to shaking them out of the bread in the morning and eliminating them from individual mouthfuls with indifferent flicks. Soon it no longer bothered me that they loitered on the table waiting for crumbs while I ate. Who knows how long I sat beside my plate to gaze at one of them with an empathic tear in my eye – a reliable sign of sinking into imbecility; watching the ant struggling to tug away, or at least shift, a cornflake far bigger that itself.

A teller at the bank began to look at me with concern. Her name badge was attached to her shirt; I said she had a lovely name and that it made her face even more beautiful. And I really meant it. She smiled at me, I smiled back, took the money and left. Outside, too, everything seemed lovely, the people, trees and cars – beautiful, alive and incomprehensibly far from me.

Day still followed day. The weekends were endlessly long, but at work I performed whatever was required of me as reliably as a robot. The more senseless the better: such tasks were just right for maintaining a bare minimum of existence in me.

And then that launch came along.

It was early June, when people do the last shopping before the summer: just the right time to put out some inspiration for culinary adventures. But that didn't help us to bring together more than the author's family and the odd unexpected guest at the Peking Restaurant. The buffet was waiting as the Chief Editor stammered out a few words in praise of Chinese culture, and an eminent Croatian gourmet shared his meditations on the flourishing of Oriental cuisine in our homes. Before we were admitted to the tasting, our heads turned when the author of the illustrations was pointed out. It was then that I saw you.

You were standing next to one of the originals effectively hung on the walls, with your arms folded, supporting your chin in the palm of your hand, and with a cigarette between your fingers. All at once I was standing on a narrow sliver of ground, everything else fell into an indefinite, mute whiteness, except for that figure, seemingly just a few steps away, which stepped forth from a gracious heavenly hand and switched off the world around her.

I stood there dazzled, without a whisp of air in my lungs and not knowing where to find it. Nor was there any room now for seeking it; she'd found me. From the depths, from who knows what inspiration, a light began to flow and made my body shiver. It was unrealistic to feel anything at that instant, but the vigilance of my senses doubtlessly overwhelmed me and was already washing me away with a roar, not giving my breakwaters the slightest chance.

Those eyes. As cold as a winter night, like wells of dense darkness, but at the same time trembling with ardour. I'd never desired anything so strongly nor dreamed that I could desire anything so much, as if I was at the very source of that shine and somehow part of it.

When the first blindness abated, I began to make you out piece by piece. Eyebrows. They arched like butterflies in flight, and when resting they were curved question marks which at the same time conveyed a reproachful comment, drew sharp borders, and wondered at the futile efforts to involve you in the event and count you as theirs. But totally human eyebrows, all the same; they didn't herald anything divine, any call of the other-worldly. But how can brows or any part of the body embody so much soul, so much completeness of being? The face beneath them was drawn with a broad hand, as generous as it was intricate, with love for every detail, without a trace of cosmetics, and covered with shadows, tiny tensions and ripples. Jet black hair which no attempt had been made to shape; once cropped, it had been left to grow into a bushy blackness so dark and dense that it cast metallic flashes. What delicate joints: every bending and folding of your limbs testified to how painstakingly they'd composed you, how much love and labour had been invested in their articulation, and afterwards the creation was covered with gossamer, in places painfully taut. Your physique was reminiscent of Thumbelina, but standing stationary you created a flame and a wilderness around you as stark as if a Bengal tiger had suddenly prowled into the building, and that made everything else seem artificial, plastic and burlesque. Yes, a tiger. There was so much suppleness in you, so much density of movement, so much hidden peril. A feverish lurking paired with coolness, a seething hunger channelled into indifference, and a scorn for lower creatures, which still managed to harass you. I watched your gaze wind across the surface of things to avoid the traps set for it; now and again it would dart like a striking snake and claim a yard of space to probe and archive. I was frightened by the idea that nothing in me could retain it and that it would look through me, too, as if I was made of glass.

Bizarrely, you looked inaccessible, as if there were no ways via which I could reduce the distance between us; but at the same time your figure was more than just an image on my retina, it impressed itself into my body like a stamp, directly, branding me with its deep and total presence. Propelling its entire aura into an excess of matter, giving it dimensions of deafening, pulsating meaning and more sense than the building's structure could bear, more than the architects of this world anticipated. Everything was at once dislocated and contourless, everything swayed in amazement, palpating this new, weightless freedom.

Not only did I do the unimaginable in fording that interstellar vacuum, but I didn't doubt for an instant what I should say to you. I felt I couldn't go wrong. If ever I was to have the grace of saying something right, just as required and at the perfect moment – if such luck exists in the world – I knew it would take shape and issue from my mouth. Perhaps in a language I don't understand. Perhaps in the form of a flower.

It didn't surprise me at all that you looked at me without surprise, expressionless, only turning your head when I came up to you. I didn't say a word. I stopped, one step away, close enough to touch you but without doing it; if I were to discover that you're made of pure desire, let this take at least another few moments. A smile darted across your face – I would get to know your smile so well, like the opening of a door to a land of pure bliss – but it was elusive, hardly longer than a wink, and at least tenfold lined with shadow.

* * *

So many had approached me with their ready-made charm phrases, each more original than the other. I'd got to know so well the words that didn't even pretend to be more than a request to enter the realm of the pleasure principle. And when they'd accomplished their mission, the whole sphere of verbality was scuppered and there emerged the terrifying banality of what had been hushed up. Agreeable words, indispensible for caressing each other submissively and fearfully, lest they be answered with a slap in the face.

I waited for my presence at the event to officially become superfluous, which it was from the beginning anyway. Everything in that place screamed out its superfluity: neckties, the perfume sprayed on necks, my illustrations and the oxygen expended, although none of those present would admit it even under torture, but that didn't distinguish them from the masses strewn across the planet in lesser or greater density, between walls no different to these.

Then you came up to me.

You neared me like the educated eye approaches a picture, trying to see something within but maintaining a necessary distance. It was new and slightly unsettling for someone to be contemplating me and seeking the picture inside. Through that same prism I thought I caught a glimpse of the place where my pictures come from. But it was only a flash, an intangible instant unable to be brought down to earth or turned into anything fluid.

All of a sudden you were here, just a step away, making no demands, nor offering anything, except for that softness emanating from you, mute and melancholic, which soon snuggled up to me.

Very soon, perhaps while we were still standing there, I knew I wasn't imagining things; although that couldn't yet be true because the truth still had to be woven, weft for weft and warp for warp. I'd been irritated and disheartened so many times by those standard expectations that I just fulfil the stereotype and nourish it with my flesh.

Words looked ridiculously small in the space between us: needless, even harmful, and of all things the most capable of spoiling whatever was on offer. Still, one had to speak, to make something of that moment which had cut us out of time. So there we were, at a table in a completely empty bar, if you exclude the barman, who was puttering around with his utensils in an attempt to conceal that he was eavesdropping; people have an insatiable hunger to hear what's none of their business. Maybe he was intrigued by there being almost nothing to hear: two freaks come in and just stare at each other. Humpty and Dumpty in black! They found each other in a ditch where they were put to keep them at a safe distance from the healthy eggs, and there they fell in love with their own reflection. They consume it with amorous eyes, never blinking, and say over and over again: Oh, what a lovely egg you are! And: What am I to do with you, one so lovely? Where am I to put you when I can hardly carry myself, when it's already so hard to keep myself together in this shell? Just see what it's like to roam the world with an egg in your pocket! Or should we break each other straight away and do away with the borders between inside and out, all the hypocrisies of the human husk? You can dress up in black all you like: in essence your garb is transparent, yellow and slimy.

I'm sitting by the wall, as I always do when I get the chance. Another advantage of an empty public space, apart from the genial absence of the crowd, is that it's easy to find a place by the wall. Of all my friends, I've always preferred to entrust my back to a wall. They say true love turns into friendship over time. Will we last long enough to build love a monument of friendship?

The main thing is to silence the doubt. Not to let it hamstring us before the starting pistol. To draw together all that is still unspent from within and open windows for it, to find space for a fresh breeze.

Both of us, without a doubt, would gladly push off into heights as yet unknown to humankind, into that which it has only caught an inkling of in fiction, far from the labyrinths where love is immured. We would like to be a weightless variation on the eternal hormonal theme. We would take our bodies up there with us, of course, because otherwise it wouldn't be fun. We would burn, and from the ashes let a new, eternal flame arise. That way we could at least emerge from the heap of stone in us: the egg would exchange its smooth monolithicness and self-sufficiency for a grain of foreign salt.

We rummage around in ourselves for things worthy of saying. We try on things which have accumulated at the back of our cupboards – will they suit us? –without knowing what the new-comer has glimpsed inside. Who are you to think you can do that? Who am I when you think that's inside me?

We've been brought together by Chinese wisdom and the sciences, both culinary and astrological. By Chinese animals painted on silk, eternalised on the bookshelves of domestic gourmets. And what did our first little quest for knowledge about each other reveal? That we have the same sign of the zodiac, and then bingo: born on the same day of the same year too! Congratulations to the winners of the remarkable twin halves competition! In a different situation I would have laughed, but this had an elemental streak of the tragic in it. Why did you have to latch on to life on that same, totally irrelevant date too: 29th December 1972? In the same city, perhaps even in the same hospital? You said there was no one left for you to ask. Did we fall in love with each other and the world back then, at first glance, and bawl at each other from neighbouring cribs about that lovestruckness, which would grow with us from year to year, like a tree with two trunks, like the shares of IT companies, like the passenger planes of rival airlines outvying each other in size until they attain the capacity to simultaneously transport entire populations enamoured in that rat race from one city to another? Was it a mix-up, malevolence or the work of a wicked fairy that we were sent off from the same crib on separate paths in life, splitting our common egg, condemning the Platonic halves to wander blindly, with the cruel possibility of passing each other by forever?

Horoscopes are one of those bullshit things you can't avoid in life, however much you ignore them. Try and be born outside the signs. Try and forget your specialnesses and what distinguishes you from eleven twelfths of humanity. That's much less than a billion! A solid foundation for the feeling of uniqueness and an insight into personal predestination! But what have the stars in store for the two of us, what victuals for the voyage to the stars? For our common astrological animal, people are a less lovable aspect of the planet. Of all company, the goat will choose rocky terrain – steep and stony – where lowland livestock break their legs. It won't climb up to reach the edelweiss (but might piss on it in passing), preferring to laugh into its beard in peace. When it's had enough of irony, it will diligently graze by the house (perseverance is its greatest virtue, along with the inability to see further than its own horns), and will diligently protect the house from guests with its stench. It's a faithful animal, happy to be tied up by the house or any other dear domain: it wants to be yoked, to bear a burden on its back. A cross isn't bad, but carrying a chapel is even more heroic. Yet it's important for it to find out who to butt horns with. Someone to share the pain and misery with, but just sometimes; for at the end of the day, what's mine is still mine. That's how we were neatly prefabricated for happiness as a twosome.

What the rational mind knows is impossible and no one in their right mind would believe – the body still believes. Trembling hands give it away and seek anchorage in cigarette after cigarette. All their composure, to the last drop of sobriety, goes up in smoke. Drunken water gurgles in my ears. Splash goes the wine, running from an upset glass over the table and my legs. Wet pants: a chance for a time-out, to splash some water on myself in the bathroom, to look out from the mirror and check if everything on my face is still there or if there are disfigurements already.

That showed me a new myself, thrown off balance, well and truly shaken up, one who'd walk the streets in the following days as if they were bomb-cratered ruins, tripping over my own shadow, bashing into public phone booths, knocking over a blind man and saying *Sorry, I didn't see you*. Marvelling at objects in my hands and their fragments on the floor. It demanded enormous effort for me not to lose the ground beneath my feet, not to let myself drop. I always found tightwires to balance on. I constantly had to check my overstretched seams. And now I consigned all that held me together into the hands of blind curiosity.

*　*　*

All that has been, when viewed in retrospect, never happened. All of human history, from the instant just spent and buried back to the dawn of consciousness, exists only in the non-existent space of memory.

How much subsequent tragedy am I interpreting into our first moments? Would they now look so dramatic and passionate without it, so charged with emotions and symbolism? In brief: how much am I lying to myself? Quite a bit, no doubt, but that doesn't matter, because what I still feel we felt together and what began between us is more real to me and more alive in my body than all the things the eye convinces me really exist; the whole universe is just one vast, painful lie compared to that.

In the downstairs area of the bar we're the only guests of the jazzers whose portraits populate the walls, beset by their gazes and the full-bodied, ebony-ivory vibrations of a piano. Syncopated saxophone motifs blast between the tables, electrifying the air, which is hot and dry to the point of crackling, enough to make it rustle beneath the blades of the ceiling fans, and burn our cheeks like a blast of sand; I'm on tenterhooks, like sand jammed into an hourglass, and every single grain is torn from my body because time has suddenly become terribly precious – not one second is to be surrendered without a fight.

You are a mirage on the other side of the small round table and one mistaken movement would be enough to make you disappear; but at the same time I can already feel your smooth skin beneath my fingers, which glow with anticipation to find yours, interlock, and keep exploring.

Everything on you is smooth and rounded. And diminutive, like a child's: your feet, touchingly curved inwards, joined at the front as if in conversation; your incredibly small hands; your shoulders so slight, as if they weren't there; your doll-like face with berry cheeks, your mouth only sketched and your nose barely hinted at. Only your eyes are too old and too big, sweeping away and erasing whatever is within their reach, and with those wing-shaped eyebrows overarching everything on your face, and engulfing all they see.

A glass model at my fingertips, begging for me to take it in my hands, a Murano miniature with space inside for a cathedral, a family of dolphins and a snowstorm; and at the same time an ultimate astuteness, a slippery darkness bordered by derision; just one step inside and it possesses me: there's no going back.

From the back room of this hospitality joint now emerges the proprietor, an international great of the vibraphone, a living legend, the main and only hero of the canto *Wine, wine, wine*, now of more girth than mirth. He trundles up to the table reserved for him on a kind of stage – the throne where he displays all one hundred and fifty kilos of his earthly manifestation to his myriad admirers and keeps an eye on all the events in the hall with the look of a sleepy toad. Since there are no other events apart from the two of us, and we're totally static, he overcomes his horror vacui by gurgling to himself something evidently amusing, causing him to giggle and hiccup, and at the same time he seems about to cry. At any moment he could melt down completely into a torrent of tears, and whatever is crushing him inside he generously gives to us, heartily treating us to a performance of his soliloquy, which he endlessly tops up from an ice-filled silver bucket.

Whatever holds this man in submission inside is stronger than the outer glitter and can't be rinsed away by his planetary glory. Perhaps that is precisely the message he's been entrusted to spread all over the world: that we reach for the stars in vain because there's no shine which won't sink into the internal mud.

But we don't hear him, at least for now. I don't know what we're saying, everything is absorbed in a mutual hypnosis, there's no other name for it, we've discovered a hunger in ourselves and seized it with both hands, and we can't take our eyes off each other. At least until the moment when the spilled wine reminds us that we have hands too, albeit unfit for handling objects, and warns us how brittle what we might build would be, and how readily the little liquid which distinguishes us from the angels brims over.

Your little red lake only lasts an instant before vanishing into the barman's cloth, but it's immediately replaced with two more glasses of wine, and several more serve as justification for the drunkenness in us which tears down the last remains of gravity, and everything accelerates and becomes more imaginable.

Even your *We can't go to my place* at closing time opens up beautiful vistas of what we *can* do, right now, because it allows us, and even invites us, to go to my place.

Outside, once we've negotiated the spiral staircase, I discover that linear, unidirectional time has ceased to exist. But in a way it still endures, consisting now of a myriad of separate, simultaneous tempi ticking inside me. The street shudders from the heat of the day trapped in the asphalt and the movements of people which have stirred it up; I see straight through every pair of eyes into people's soul, that's what I feel; with all my being I understand what makes people the way they are and what it means to be that little piece of the universe. I instantly turn into what touches me: the title of the book in the shop window, the smell drifting over from the toasted-sandwich kiosk, a fragment of the sentence which brushes us in passing. I no longer cower in myself but am my own bright, luxuriant, sparkling explosion; I exist in an unlimited number of dimensions, and they keep extending and I'm present in each of them with all my being, and every segment of the world is open for me to read in deep perspective.

Now we're in the car, beneath the horse chestnut in full bloom. It's not a big car but could fit a whole flock of folk your size because you take up only part of the seat; at the same time, this is no longer the car I knew, its purpose and potential are as yet undefined, and a tension reigns like in a spacecraft before lift-off. But my hands and legs do their job; some force tells them what to press and pull, and the scenery glides past and the intersections roll by in a recognisable sequence. Every time I dare to look to the right I find – incomprehensibly – that you're still there. With those eyes which hardly fit into the car, black fireflies glowing in the dark; for some reason they haven't flitted away but tamely escort me home.

I unlock the door and push it open, and still on the doorstep, without turning on the light, we're seized by a fever and reach for the other body, which immediately refuses to remain foreign, and in it we recognise the other half of ourselves; like a switch, this sets off a trembling in both of us, and our two halves inflame it further, stirring and fanning the fire in each other; our halves understand each other perfectly in their own language unearthed in regions of our being which have long languished in ignorance; we had no idea that we possessed them, and they us; our body takes us over completely, lifting us out of oblivion into its arms with a love swift and sudden, and we would instantly surrender it all we have, and that is now so much, more than can fit into the sum of our earthly existence minus this instant; it is one immense microcosm, it merits that we stay in it forever and ban other forms of existence, more of which arrive to vie with each other ever more frantically and destructively; which to choose, perhaps the one where it becomes certain, irreversible, that our lips will adhere; it already exceeds all my hopes, the horizon of my life's combined expectations, to think that the closeness of someone's lips would bloom in me into such splendour and riot, but they don't stop at that, they really do touch me, all of me and all at once; I tremble from head to toe from one single touch of that tiny, downy body because it answers every tremble like a mirror with a trembling of its own, and that mirror shows how much I've missed what you are, what now bedews your lips; I press myself into them and they absorb me whole, all that remains of us is a common mouth – a source and an orifice at the same time; all else is swept away by the darkness revolving around us, we're buffeted by a whirlpool and are at the same time its heated, delirious heart, freed of mental grime, and our fingers and mouths conquer centimetre after centimetre more of that naked throbbing, wherever I touch is terribly vibrant, it burns, renders, dissolves and draws me into itself, it can't stand clothes a second longer and we cast them off like fetters, it's inconceivable to ever wear them again, such an insult to the skin, it's unimaginable to touch anything except your skin; yours and mine have been tailor-made to press up to each other, envelop each other and enter every recess, to grind each other's presence into the grooves; all the separation we've endured now gushes forth, rushes to recover what is ours, all of life has marathoned and moulded us for this moment, with Spartan austerity for this eruption, whatever we experienced before was only for comparison with this, for the sake of euphoria at discovering the original; bare skin takes on the role of lungs, inhaling the heavenly manna from the other skin, drinking it without breath, with elemental passion, as if possessed; pedantically I sample one morsel after another, only to return obsessively to the epicentres, tirelessly drawing from the chambers of relish, from your breasts and armpits and groin and all the folds, furrows, openings, cavities and dark spaces; I penetrate, press, plumb, probe, plough; you tremble beneath me and rise up, fit flush against me, squirming, moaning, gasping, striving to break through the membrane which hampers complete osmosis, the fusion of the sexes, of shorelines and skylines; we'll stay uplifted in the stratosphere, the eddying elements, we'll blindly seethe in every segment of ourselves and hide in the astral expanses from all that is perishable and one iota less than intense, integral, hypnotic and boundlessly arousing; that's all we can do, it's the only place, there's no further than this.

* * *

I was one of those women who would readily claim, because you have your expectations but nothing more sensible to say, "Really, it's pleasure enough for me when you come". And that was almost the truth because I was never crazy about orgasms. I mean, the whole concept of 'doing it', like some assignment, with that one goal in mind – no thanks, I'd rather not even start. I don't mean to say that, for me, orgasm was a planet in some virtual galaxy. It did visit me here and there, more like an exception to the rule, independent of the effort invested. Sex was an absolute must for me in every relationship; at the same time, sex was no good without a relationship. But I didn't go asking *Cosmo* how many times a week I had to come; it's a bit strange investing effort in a passion, honing that skill and counting the number of times 'it' happens.

One thing is for sure: you didn't demonstrate any special tricks or unprecedented mastership. But I 'climaxed' already during what some call foreplay. And once more soon afterwards, which is a bit of a contradiction, but let's not be pedantic. I was in wonderment, spiced with irritation. At the same time, that shuddering was now deep inside me and effusively demanded feeling. Which box to put it in? Where did it come from and how was it able to seize me so quickly? I thought I saw far enough to be able to trust my instruments and was immune to surprises. But now something not only pressed the buttons in me but came up with new ones too.

Wasting no time, that feeling turns into a state of countless nuances, high and low, ranging from the thrilled and the anxious to the blissfully blunt: I get to know it in detail and learn that there's no box to put it in because there's no space in me it hasn't already occupied. I see it *in place of* what I look at, I can't find a suitable spot for myself because I'm always somewhere else; I spend the same number of hours in front of my canvases but keep forgetting why I'm there, every now and again I find myself messing around with my paintbrush, but the patterns it leaves are childishly silly; orders come by phone, I diligently note them down, and a few hours later the piece of paper no longer exists; I promise to come to events and remember them days later, if I'm lucky; the nights are jungles of fruitless thoughts, and I spread their branches for hours in search of a little oblivion, and as soon as it comes over me I open my eyes wide and continue living where I left off, equally eagerly, the dark is dispelled by a deep vigilance, as universal as it is hysterical, but during the day it's reduced to an easy expectation of the evening; we skip a few for fear that the constant friction will burn us, our bodies won't allow anything else when they come close, so we take these forced breaks, insert 'evenings off' but go crazy from the lack, which we patch up over the telephone line, drifting half the night on the telephonic raft; during the day we call each other for silly little reasons, or without them, it's funny how little we say to each other and prefer just to listen to one another's breathing, it's funny how substantial that sound in the receiver can be; I miss it as soon as I hang up, and instinct makes me check if a mail or text message has come in the meantime (as if any time had passed!), and mostly I'm not disappointed, there's another chain of self-infatuated letters not talking about anything else, and it's incomprehensibly hard to exist outside them, to find the calm for any other activity; everything else sounds incomplete, ignoble, indecent.

At the same time, it covers me like a capsule impenetrable to the eyes of others and impervious to atmospheric events.

Father's suffering now just glides along amiably beside it.

You're inside it too, occupying the whole space before I realise; if anything coherent can be squeezed in, it's as dialogue: I have to explain to you and discuss with you whatever goes through my mind, to ask your opinion, even if it's just about a choice of teaspoon; my eyes now serve exclusively for searching for things worth sharing with the you in me.

But when we're together, it's hard to arrive at words we haven't already shared through our touches and gazes, or purely through our closeness. That's a bit scary, but there's no time for far-sighted fear or anything less immediate than embraces. Besides, it feels so much more real and satisfying to be cloned – that togetherness in everything conceivable.

Of all the tenses, only the present is left. I don't know which of us suggested it, or if we broached the issue at all, but we both wholeheartedly agreed to an embargo on whatever was before, an agreement of silence about the past. What good could it do us? I know too much about my own and will happily give it away to the first bidder; I want you here and now, without a single bit stuck in other dimensions. How pretentious, how childish, to expect that we would purge ourselves of everything which prevents us from reinventing ourselves from zero and tailoring ourselves to a totally new measure. But whatever knowledge we've gathered so far is of no use – there's no room for anything except immoderate expectations and childlike wishes.

From evening to evening is an ocean-wide gap – plus there are those we bravely miss out to cultivate yearning – and the days are like a dive with my breath held. When it's time to come up for air, nothing can hold me down: I happily take the tram out to the terminus, then three stops with the bus through the outskirts. And as soon as I get out and am on the footpath I feel well enough to want to stay, I don't need to take a single step more towards happiness because it's already immersed me from inside, I float along on it, saunter and give it time to settle; I've felt at home in this neighbourhood from the very beginning, as if I grew up here. In just a few days I grew propellers and roots, acquired an earthing in my own body, so that my body and the other twelve grams feel they belong here. And I'm hardly heavier on my legs as they carry me to your house, perfectly camouflaged in the emulsion of suburban stagnation among hundreds of other equally shabby houses. There is nothing here to comfort the eye, let alone shape the desire for earthly duration, for putting out the tentacles of one's family; yet so many have dug themselves in. They tie themselves to a clod of soil to call their own as evidence of their human self and its prosthetic devices, animal, vegetable and material, which they've crammed into their courtyards to adorn the plots of their existence, and how right they are to do so: it's the culmination of wisdom to stir up one's tribal instinct, to nourish it with durable foundations and day-long pursuits, with gardens and kindergartens, or at least balcony-based evocations of Paradise, to enclose one's biotope and colonise it with human hubbub; all that is perfectly com-prehensible and compelling, in fact it's the only way; and it's with that inside me that I ring your doorbell every time.

And then it disappears as soon as I'm through the threshold, it's like I'm in a submarine, a craft undetectable by earthly radar; your hands erase the outer world. How can you say they're no good at anything in particular, how else can my every thought be transformed into the desire for you to touch me? It intercepts and grounds our attempts to fill the space between us with words, to see what fuses us together in verbal contour and at the same time maintain the air between us with words; we can't live for more than a few seconds if we're an arm's length apart; already we're in under each other's T-shirts, each other's palate and all the arches of our physical existence. For the life of me I don't know why I go faint so ardently beneath those hands, but it's blindingly easy to follow the way they shape me with their touch, the way my contours emerge from the sweat we pour on one another. We wring each other down to the last drop and afterwards we still have more; the nights are getting hotter and we pour yet more heat into ourselves, but wine has no particular part to play in this, the wine in the pauses is only a brief distraction from our serious stupor; the sheets beneath us are drunk, flooded again and again by our fluids, all crumpled, then smoothed out only to be creased and kneaded once more, my whole body craves again for that kneading as soon as our raging rivers subside, I need your hands everywhere and ever deeper, and your lips which you immerse in me; you always meet me with that wet smile and a tenderness which turns me to water and begins to control my movements already at the doorstep, I have to press myself up to it straight away with my breasts and belly and thighs, I bury my face in your skin, and immediately we fall into a bewilderment, where everything is interlocked, stirred up and fuses in the same impassable, pulsating second; a hundred times the same, simultaneously, we press crotch to crotch, chest to chest, I rub my breasts against your bare back, your belly, they stay in your mouth to the edge of unconsciousness, and you in mine, hot, smooth, supple and slippery; you slide easily down every valley, the channels are velvety and moist, full to bursting with delight which has to be flung from my throat with a scream; I want to suck all of you in through my throat, fill my lungs with you and seal them, and it feels you'll melt me with your lips, every last bit of me will flow into your mouth, and we'll be wedged in each other so inseparably that we'll have to be smelted down; you'll finish me off with powerful thrusts, my groin will burst and all the threads in me snap, my heart will rush out through my forehead, I'll just gasp my dying breath, and I won't care. Yet

I dread how things will be afterwards, how to walk the earth after that, how to repeat it, or at least come close to it, but this fear is needless because even before the sweat has cooled from our skin we're there again, equally hungry.

*   *   *

That light bulb had long since given up the ghost like all the other similar things I've neither fixed nor removed: I consummate my acceptance of the situation by ever more skilfully avoiding them with my gaze. The next evening is awash with the flux and tide of uncertainty as to whether you'll say *I'm sorry, those were a few seconds of foolishness, you know the rest yourself: what happened was all just in your imagination.* Finally I more or less steel myself for the blow; I pick up the phone, type in your number, hear the first ring, and suddenly the light bulb comes alive and dazzles me with a blinding beam of light, like a spotlight from above.

The bulb hadn't gone, it had just lost contact. And of all moments, it chose that one to reconnect. Quite a trifle, really, with no value outside the context, but in cooperation with the rest – a Messianic annunciation. It began with the realisation that we were born on the same day, of all days in the history of humankind. That already holds enough seismic potential of its own, rousing me wide awake and demanding serious meditation, but it produces nothing of benefit, nothing applicable, more just fear and trembling at the sense that what I have in my hands is finer than a spider's thread and at once more precious to me than my own birth, and sent down to earth in only one single copy.

Discussing our favourite books, films and music confirms, if there was any room for doubt, that we've lived in telepathic twinship without knowing it and have together created the archetypal match-making TV show; a fiction about love à la carte; it was our overlapping which inspired the fantasy about entrusting one's partner-search to a well-informed agency with a global database of potential candidates. It's almost funny how many crucial pointers, bases and sources both of us have visited on our separate orbits, how many similar traces have been impressed into us, how many identical inter-pretations, feelings and landscapes of the senses... What congeniality our destinies have blindly concocted in these two vessels!

It's not easy to live with that because the thrill of discovery gradually turns into a search for something we can't hear and, being silent, we can't know in advance. Being so close that there's no need to seal up the gaps between us is certainly satisfying, but it distances us from everything in the external world. Starry-eyed at so much inner beauty, we're imprisoned in that vacuum. In the air, the flowering chestnuts of May are replaced by the fragrant lindens of June, and still our mutual enchantment lets nothing else into our field of vision, no step out among the mortals. I live for the moment when the doorbell rings and whatever has called me during the day and assured me of its existence dissipates when I see you at the doorstep.

And the same scenario is repeated. We fall into one another, into oblivion, revolving in a vortex of vertigo. It's even a little reminiscent of a turntable and the stylus in its groove – it has no sense of duration, all that happens is circular; we copy out page after page of the same moment, one over the other. The only trace of time are your cigarette butts which fill up the ashtray; your lighter is in your hands as soon as you take them off me; that sight is at once like a hand placed on my shoulder by a different time, but it's enough to shake it off for it to disappear; when you go I send a draught of fresh air through the whole mélange, ashes are returned to ashes, yet the veils of smoke in the air keep you for several hours longer, and then I hold my breath until the next evening, which we'll again set on fire.

The material world between us is now only still embodied in wine. For lack of oenological education, in the supermarket I let onomastics decide: I bow to nominative determinism and take a bottle of Macedonian red with the label *T'ga za jug* – Longing for the South – and the move turns out to be so fruitful that we never even think of changing or experimenting with variations; a bottle of this brand, filled with the optimum blend of longing and the south, a formula which ferments in us into all-evening euphoria, gives the south wings on which to flutter here and lends longing an aesthetic, epic dimension; not a single evening reaches the end without us extracting the soul of the genie in the bottle.

But the shelf-life of oblivion and the ignoring of the past is limited. The less alluring face of longing returns too, that countenance which no one would take off the shelf or invite on an endless summer holiday, but there you have it, far-thinking God included it among the prizes to create a little suspense and give the true long-term winners a chance to stand out. Whatever I feel when I see you, however certain I am that this is our common truth and with however much desire you show me that it will never ever be different, I start having bouts of what I call longing just so as to cover up the Unnameable. It strikes root and gains ground, at first only in solitude but soon also when we're together.

I hide, but it becomes ever harder. In those moments, which grow to swallow up ever greater slices of the day and cut to the last credible explanation, I gasp for words on the phone like a fish on dry land, and I put an end to my anguish by inventing things I desperately need to do just then. When we meet, I respond to your increasingly questioning looks with whatever pretexts are at hand: insomnia, stress or headaches.

But each masquerade works only once, and the guise is already crumbling. Reflections of the Unnameable settle flake by flake on your worried face, amidst nervousness and anxiety. I watch this from the inside, and I would scream, I would let myself be crucified, if only it would stop; but I do nothing.

The chemistry and mechanics of the body never fail. As soon as I touch you I'm reduced to prehistoric instinct. A vitality seethes up within me, seeking release, wanting to fill you everywhere like fingers in a glove, to dig into your skin in a frenzied thirst for your smells and tastes, and I can't get enough. Although I search you with my tongue from your mouth to your toes and the depths of every concavity, I can hardly taste a hint of humanity. As if you weren't a warm-blooded being and your molecules in no way tainted with flesh, and your elevation into the ether is so effective that it almost evokes a nostalgia for something animalistic, or at least savage, but in vain, it's inconceivable, nothing less tender than tenderness can flow between us, not even in thought.

And every time that leads to what I sensed at the very beginning and what soon emerged in full glory to petrify my gaze: that I can only watch as everything precious I take into my hand shrivels before my eyes, that your burning, all-embracing closeness won't be able to bridge the gap which separates us, and that not one bold launch towards fusion will prevent us from becoming mere objects for one another again. That's how it is, although there's nothing on you I don't love, and although every little piece of your being is still equally alive in me today, tangible in its plenitude and untouched over time: if I move one little stone I'm buried by an avalanche of the others.

That butt-end of a smile you greet me with, without words, your head just leaning towards your shoulder, a slight twitch of your lips... Your eyes for an instant deep in mine, dark and piercing, with an insatiable glimmer... The thought which first flashes across your face and only then, painstakingly weighed up, crystallises in the air, shallow reefs and shoals... There are hundreds more which don't come beyond your mouth, except as sighs or pouting like an angry duck. The shrill voice which escapes your mouth at the end of the sentence like the aliquot tone of a musical instrument... The ait of fine downy hairs beneath your ear... A traverse streak on your nose when you're tired... Your calves outstretched across my belly, and I caressing them... So much joy beneath my fingers that I choke on tears, feeling that eternity is sneering at me, and I only stare at it through a sheath of ice, I don't know what else to do.

It's similar outside the cocoon, too. While we sit in the theatre, our fingers intertwined, my hand roams all your accessible places, I explore down your neck into your unbuttoned blouse; the woman on the stage beats the air with her fists and crawls on all fours with her veins almost bursting – on the whole it's not so irritating that someone would get up and walk out – but my only thought is the time wasted when I'm not looking at you. In the bar afterwards your beauty is so sparkling and so deafening that I feel like going from table to table and asking the visitors to forgive you for it making them feel ugly in comparison, but they don't hear because they're busy talking. Yet I don't say a word to you about this, I keep it all inside.

The evening social do – how absolutely spiffing! The participants include contemporaries endowed with canonical sway, lucid insights into the functioning of the world and a gift for its humoristic recycling, even with unadulterated charm. Some seem happily replete with their own ego, in euphony with the environment and embraced by the fulsome resonance of their own words. And me? I take delight in comparativist ping-pong, after you I start to see a buffoon in everyone, about one fifth the size they believe themselves to be, with a wind-up key on their backs, engrossed in the gross bubbles they blow with their spit.

At your joint exhibition together with three other artists I feel I've come loose from the floor and am budding with pride because their attempt to drag you back to earth and break you down to their size is so ridiculously unsuccessful; disproportion is the main event of the evening, even for someone artistically illiterate like me it's as clear as day that only your paintings have that inner glow, and in your eyes there's a glow for me only, it flashes with anticipation that we'll rush home to my place and let rip, with the whole evening ahead of us; we've brought quite a drunkenness with us but still open another bottle of Longing, and a bag of laughter in ourselves; everything revolves with us in the heat which unceasingly pushes back the borders of the possible, the air itself is pure fire, and we laugh in its face, rub body against body until the last bridges are burnt, and with them the very idea of returning to humanity.

But that other truth ripens at the same time. The next day, and now almost every day, I stare with terrifying sobriety into Nothing. It's there, sneering, both in inhuman distances and in tame, everyday objects – a spoon or the fin of a radiator is able to hypnotise me and cast me into my inner well. The couch is constant, kindly and full of understanding, but as the hours pass it numbs to me. I get up at night and sometimes spend half of it sitting on the balcony faced with the childish, theatrical, but unanswerable question of how to keep on living. That should be indescribably easy because of you and with you at my side, but I'm ever less able to get myself together. I just watch, day after day, as the seasons sail by on your face.

*   *   *

It was like observing a freshly painted picture and the way it changes before your eyes. Its contours distort into something deplorable, even taunting, and the colours fade away. You still recognise it, more or less, and can link it to your work and that part of you to which you've given material form. But not a single brush stroke has left the mark you intended, nor can anything be corrected. Every detail has got out of control and the work as a whole seems strangely arbitrary; and that hurts.

I seek in vain to understand what happened. No sooner had we risen to lofty heights and inhaled the zephyrous breezes, than I felt a solitude in my lungs. There wasn't even time for anything to get spoiled. I don't remember a single harsh word or either of us raising our voices. Or anything like a cloud on the horizon. But I watched as it deflated day after day, floated back down to earth and withered away.

Viewed from here, everything we had looks like a thimbleful of air. Whatever I saw – our ethereal unity and fusion – was perhaps an image painted on a non-existent canvas by the wish that it be true. And it was, for that isolated instant. But how much truth can there be in a scene which so thoroughly melts away?

Your enthusiasm lasted about as long as a child's when given a new toy. It's true that your Peter Pan syndrome fascinated and beguiled me. But it quickly became clear that there was a less inspiring, highly impractical side to your being stuck in boyhood. It was plain that you didn't know what to do with me.

Consciously or not, you stripped everything from me. It came off in fine pieces of husk, but steadily, totally, down to the bone. And I don't have unlimited patience. I tried hard to understand

and to move things along and to wait for the problem to pass. But I never caught a glimpse of what consumed you so quickly, squeezed the life out of you, and then started working away at me with equal devotion.

I can't imagine any ill intent. But you really do deserve someone who will respond to your declared feelings by sighing and biting their lips, who will swiftly depart when anything resembling perfection is born in you, who will join in your joy with a pained face, and who will assiduously nourish the insight into your inadequacy and your inability to counter whatever exasperates them.

Unfortunately I already had a patient like that at home. The two of them overlapped ever more unpleasantly, they added up and aided each other in irritating me. With the best will in the world and all the understanding I could muster, I just wasn't able to overcome my expectation that the one I love would at least reach me his hand out of his prison.

I've never met another person so divorced from their feelings. The emotionally stunted are easy to sort out. With you, your feelings began to sparkle and for an instant showed wings and a palpable refinement I was immediately drawn to. And then they disappeared behind stockpiles of who knows what past evil, behind all sorts of junk which loves the limelight. And soon they almost needed pulling out of a well.

I don't know what irritates me more than your romantic gesticulation and tokenism, the words you stick like stamps to your suddenly unique being and the emotional boons which come as by-product of our interaction, as if you and they were all from some Toyland post office. And so I found myself in the role of spokeswoman, animateur and B-girl forced to plead for a smattering of applause.

And, at the same time, all you didn't say and all I waited for in vain to happen quickly left a bitter taste in my mouth, although the opportunity was there and begged us to take it. Strangely enough, I couldn't but take it personally that you just watched, without a word, as each of us withered in the other and the silence between us mounted. And that you didn't prevent it from gouging a wound in me and tearing it open again every day.

Even now I don't think I should have protected myself from the way things were going, with you creaming off all that was pleasant – the aesthetics of it and the fun – and letting the rest go down the drain. Whatever I was so lucky as to filter out by non-verbal, telepathic means, I absorbed like a good little sponge. And over the phone I was like a soundboard for what your voice couldn't or wouldn't express. So we tele-pained together, and our suffering easily bridged the rift.

Which of the flourishes of your fading should I single out? Your shoulders bent beneath a burden of existential absurdities, antediluvian but addressed personally to you? Your misty eyes lost in the abyss which opened up in the middle of the floor? The ability to forget what I'd told you half an hour ago? To sit the whole evening in company just answering questions, in a mumble? Or the outright lies – though I called them by a different name so as to swallow them more easily, when you started avoiding me?

But my favourite was your slow, pained *sotto voce* in the receiver. All at once it ran dry like batteries going flat, and ones like that aren't made any more, what bad luck. From then on your voice only brought words like the wind carries an echo from afar. You sobbed and choked, but whatever remained in your throat could no longer be spat out and there was no way of extracting it. OK, never mind, speak to you tomorrow.

You took my alarm signals pretty well: my protests and silent Masses, my attempts to give you a jolt, or at least a shake-up, and to stick comical moustaches and beards on phantoms. And then there were the pains which started to spring up in unusual parts of my body – elbow, jaw or rib – and sometimes last for days, making me go for an X-ray in the belief that something was broken. Not even my avowals that I couldn't go on like this inspired you to anything more than awkwardly stare at the floor.

I searched myself for blame, trying to find things I should feel guilty for. Perhaps for not having big tits in my bra and lacking four to six centimetres on the vertical? Or for not sympathising profusely enough at your moans of self-pity? Or because you secretly craved for a blonde, a redhead or a platinum bimbo? Or because you actually need someone who'll use you as a doormat and spit in your face to remind you how wretched you are? What a shame I have absolutely no talent for that.

All that was missing, now I'm sure, was your ability to keep me in focus. For as long as we touched, everything worked wonderfully as if there was no chance in the world of it ever stopping. Even when we were with other people we never stopped touching each other, holding on to each other and intertwining our bodies. Our physicality had a life of its own – insatiable, unquenchable, indestructible – but ever more out of step with everything else, and keeping it in view became ever harder.

*   *   *

It smelt of proper autumn that morning when the chilly air drifted from the dew-covered grasses and flowed through the rust-spotted, insect-gnawed crown of the walnut tree, which had now grown into the house so far that its branches brought every wind inside, flailing at the furniture and raining leaves on the floor. The Samobor hills on the horizon were still a chimera behind a wall of pea-soupish fog; a tremor of dawn remained in the air and, as usual for that time of year, the distant smell of the first days of school came wafting up. Walking on my tiptoes so as not to wake Mother, I carried out my luggage and locked the door. Only on the stairs did *the true state of affairs* come home to me with a jolt and a realisation of the relativity of death, or life; while Mother had been alive I'd hardly taken note of her, at least in the last few years, but now she appeared to me most assiduously.

I drove to pick you up. My stomach tightened a little at meeting your father. Answering his questions, be they inquisitional or polite, and even just hearing his paternal advice, words of encouragement and best wishes rather wearied me right at the outset. What was more, given the situation, entering the house had an uncomfortable sense of abduction about it, of taking the sun away from a person who's deathly cold, or plucking out their vital organs. But it went smoothly without a hint of friction; his eyes were a touchingly faithful duplicate of yours but too extinguished to take any real note of me. As we shook hands goodbye, the premonition pained me that I was seeing him for the last time, because very soon he would die, or I would, or we were both dead and had simply not yet registered the fact.

In the car, there was a tangible thread strung between joy and anxiety. On the first leg of the journey, to Karlovac, my hand travelled in your lap, with you snuggling up to it with your face and breasts, but this blessing also contained a fear of drowning and an inkling of the coming flood. We were going on a seaside holiday after the summer because, despite my eight years at the firm, I hadn't advanced to be one of those who could take their annual holiday when it suited them. But that didn't bother me; on the contrary, the sea was now even more appealing, decontaminated of the package pleasures of mass tourism. But those three weeks of complete mutual devotion came around a tiny bit too late for us, at least that's how I felt. As if all the years of waiting had eradicated my ability to take what I had lacked for so long. I'd lived for too long without love; in my thirty odd years I hadn't really learnt what life is like when you truly love someone. My lovestruckness was created by a chemical reaction, incomprehensibly powerful, and for some time it held me in a state of shock like that caused by acute pain; but when the anaesthesia wore off and I simply needed to *love*, I didn't know how to. That was a very dubious thought. Or rather, of all imaginable thoughts, it would be hard to find one more stupid, pathetic, and also more malignant; but I didn't know how to hide from it.

Something else travelled with us too – a remnant of the evening before. The lady colleague who had worked in Marketing until she disappeared overnight, both from the firm and from my semblance of a life, had suddenly spoken from the receiver after several years in limbo; she was as nonchalant as someone continuing a sentence after they'd just had to get up because the kettle had boiled. She didn't have anything noteworthy in the way of news, nor was she calling to find out what was new with me, but was inspired by the idea which had just shone forth that day and hurtled like a comet towards my fragile planet: that it would be great to revive our old affair. While I listened and detected her intention creeping up through all her waffle – the question if I had any plans that evening – I knew very well what I would answer: that my plans were to prepare for a trip with a person of my choosing and that every other female was an alternative; and when the moment came, I just said no. But several hours later, in a mental blip which my conscious mind found a way of bracketing out and rendering impenetrable to thoughts like *What are you doing?* and *What's the point?*, I was standing at her door and ringing the bell. The same boy opened as before, now a whole head taller and only really recognisable due to the door situation. After looking hard for a moment he recognised me, was happy to see me and made a long face when I said I wouldn't come in. He couldn't tell me where his mother had gone, he only knew she'd be back late. Her decision to continue our romance was of no great duration, however long it had been in the making, and I accepted that with gratitude. Though not with relief, because I knew that if it had restarted I would have felt so immensely guilty. And I couldn't think what conceivable good there was in it.

Leaving the car at the ferry terminal was also a mistake, albeit a lesser one, and things probably wouldn't have ended any differently if we'd taken it to the island with us, but its lack helped turn the stay into a form of imprisonment. The internet hadn't quite given us a clear image of the little town we chose specifically for its lack of inhabitants; we didn't know, for instance, that the only shop there was closed in the off-season, and it was half an hour's hike over the hill to the next one. Or that the cliffs which the only beach was nestled between were so sheer and jagged that it was impossible to walk on any further along the shore, let alone seek a secluded spot. Or that the off-season isn't the same as after a neutron bomb – uncultivated folk compensate for their small numbers with extra decibels and a tight family ethos. In other words, we had little choice but to spend the evenings on the charming, shared terrace of the apartment building in collective merriment which not even the orchestra of crickets with its numerical superiority could drown out; we were flanked on the left by two fanatical Slovenian card-playing couples with great lyrical potential for genital expletives, and on the right by a Bosnian businessman and his family; Mr Big had a thing to two to say to his mobile phone even after midnight; his speech was linguistically less exacting since he was a passionate devotee of the immutable, all-purpose phrase he liked to spit out with every single sentence: *Fucking hell!*

Approaching in a vintage bus, which strained and chugged on the one, morning route of the day, we spotted the town from the crest of the island. It fairly took our breath away: far below, amidst a lunar rockscape already so sun-scorched that it quivered, as steep as a wall, we saw a handful of houses just pinned to it, as if it was only a matter of time before they succumbed to gravity. Right at the bottom they were promised a treacherous blue softness, seemingly introverted and immersed in smooth meditation. When we'd wound down into the town, that precarious little pocket of resistance to free-fall, everything looked skewed, like a crookedly hung picture gradually giving way and slipping; one careless step sent stones raining down the slope; buildings rose up and thrust out their balconies, almost shutting each other off like flytraps; stunted trees between them flung out their branches in a futile search for support, and the parked cars provoked seasickness; the whole set-up was crying out to be secured with heavy chains.

The beach was designed by Federico Fellini. It was actually a combination of a beach and a pocket-size fishing port, although no fishermen were to be seen, only two rowboats baked in seaweed and three worn-out fishing traps at the pier. Next to the pier, you could see a bicycle in its resting place at the bottom: a real antique with dynamo light and basket, although surmounting that steep slope on a bike was inconceivable; that being perhaps the reason why it lay where it did. Because of the dizzying incline, families came to the beach and stayed all day, well equipped with cooler boxes and aids for active recreation. If they forgot anything, their beach neighbours usually had it. People knew what the others were having for lunch and the clue they were stuck on in the crossword thanks to the amphitheatrical acoustics which the rock-sheathed walls lent the beach; nature had anticipated fast food, too, by hollowing out a hearth in the rock face: *Eh, this one here's burnt, bloody hell.* The inland part of the beach was reigned over, in absolutist manner, by three or four pre-school children, to all appearances from the same family. Whenever one of them needed to do a poo, the job was done with collective support in the corner. The sea front, on the other hand, was constantly guarded by two rotund forty-year-olds enthusiastically playing keepy-uppy and highlighting their achievements in that endeavour with resilient cries of *Great, mate!* Plus there was a bodybuilder of competitive calibre, one of the sort you think only exists in comics, with arms dangling down to the ground and a Hitler hairdo, albeit without his equipment and now completely devoted to floating on an air mattress. The only thing missing in this menagerie was a circus midget who would settle down in the middle of the beach and calmly masturbate.

You could go out early in the morning or at dusk. But the

early morning pleasures are best appreciated by those who had a reasonable night's sleep, and as far as dusk went, after ten days or so the beach began to seem further away, edging beyond the border of reachability. By nightfall, the bulk of my mobility and potential for uprightness was exhausted and I would become part of the deckchair on the terrace. I must say it was quite all right on the terrace, especially in the mornings when the card-players and the neanderthal with his mobile used to gather down at the beach, up until when the sun took over, beating down with all its might as it sailed across the sky. With a book in hand and my legs stretched out over the railing, I was in my element here; cascading rooves bowed to us from below, stone walls promised indestructibility and immunity to storms and earthquakes, there was as much greenery as you like to cool down under, oxygen blew in from the open sea, and the sky met the water in a distant blur of azure. And above all, you were constantly there for my eyes to behold, filling them with immeasurable delight.

Carefully peeling back the sheet, I would be stunned at my discovery: I find you curled in the shape of an S, a body I already know in every detail and still can't conceive that it wants to belong to me – why me? Your face rippling with peals of laughter yet immediately calmed with a finger to your lips; the resolute line of your chin and the meditative shadow beneath your cheek, in profile, as you chew on your pencil over a sketch of the inlet; your dress the colour of sand, clinging to your sweet prominences, glades and hollows; tiny toes, touchingly child-size, which seem lost in the middle of the bed; calves freshly depilated, and I hear the rustle of silk as you feel them to check the result; armpits which, as you dry your hair after your shower, I want to bury my face in and remain there for the rest of the summer holiday, nay, for the rest of my working life and retirement.

Countless flashes like that shook me in sweet pain. And I was stupid enough to be silent about every single one of them.

My body sought and was rewarded: in the morning while still half asleep, gladly once more before lunch, and again after our afternoon rest, or instead of it, or instead of lunch; our hunger took care of itself and soothed our overstimulated skin with intoxication. But towards evening a languor would set in; my stomach swelled up and the stale sediment grew, bitter clouds rolled in, the contours of things blurred and everything in me turned to mud. Time would refuse to pass or go anywhere of its own accord, all snotty and clogged up, like a curtain of mucous in the air; every second was a painstaking struggle. It became indescribably hard to be me – incomprehensible that I was anything less than sixty years old! With my current level of energy, it was unimaginable to fill the shell which represented me, to climb up into it out of my dark shaft.

In one of those twilights we climbed up over the hill. From the highest point of the island our gaze shot out dramatically far and met pitifully little; a blood red haze mirrored, or perhaps heralded, a mute bang – the faint trace left by the collapsed core of our galaxy. Our temporary home, together with everything we'd brought with us, looked pretty insignificant from there. The little town crept down the other slope, reluctantly, like into the gaping mouth of a cave; its upper reaches were overgrown with brambles and thorn bushes like the neglected interior of the island. In the blackness behind the last houses we glimpsed the remains of vineyards which had reverted to scrub, and further, towards the interior of the island, the signs of a century-old exodus. If the darkness had been slow in coming, in the end it proved mighty effective; the off-season hadn't extinguished all illumination. The few half-hearted specklets of light only irritated the eye and made the steep sidestreets and paths even harder to negotiate; they were eroded with potholes and trenches, with pipes jutting out of like broken bones as if the island was in the throes of trench warfare between rodents. The shutters were all closed tight like the lids of blind eyes. Even more of them were simply missing, as well as the window frames, doors and everything behind the façade which normally constitutes a house; the dominant form of architecture was the stone skeleton with a fig tree growing through the collapsed roof and with rubbish and excrement thrown inside. But it became ever more questionable as to who could have done that because the only living creatures we came across were a few emaciated cats, as thin as rags, who saw us off with their bony heads as if *we* were the last residents and not them and their realm. And then, out of nowhere, a little girl popped up in folk costume, trailing skirts and lace, and then another, confirming that some of the population had indeed survived the mildew epidemics, urbanophile migration and government-condoned robbery; humans are a hardy breed, especially those from the islands, and they even celebrate their history if their present is going nowhere. The girls told us that a folksy gathering was to be held at the church, with the locals flicking off the Euro-tourists and presenting their authentic, conserved, off-season selves, purely for themselves. Uninvited, we just let ourselves be directed to where we could find food. At the tavern they were pleasantly surprised to see us, admired our youthfulness and what remarkably beautiful twins we were, and wanted to prattle on to us about all sorts of things. But they were far from diligent in the kitchen, and if there hadn't been a basket of bread on the table we would have sunk our teeth into each other. When they finally had mercy, there was no overlooking how sick you were of my face and my carping, let's call it my crap, and you lit up after hardly touching your octopus salad. I sat picking the bones out of my fish for a little longer while you, with ever more caustic lips, poured some more from the carafe and rent the air beside my head with your gaze; and then, without a word, we set off wearily down the hill, plunging into pitch darkness.

The next day dawned a doldrumish grey. Not a breath of air, no movement or activity – everything seemed stifled under that leaden hood. You went to the beach alone for the first time, without asking twice and without inquiring what it meant when I shrugged my shoulders. I spent the whole afternoon feeling the contours of that separation, how the space you vacated now prickled and hummed, and I tasted the soulless and bitter futility of time deprived of you. It turned out that those two weeks had created a narcotic addiction in me and my body no longer agreed to be without you for several hours. But when you came back, I didn't so much as mention the wave of warmth which engulfed me. I promptly forgot that feeling and sank back into my quagmire of quiet, staring into it and not finding anything to say. I didn't have the hint of an answer as to where this bog came from, and what came first, the chicken or the egg, and if the few grains it pecked amounted to a kind of depression, which I only call depression out of kindness towards the hippocrats who swear that everything has to have a name. Or was this bog a product of the realisation that even when I'm suffused with love I see its image in the negative, starker than stark, which permeates and poisons everything damn fast, and is not aided by my playing the hypocrite and wrapping it in sandy or muddy metaphors?

The next day, equally grey, muted and anaemic, that (Polish? Slovakian?) couple with their child appeared on the beach. It had that syndrome which reminded some people of Mongols. While it's certainly a healthy parental approach not to stress the condition and put on a big fuss about the child, they tied its hair into a pigtail and put it in a tanga. Set aside in the sand, that baggy being perfectly portrayed the warrior resting after his ride over the endless steppes, oblivious to the play of the heavens and the squeals of children. He didn't need playthings or the attention of others; somewhere far from the beach, beyond the coordinates of Croatia, he was preoccupied and kept blissfully smiling for hours by the discovery that sand comes alive when you take a handful of it and let it gradually trickle through your fingers, and by the realisation that the event is inexhaustible: as soon as your hands are empty you can take two more fistfuls and return it to life. Some try to shape the sand into towers and little castles, at least until the first breeze comes; for the majority it's just something to sit on; but that little nomad, in pouring it to and fro, had unwittingly found a refuge from earthly decay.

And then the beach was raised to its feet when one of the children pointed into the water and started to scream *Shark! Shark!* And sure enough, fifty metres or so from the shore, a black fin could be seen cutting the surface. All in a row, admittedly two or three metres back from the wet line of sand (you could never be sure what those monsters of the deep were capable of!) we tensely watched as it drew near, lazily but steadily, the condensing of an enormous smudge immediately beneath the surface, until it floated almost straight up to our feet. It came like an epistle in fish form, a message to us from across the sea, and silence prevailed as if in expectation that it would speak and spit our verdict out on the sand. And when the creature finally beached itself, people agreed that it was a dolphin – and may always have been – but weren't relieved. The beach was now homogenised in pity and mourning, which remained hanging over us together with the stench of decay, even after the carcass was towed out to sea by a dinghy. Everyone read what they wanted into that watery message, using as many tragic metaphors as they could. These premonitions stayed with us throughout the next two days, burying the beach and shrouding the apartment in dead silence. On the morning of the third, when I came down from the hill lugging food from the shop, you were gone.

* * *

I wanted to go, and should have already left at the end of the first week. It was as clear as day that no miracle was going to happen. But when you want to believe in something, you find a way of ignoring all the evidence to the opposite. You cling to it even after it's evaporated in your hand, until the lack of it starts to affect your body with the inability to maintain the illusion any longer.

When we left for our holiday, my disappointment was so enormous that it well nigh filled my suitcase. Virtually the only thing still left alive was my promise to you that this was different, that it could cancel the world which had existed before and therefore had nowhere to disappear to. The first half of the promise came true on the island: I found myself amidst a scene of natural devastation in its geographic manifestation.

Just as you're richer the more you give away, so I was impoverished by what I gave into the void. I was drained by my very own energy since it was devoid of any practical use. Whatever I tried to give came back at me, fierce, hurtful and hungry for my flesh. There were moments when the passion still smiled, but the rest of the time it devoured me.

For days I was my own cage. The island mirrored it in three dimensions. Inside, I was unable to think of anything other than confinement and suffocation. Ever more constricted, I languished between the bars until it made my head spin. For two sleepless nights the need to pull the bars apart condensed. In the third, just before dawn, I was out of it. Irreversibly.

Rugged up in a blanket on the terrace, shivering a little in the dew, I waited for you to wake up. When you went off to the shop, I crammed together my things. During the night I'd thought up at least twenty-seven versions of my farewell message. And all of them sounded equally superfluous in the end. On the way to the bus stop, I didn't even look back.

When I boarded the bus, a long time later, I finally felt I could breathe again. I was free of the stone which had been dragging me under. There was almost a taste of victory, however bitter. Inside, I was already busily counting and ordering the fragments of my life. I suppose that's roughly how you feel after donating a kidney to save your own child.

The bus passed you on the uphill road out of town. At first you were a shapeless stain, appearing in the distance after a bend. Your moment as a full-scale human figure, preoccupied with the downhill slope and the heavy rucksack, was terribly brief. Then you plummeted back into shapelessness. The next bend wiped the stain clean away.

I watched this from my seat like a documentary film, and now the reel was empty and being taken off the projector. The settings of the tragedy far below were already being taken to the archives. The sun sparkled and there was a surprising freshness in the sapphire sea. The trip almost felt like a school excursion.

It stayed like that for most of the way. I bought a *Vogue* and read about the ultimate nuances of nails. I ate a greasy pasty with delight, dropped off to sleep and was dead to the world. When I opened my eyes the signs said Karlovac and an old lady framed by a headscarf was sitting next to me. She smiled and immediately started talking about one thing and another and offering me fruit; she took my hand between hers and marvelled at how smooth it was. And at that instant my tears started to flow.

I cried for the rest of trip, telling her the whole story, and she despaired with me and was soon crying herself. I wasn't crying hysterically and could almost talk normally. But my head turned to liquid and ran out through my eyes and nose. And it didn't stop afterwards in the tram, nor at home. Only towards morning was it interrupted by sleep.

The following days were similar. Tears only came on and off, and I spent most of the time lying motionless. Getting dressed or going to the bathroom for a glass of water were huge challenges. For each, it took me hours to gather the strength. From being teary and half-asleep I would drift off fitfully into the unconscious, to be returned from there again by the discomfort of a tear-soaked pillow. The change of day and night could vaguely be glimpsed through the roller blinds.

But there was also a good side to that: finally I didn't care what Father might have been thinking and whether I was in danger of traumatising him. That feeling was a huge achievement it itself. He made something of an effort within the limits of his abilities: he stood a little in my doorway, mouthing the air; he turned his hands upwards, let them fall to his sides, and went back to the couch.

The first thing I had to do, when movements with a particular goal became feasible again, was to get rid of the sketches with their malignant aura lying unpacked at the bottom of my suitcase. Landscapes, portraits, images of the naked sleeper – I tipped the entire contents of the folder into a black garbage bag, where it was joined by my entire artistic production of the last three months, after a cursory glance had confirmed its utter worth-lessness. I donated everything to the Refuse Collection Service.

Then the decision came to me, as unimpeachable as the word of Moses and Gabriel: I had to move out. No amount of scrubbing and scouring would cleanse this container that was me: it had to be substituted. I had to cut off the dead meat, all of it. Three days later I had an immaculate new address. I didn't even take my painting equipment. I bought everything new, right down to the last piece of underwear.

I started working that same afternoon. I didn't perceive it as work. I sat down on the floor and began drawing lines, filling in one sheet of paper after another until my body sagged and I collapsed into bed; but as soon as I opened my eyes I continued. All the while, I was about as cerebral as the parquet floor under my bum. My hands were in the grip of that fever, but it was only local activity – the rest of me was under anaesthetic. Until the business with the woman from the twelfth floor. But four days afterwards I went on as before.

Only some weeks later did a little space for other activities and people open up. I started dropping in to see Father more regularly. Or had a quick coffee with someone for twenty minutes. Gradually the smells of late autumn reached me, the sounds of the neighbourhood, and the wish to go for a walk in Maksimir Park. I enrolled in a yoga course and tried hard to feel *the spirit of the group* during the exercises. Now and then I even turned on the TV without sound, like an aquarium.

Not that I never thought of you. It happened too often at first and brought on bouts of rage and bitterness – I don't know myself and can't stand myself when I'm like that. But when the storm subsided I was able to almost calmly recall a shared moment, a detail of your body, or imagine what you were doing. Even – in my head – to dial your number. But in reality that was quite impossible. In this life, there could be nothing more between us.

* * *

The terrace is quiet now. The entertainment potential of the situation is acutely apparent to all. Even the mobile phone avoids ringing so as not to miss anything. Pretending to be disinterested, the others oppress me with their looks, demanding a dramatic outburst. I realise I'm disappointing them, but I'm not going to withdraw. I stay sitting on a plastic chair with my eyes glued to a bottle of mineral water. Whatever they think about this is far from the punishment I deserve. It hasn't even begun yet.

I can't go anywhere until tomorrow morning. For now, I have to work on extending time. I take a book – a reflex which reveals its full naivety after just ten minutes. I crouch on the bed rocking, with my chin between my knees, for who knows how long. The terrace is deserted. I stick my legs out over the railing and then go back to the bed. I pull hairs out of my forearm with my teeth. Wasps are getting agitated around the watermelon in the plastic bag on the floor. I need some fresh air and head down towards the sea with large steps. My foot slips on the gravel and I go flying into a blackberry bush. It takes a lot of effort, and self-deception, to extricate myself. In the same instant, voices from the beach turn me around and send me uphill. Now I notice blood running down my left arm. It looks the way it should. I don't stop at the houses. I rush to the peak and over the other side. I sit in the tavern at the same table. They have cigarettes, so I order a few together with an octopus salad and a carafe of red wine. When the plate arrives I already feel so sick that I would vomit if I took a single bite. I stagger through the semi-ruined city. Little peppers and kale still grow in a few of the courtyards. From somewhere I hear the braying of a donkey. On the square in front of the church a travelling salesman has laid out the content of his van: flip-flops, plastic sunglasses, enamelled pots and make-up sets. I see the darkness coming on as if someone has thrown it from an ambush.

I crouch on the bed again, rocking and biting my arm. I walk around and around in circles on the terrace to the edge of unconsciousness, sit down for a bit, and then walk again. Just before dawn there comes the smell of lavender, anise and overripe figs. The bus arrives completely empty. The ferry is tilted by waves whipped up by a stiff southerly wind. In the car my headache progresses from painful to acute but I light one cigarette after another. I press the accelerator to the floor although I see no need to hurry. On the contrary, it takes me great effort to think of the journey's destination or anything planned afterwards. The white lines rush towards me and landscapes whistle past on both sides, but that could last forever because there's nothing ahead. All of a sudden I feel I as if I've run out of petrol. My body refuses to take part in the trip any more. At the next lay-by I stay sitting with both arms braced against the steering wheel and face straight ahead as if expecting the car to race off again by itself. I get out and walk around it, shivering all over although the sun is high. I drive on, and soon my pounding heart forces me to stop again. I park with the right-hand wheels in the grass and recline my seat. Spasmodically I black out, my wires lose contact. The car shudders whenever another rushes past. I wouldn't call what I feel fear; it's more like the anxiety before an exam.

I get home at five fifteen. The air is incredibly thick and I have to chew every breath of it. I sense great, destructive things wanting to happen in the hours ahead; just pull a string and they'd explode. Still, I stay sprawled out on the couch. Simply moving is inconceivable. I don't have the slightest idea what to do with my time.

An indefinite number of days pass. At work I'm as amiable as ever before. Whoever approaches me speaks in a soft voice. Their eyes linger in mine for a second longer than necessary, but they refrain from comments. At home I rarely turn on the light. There are no more food items in the cupboards. Whatever I pick up has to be shaken free of balls of dust.

I sit on the floor for at least half an hour with the telephone on my lap, or maybe it's three hours. Then I call her. It rings five times, I hear the click and then I quickly hang up. I topple onto the bed and go out like a light. At the office I have to constantly fight off the desire to shut down the computer and leave because I've picked up a virus or my ulcer has started playing up. I drive straight to Medveščak Street. Your father peers down from the balcony. No, you're not at home, and he doesn't know when you'll be back. He leans against the railing of his observation point and watches me as I go. At home I put down my bag, wash my hands and open a tin of sweet corn. I strain it, eat one spoonful, and get up again. This time I park on the other side of the tram track, exactly opposite your courtyard door. Now and again a chestnut leaf falls onto the windscreen. You could have come back in the meantime, but then the window in the attic would light up sooner or later. I count the trams as they pass, and after forty-nine I reach for my mobile. *The number you have called is temporarily unavailable*, it tells me. The trams now become few and far between. I'm woken by the cold. The glass is milky with dew and my stomach heaves at the bitter nicotine stench. It's too early for the office, so I drive to the bus station. In the bistro, I unnaturally prolong my coffee and croissants, and I manage to arrive after one of the secretaries. I don't take a lunch break because I have to leave a bit earlier. The attic window is open, but it's still a while until it will perhaps come alight. The person we've called has turned off their mobile device. I consider the possibility of climbing up onto the roof via the drainpipe. Even if I found the ability, it looks pretty decrepit. The night is already quite black but the window doesn't light up. I take my mobile and order a pizza from the number I know by heart; Quattro Stagione with an extra portion of olives and a can of Zlatorog beer. Without removing his helmet, the delivery boy eyes me with amusement as if I was an exotic, ill-starred early version of the human product I'm proud to belong to. While eating, I listen to the evening news on the radio. After the weather forecast I turn it off and recline the seat a little. My back hurts; I fold my arms behind my head, making sure to keep the approaches to the house in view. The mobile device is turned off, like before. A drizzle sets in.

It takes me a few seconds to recognise you. Or rather, to think what to do with that information. I jump out of my car but have to let a tram pass before I can dash across the street. Only now do I perceive the male figure who has stopped at the door at the same time as you, although he's almost twice as tall, or perhaps precisely for that reason – it's hard to convince my eyes that he's of the same species. That doesn't prevent him from pressing his lips against yours, while coiling like a cobra. Enormous limbs crawl everywhere, doubtless seeking the softest spot for the bite. You hug that hulk, at least as far as you can put your arms around him, and press your face into his belly. You wait at the fence for him to turn round and send you another drop of venom with his fingers. In return, you lean your head towards your shoulder in that painfully familiar way. Then you disappear.

I imagine following him, keeping ten metres' distance. That isn't hard, although he wears the largest shoe size; he's not in hurry. Rather, you'd say he's maintained a healthy attitude to time. Is he one of a race of perverse giants who go around collecting Thumbelinas? Are there any more on his list for the evening? The rain doesn't bother him. He's probably a water-polo player and water is his element. He crosses Ban Jelačić Square diagonally, in just a few steps, and enters the Bulldog Pub. The acorn returns to the oak. I find him underground, in the catacombs adapted to the consumption of drink. I sit alone behind one of the partitions. He doesn't see me, preoccupied with writing in his notebook. Devotedly, with evident elation and inspiration, he fills one page after another. He raises his head and immediately lowers it again, only looking up again when the waiter brings him his Cockta. What, a soft drink?! He brings me a vermouth, although I've never had one before. For a while I look at the virgin glass; I exhale all the air in my lungs and follow him to the toilet. I stand up on the toilet bowl and climb up onto the cistern, and there he is. Back in the bar, I wait for our eyes to meet. There isn't much surprise in his, perhaps a touch of melancholy. He doesn't try to protect himself and keeps both hands on the table even when a red bud blooms on his collarbone and is joined by one on his chest. And another on his forehead. His head just sinks against the back of the chair. I discard the gun like the core of an apple and leave with a step both resolute and calm.

The rain has intensified. Gusts of wind bend the branches. Chestnuts drum down on the roof, even whole burrs. An umbrella stops in front of the courtyard, goes inside, and only now do I realise who's underneath it. I yell your name from the tram track. Despite that tremble, you only manage a glare. Your eyes are compact, armoured and cold.

'Can we talk?'

'About what?'

I can't squeeze it all into one sentence and only just persuade you to listen to a few as we sit down in a nearby bar, although it doesn't deserve that name: the low building concealed in a park behind residential blocks successfully conserves the communal aesthetics of communist Yugoslavia. Wood-panelled walls and ceilings, rustic carvings, chequered tablecloths and an overweight, moustached waiter in a white shirt open to reveal his hairy chest. The woman in the speakers miaows about her man having cheated on her, stolen from her and beaten her, but she loves him all the more. Encouraged by such kindliness, I launch into a confession of my guilt, *in extenso*.

'You're all mine, I'm deeply aware of that, and also of all I've done wrong, or failed to do. And all the pain I've caused you, and the terrible loss, for both of us. If anything has ever been clear to me, it's how much guilt I bear.'

You tell me I sound more Catholic than Radio Maria, but I pretend not to hear.

'Only one thing is worse than the damage inflicted: the possibility that it remain unredressed and knowing we have to live with it until the end of our days. *Under* it, to be precise: crushed and ground. How can we live with the memory of something so exalted and magnificent as our love, and its consequent absence? How can we stop staring into that cleft when it's as big as life itself and can't be diminished even by the sum total of everything else experienced? The rest of my time would be a flat, empty road without a goal if I had to spend it without you. The only way out of this sorrow would be sorrow for myself. I would inevitably see my lack of you everywhere and in everything, and I would view everyone by how much they differ from you. I would no longer find a shred of feeling for people because all that I'm capable of feeling belongs to you alone; I can't exist without you. Please just let me live, for you, because I can't live any other way. I'm saying this because I know your desire hasn't disappeared, I know it in my bones, in my every neuron. Otherwise I wouldn't approach you like this. I'd vanish from the face of the earth in shame, and also so as not to trouble you with my presence – if I wasn't absolutely certain that we belong to each other, that we were made for each other...'

You say something about there being a similar bit in Woody Allen, but still I continue...

'...to be there for each other. To give meaning to the other's existence. So we can learn what the real meaning is. You'll say that's cheap or even vulgar, but it's true: only now do I feel with all my body how much we're connected, when you're wrenched away from me.'

You tell me I'm being histrionic...

'If only you knew how base even the most dramatic words are, how far from what's inside me! How beautiful that is, although it hurts insanely! Oh, don't get me wrong, I'm not a masochist. But I wouldn't give up a single bit of the pain if it meant being robbed of what I see before us, from now until our final day. This isn't coming from my loss and longing; it's all been inside me. It just couldn't find a way out to show itself, to really come awake, to overpower what's smothering me. Maybe it had to be like this – maybe I needed this to happen so I'd know what it means to fight.'

You claim not to have needed it at all, whether I did or not...

'Please give me just a little longer, a scrap of space at your side, so I can show you a different part of me. Please don't discard me without giving me one more chance, I beg you. I understand, at the moment you think your feelings for me can't return. But what now burns inside me is a hundred times, a thousand times stronger than what you've seen so far. It far exceeds what any human being can feel. It's not mine, it's not personal any more, I'm only the medium it resonates in because I've picked up the frequency. I've opened myself and surrendered to love in its purest form, the love which has existed since the world was born, which created us and is all around us, but we're unaware of it because it's beyond belief until something happens; only now do I realise how blind I was.'

You say that's a shame, get up, grab your bag and umbrella, and disappear.

A van drives past with the picture of a rotisserie and the name *Balkan Grill* on the side. I enter the number and let them recite everything they have on offer. Then I choose shish kebab. They haven't got Zlatorog, so I accept a Stella Artois.

The morning is wet but the sun has risen and the sparrows are lively. I call the office and report that I'm stuck in bed with the dreaded lurgy. I imagine lurking outside your father's house. Finally I see him returning home with a shopping bag on wheels. I step over the fence and hide behind the cypresses. Here he comes now, groaning with every step. He needs time to fit the key into the lock. While he pulls the bag in behind him, I grasp the door and then lock it from the inside. He trembles with rage but doesn't dare to shout. We'll talk upstairs, I say. He doesn't offer me a drink or say a word. Seated at the kitchen table, he just follows my steps as I pace around in semicircles. I tear the wire out of the telephone. With three strides I'm up in the attic. Innumerable objects but an impression of orderliness, the sofa bed is folded up. He doesn't move; a bottle of milk protrudes from his bag. The fridge is hardly inhabited: margarine, a piece of sausage, a mouldy beetroot in a jar, and something cooked but intended for animal food, judging by the smell. I find a glass in the cupboard and pour myself some water at the sink. I drink slowly behind his back. His skull is stately and bald at the top; one blow with a stick and it would burst like a watermelon. He protests but doesn't resist excessively when I tie his hands behind the back of the chair with telephone wire. He endures it all bravely, with a minimum of yowling, and answers me only with scornful glances. In vain. He's of the breed of parents who would *really* step in front of the bullet meant for their child.

Waiting out in the car again. I run out of cigarettes but don't dare to be away even for as long as it takes to zip over to the kiosk at the corner and back. I manage to recruit a boy from the neighbourhood by promising a fat reward. The guest on Radio 101 is the manager of the crematorium. Radio Three is playing opera music. The search button only leads to advertising. *They're taking me down, my friend,* says a very deep male voice, *and as they usher me off to my end, will I bid you adieu?* I quickly press it again. There, on the pavement, fifty metres away: I recognise you by your walk, although the details have yet to get past my short-sightedness. A light-coloured velour jacket, black pants and a bag over your shoulder, both actually grey compared to your hair. You unlock the courtyard door and then that of the house.

Times passes. Sweat from my brow drips into my eyes. I notice my middle finger is tapping hard and fast on the steering wheel. It doesn't stop even when I cast it a reproachful glance. The door of the house opens. I bend my head down to the gear lever and wait. Now you're at the tram stop for the city-bound trams, with your back to me. I still stay nestled in the seat until number fourteen comes. It moves off again and I drive along after it. Panic thinking is no good for coming up with instant strategies. Only when we reach Ribnjak Park do I realise I'm not going to be able to follow the tram further than Vlaška Street because of the one-way system. With squealing tyres I veer off into the street on the left to the honking of oncoming cars. There's nowhere to leave the car and I have to double-park in the hope they'll find their way out somehow. I run after the tram like it's the last ferryboat to ever leave Hades but the gangway has been raised in front of my nose. When I reach the interchange, I grab onto a metal post to get my breath. You're gone – no, there you are, at the top end of Draškovićeva Street. I lose sight of you for a moment as you head round the corner to the right. I give you a fifty-metre berth. We walk along, past Kvaternikov Square and a major intersection, and then you disappear into one of the buildings close by the road. I look at the names on the doorbell panel next to the Meblo furniture shop: yours isn't there. The door is locked.

The car has been reparked for me, the autosnatchers confirm on the phone. I go back down to town, hop into a number eight tram and set off on the mission of redeeming the car. A ticket inspector comes. That's almost comforting – some divine eye is still overseeing and organising things after all.

The name Meblo stays beneath my closed eyelids, a flickering orange, until its letters slowly fade. I repeat the game, who knows how many times. From 11.30pm till midnight Radio Three presents a French critic's essay on the political economy of music.

You appear at the door at nine fifteen. I head across the street; you've already entered the bakery at the end of the building. As you leave, you see I've found you and flail back with your bag. Without any other comment, you let me follow you down the corridor and in through your door. After the dark of the basement, the windows are blinding. Not waiting for your permission, I flop into the armchair. You stay at the doorpost with your arms crossed. I feel very awkward in my raincoat with the jacket underneath but don't feel it's right to take anything off. The pincers of your gaze, the gallery of ghastly yet vaguely familiar faces on the canvases standing by the walls, the light in your eyes from through the barred windows, my raincoat – I feel like a police inspector brought in for questioning, caught in a web of his own lies. My time is ticking away, but nothing more than a mumble passes my lips. Instead of everything I've thought up, phrased and finely honed for days, I burst out crying, loudly and fitfully. I tremble from head to toe as I saturate my clothes, the armchair and the carpet with tears. Now some words do begin to come, breaking out in little spurts as I gurgle between sobs, and a whimper is suffixed to every utterance.

'I'm sorry, it wasn't supposed to turn out like this,' I barely manage to pronounce, 'I really didn't mean it to be this way.'

'There, there. Come on now,' you say. You help me get up and tenderly see me out.

At work I intercept multiple police-like glances; there are conversations which abruptly break off as soon as I appear. My eyes send out threats to everyone, and it works. Just leave me alone.

I ring. You hold the door for a moment, and then open.

'Tea?'

I'm perfectly composed, upright and confident as I twirl the teaspoon in the cup and place the squeezed-out teabag on the saucer. A subtle, highly aestheticised scene of Kieślowski quality, or perhaps even Greenaway. We both smile quietly; what grace, are we going to exchange bows like geishas next?

'Promise me something –,' I finally say, 'just one thing, and then I'll never darken your door again. Promise that you'll get in touch if you ever desire me again. Purely hypothetically. It doesn't cost you anything, it can't hurt you, and I need it in order to stay alive. I need at least the *possibility* of that happening, whenever it may be, even if it means I wait in vain for decades. Without it, my life is completely worthless.

'I promise.'

A close-up of tea in a cup, a pregnant atmosphere and the mysteries of the murky liquid.

Outside I deeply inhale the fragrant air. I extend my hand to stroke a passing child's cheek. I walk round the building, unlock the car and settle comfortably into the seat. I open a bag of pistachios and shell them with relish. The parking lot is small, embraced on all sides by buildings – very cosy. A joint extension of living rooms, where their sounds meet and flow together into a symphony, a unique and irrepressible ode to life: televisions, vacuum cleaners, birds in their cages, the clangour of crockery and kitchen utensils, laughter, burping, the scolding of children and domestic pets. This nascent botanical garden wedged in between cars is just like a vase on the table.

I ring. You hold the door for a moment, and then open.

'I'm dead. There's no one inside any more,' I declare. 'That wouldn't be anything special – I mean, it's like that with the vast majority of people, and they show no signs of it bothering them – if I hadn't felt for an instant what it was like to be alive. I was dead before, too, but I can't take it any more since I know what it means to be uplifted, freed of everything which rivets us to the ground. Isn't that the essence of what we all long for, consciously or not? To break out of our imprisoned selves, the armour of our own egos, to crawl out from beneath the burdens which crush us? Let's detach ourselves from earth-boundedness, the two of us, and, refreshed, rise up to stay in levitation forever!'

Carried away, I take liberties and lift you in my arms. You don't weigh a gram.

'Put me down. This instant!'

'You see, I would carry you for as long as I have arms,' I say. 'Never would I let you fall. Not with what I know now. It hurts too much not to have you: it's such a hard lesson and I can never forget it.'

'The most I can do for you is to wish that you capitalise that wisdom in some other relationship.'

'There can be no other relationship,' I avow. 'There can't be anything else after you. One moment of you would be enough for me to crawl around the world on my knees.'

'Doesn't saying pompous blah like that make you sick?'

I guard the dark at the door like an ancient sentinel, a standing stone. In the end my legs give way and I let myself slide to the floor. I sit on the doormat with my back against the wall. Gradually, at the other end of the corridor, a pale and then ever brighter rectangle is etched. I 'm torn from my doze by the door opening and a shout of surprise above me. You step over my outstretched legs, then once again in the opposite direction, rustling with a plastic bag.

In the bakery I buy a cheese pasty and a cherry strudel. Oh, and I'll have one with apple too, thanks. I eat them in the car, taking care that not one crumb ends up outside the paper bag. One of the topics on national radio's news and current affairs programme is suicide. Today is World Suicide Day, or something like that. The announcer enlightens us with the remarkable fact that depression is one of the leading causes of suicide. Here in Croatia the statistics aren't alarming, thank God. Even post-traumatic stress disorder hasn't significantly spoiled them, contrary to appearances. Research has found that the Croats are not a suicidal nation, he emphasises triumphantly (a million homes heave a collective sigh of relief and fireworks are prepared for that evening). True, it happens here sporadically, but almost exclusively in the northern part of the country. The announcer mentions that the rate is a little higher along the Slovenian border. Slovenia is part of the civilised world. And in this respect we can see how much we lag behind it, although there's a little influence from across the border. The paper *Jutarnji list* reported a year or two ago that an Australian doctor by the name of Nietzsche had patented so-called *exit bags*. Dr Philip Nietzsche chairs the association Exit, which distributes free plastic head covers with a personalised elastic neckband – but only to trained users who have acquired a diploma at a corresponding workshop. Zagorje and Međimurje counties in the north of Croatia are famous for their shrewd entrepreneurs. They're already flocking in droves to Brisbane for agency contracts, aware that the system doesn't have to be free of charge.

The light has gone on behind the drawn curtains in the basement flat. The door of the building is locked. The mobile device is on, but it rings in vain. I press a few doorbells simultaneously. Pest control, I say, could you please open? Downstairs I ring twice, three times, knock, and then lower myself to the doormat. Every now and again there's the clack of a door somewhere further up. For something to do, I test myself to see how many of Cioran's aphorisms I still know from memory. Surprisingly many. At the peaks of despair, *the awareness of death's immanence in life creates an atmosphere of constant dissatisfaction and restlessness that can never be appeased.* Some are quite matter-of-fact: *There are experiences which one cannot survive, after which one feels that there is no meaning left in anything.* Or this one: *If I obeyed my primary instinct, I would spend my days penning harsh epistles and letters of farewell.* Oh, if only! But people are so damn corruptible. With professional marketing, or PR as they say today, tertiary things can easily sweep the primary and secondary out of people's heads. Hmm, that begins to bother me, so I start counting the number of clacks. I like the number 69, it evokes pleasant images; I'd like no one to pass now for as long as possible. But now a fine crackling sound begins in the lock near my ear, and a stethoscopic scraping punctuated with pauses goes on for a long time. And now the door abruptly opens, only a little but enough for me to put my foot in the gap.

'There's nothing to be afraid of,' I reassure you because you tremble as I sit you in the armchair.

'I'm not afraid. Just go. Leave me in peace.'

'Unfortunately that's not possible,' I say, kneeling down. 'If you want, I can simply die. I'm prepared to, if it's for your good. There's no other way to get rid of me. I'm not going to leave here without force. Whoever you call, they'll have to deal with me. That won't be hard – there are few weaker than me. After all, I won't return their blows. But tomorrow I'll be at your door again. If you call the police they'll take me away, but no one can prevent me from coming back. There's no law to prevent me from standing at your door. As a last resort, they could hold me in custody, but not for life. As soon as I get out, even if it be years later, I'll be back. Day and night. You can change your address as much as you like, but I'll find you each time.'

'You mean I really have no choice?'

'Heaven wants it to be like this,' I say. 'I'll lift you in my arms and carry you through the whole city, all the way to my house. We won't set foot in the outer world again.'

'How can you be so selfish? That's got nothing to do with love any more!'

You wriggle free, get up and storm off into the kitchen. You resolutely push away the arm which tries to embrace you. When the other comes to its aid, you can't prevent them from carrying you away into the room and lying you down. The bed isn't wide but is more than enough for us. We're fused together – you turned towards the wall and me wrapped around you from behind. You don't struggle any more and have stopped scratching and kicking; now you just cover your breasts. Needlessly. I seek no more than the softness of your neck, that sweet-smelling warmth I bury my face in.

'I won't do anything violent,' I assure you.

'This is violent enough! Let me go! LET ME GO!!!'

There you go again, although we've breathed as one again and so much tenderness has flowed between us. I'm forced to grip tighter.

'Please don't do that to me, don't make me push your head into the pillow,' I say. 'You'll only get hurt. Look, you've already got bruises on your knees and elbows. Can't we stay at peace? Rationally, without strife, to share what we have now, if there's nothing better in store? Only please don't be curt with me. Don't you start, and neither will I. We'll lie here like this until nature has its way.'

You cry voicelessly. One after another, pearls emerge from the corner of your eye and spill. How callous I would be to coldly watch them fall; I kiss them, drink them, gather them down to the last trace with my tongue. You don't resist. You do nothing to show you're alive any more. Your arms lie listlessly by your sides. Added to the grabbing and friction of just a moment ago, that becomes too great a temptation. My abdomen is still flush against your back; my erection is so explosive that it rings in my head. Something far stronger than civilised scruples seethes in my blood. Your zipper gets caught, so I tear it apart. Your panties are black and find their way to your ankles almost by themselves. You bite my hand, probably to blood, but I feel no pain. Whatever happens, I won't hit, I promise myself. The problem is more that I keep blacking out for seconds at a time. Your knees are squeezed together and your thigh muscles strain almost to bursting, but I just need to press with the weight of my body and your thighs yield and spread wide like an oyster opened with a knife. Almost regretting that the resistance is over so soon, I clasp your butt with one hand and pull you onto my member, as easily as a custom-made sheath. It's smooth and tepid, and I hear the squelch of flesh on flesh. Your sobs are replaced by a sound like a death rattle, deep and protracted. I have visions of muddy puddles, silt and animal dung. Ejaculation happens but seems somewhere outside of me. All at once I'm founded on that sweat-soaked, bespattered, denuded body. I turn over onto my back, do up my flies and stuff my shirt into my pants in the hall.

'I bet you didn't think for a second that I'd be capable of something like that?'

'What's the film you've made your intimate myth from – *Boxing Helena*?'

'But even there it turns out that everything's fiction. Besides, I only love that film, along with lots of others, because the actress reminds me of you.'

'Bullshit! What about me is similar to that woman?'

'Your eyebrows. But totally contrary to the metaphor of amputating limbs and shutting someone away in a box, I wish for you to grow, develop and blossom – as an artist, an individual and a woman, and I can aid you in that.'

'If only you'd let me get up. My shoulder has gone numb.'

'Then turn the other way.'

'I have to go to the toilet.'

'I'm going with you.'

'I'm hungry.'

I get up to bring you a glass of water from the kitchen. A long, serrated knife by the breadbox catches my eye; it lies there like an evil forefinger – an invitation. I meditate over it for a moment, then I cut. From my left shoulder downwards, around five centimetres, but deep. I put my arm in the sink, taking care not to drip blood on the floor. I wait. Finally you peer in. I cut another five. Only one thing can stop this, I say. Without blinking, you turn, take your jacket from the coat-hanger, the keys out of the lock, and call over your shoulder from the doorway:

'Just pull it shut behind you.'

At work the bloodstained tea towel shows through the sleeve of my shirt.

'What happened?' they ask.

'A shaving accident.'

Through the window, from my chair, I can see a little piece of blue sky. One of those bright December days which wipe away all the decay of late autumn. The coffee in a paper cup warms my hand like a friend. I look forward to the working day ahead and apply myself with more élan than ever before. The bundle of paper on the table is a Croatian translation of the book *Seeds of Deception: Exposing Industry and Government Lies About the Safety of the Genetically Engineered Foods You're Eating*. An electrifying read. It grips me to such an extent that I stop worrying about typos and redundant commas. I devour page after page, crying out *Unbelievable! What utter bastards! So many people aren't aware of this at all!* At the end of the chapter 'You Say *Tomato* – I say *Not Any More*', I decide to devote my life to the struggle for a permanent global ban of aspartame, alpha-amylase and cyclodextrin glucosyl-transferase.

I don't know what I found in you. Your ears, for example, are clumsy. The lobes are too thick, without refinement. Who can like you with ears like that? Besides, what am I to do with a pony of a woman? There are so many pint-sized ones around! I've already almost forgotten the smell of your skin. In a few months I won't recognise you on the street. Any other woman will fill the gap immaculately, down to the last millimetre, as if we were talking about Lego blocks.

The Boss calls me in for a chat. Oh great, so this is it then. It was only a question of time, I didn't even try to camouflage it any more. I must say, at least he had the human decency – that's how it probably looked through his eyes – to wait until after the Christmas break. I try to put on a smile like his, and I even succeed. I've always had nothing but positive feelings for him. I'm sure we'll embrace when we say goodbye; I'll carry one of his cigars in my jacket pocket and light it years later, when nostalgia befalls me.

It's to do with a capital project, he tells me, immediately getting down to business – our most important project in the year ahead. We're to publish the collected works of an eminent theoretician of literature, a living legend of Croatian literary scholarship. This is a great honour for us, but also a responsibility to perform the task properly. To make sure things go swiftly, he's decided to entrust it to me despite my lack of experience as an editor. He's attentively followed my work over the last few months and established that I'm ripe for the task. The moment has come for me to be promoted, to move up a rung. And later, if I prove myself... who knows?! He feels I have what it takes for big things – and here he leans forward and winks – if I know what he means. But more about that later. Now I have to roll up my sleeves. He reclines into the back of his chair and carefully puts the tips of his fingers together; a vertical furrow appears on his forehead like the one on the portrait guarding his back. I'll have to revise all the texts most prudently. With all due respect to the author, some of them perhaps need to be... brought up to date a little. In cooperation with the author, of course.

That's why I've been chosen. Because of my sensitivity, or rather humility, which will certainly mellow him and get him on side for the small cosmetic alterations. My very first look at the material reveals the unusualness of the project. The earliest texts were written in fifty-five, and the literary theory in them is only a screen and a springboard for reckoning with Stalinism on the one hand and the decadence of Western materialism on the other. He becomes fiercer over the years.

Success sharpens the scathing pen of this well-read critic, and everywhere he scourges the class enemy, the ecclesiastical clique and the demons of nationalism; he recognises the unity of the emancipatory aspirations of the exploited and disempowered which runs as a thread through world literature, and in the history of regional literature he discovers proof of the age-old brotherhood of the Yugoslav peoples; and so on up until the nineties, when, in keeping with the times, he celebrates the resurrection of the Croatian pastoral novel, the opulence of Croatian baroque verse, and crowns his scholarly career with a study on the Ustashi politician and folk writer Mile Budak, whom he considers a precursor of post-modernism.

Since the old man is hardly mobile, we agree to pedicure his opus at his home, however many working days it takes me (the Boss is generous). But it immediately turns out that my endeavours to institute aesthetic changes have no chance whatsoever in the face of this littérateur's tide of evocations. Whatever we touch on instantly casts us into a well of associations. Starting from his participation in the national liberation struggle, where biographical pedantry would indicate he was just twelve at the time, and despite the fact that he sometimes mixes up that war and the Croatian War of Independence of the early nineties. Therefore I resign from all technicalities and let him sail spontaneously through the book of his life, only occasionally interspersing minor questions like little lighthouses when he drifts off course. We spend pleasant hours together. He's a nice, agreeable fellow, and evidently I arouse his paternal feelings. He's also an inexhaustible, although lugubrious narrator. All his reminiscences, even those from early childhood, lead him back to the same topic. His muted voice and misty eyes clearly show that all other baggage, ideals, books and people pale to

insignificance beside it: the woman of his life. His wife recently passed away after forty years together, without children. And here he is now, alone in that enormous, dark flat, in the quicksand of his own useless mind. Since his stories were rather elliptic, it took me a dozen or so sessions to establish that the main heroine was actually from an episode which took place in the nineteen thirties, before he married.

Overall, the weeks slip by pretty smoothly. With only one excess, at our webshop editor's birthday party in the bar across the street. Domestic disco music is doof-doofing away but the vociferous female colleagues have warmed up with colourful cocktails and manage to outshrill it. A twenty-year-old couple sit at the table in the opposite corner. Leaning towards each another and smiling, they whisper alternately in each other's ear and caress each other with glances indecipherable to the rest of the world. She takes his hand and rests it on her cheek. Tears begin to run down mine. I'm discovered several seconds later, giving me enough time to start frantically turning all my pockets inside out because I've lost my wallet with all my documents and the pay I've just picked up. The girls devote themselves to the search and produce it out of my coat pocket with noisy jubilation. But I'm not greatly compromised.

I still can't get through with my mobile. I call from a telephone box, and finally:

'Hullo?'

'I know what we're going through isn't at all original,' I say. 'It's happened to thousands or millions before us: two lovers sooner or later find themselves, how should I put it, out of step with each other; emotions tip a little one way, and the other feels they're strangling him, and that can sometimes drive normal people apart; but we are so far on past that danger, how trivial and tiny it will look to us, how we'll laugh at it when...,' and now I notice that I'm alone on the line.

The lights behind the curtains of the basement windows go on, off, on, off... I gradually become friends with the caretaker of the building. She's distrustful at first, which is natural in her position, but she grants me her trust and even opens up her heart. She drops in almost every day after walking to Mount Sljeme and sits with me for a while. We talk about the weather, prices at the market, and things like that. Sometimes she brings me a piece of cake she's baked, and I offer her dried figs, chips and bananas. She shows me photos of her grandchildren and tells me about each of them in great detail and with love. As well as bursting with vitality, she has only serene and complimentary words for her co-tenants, what life has given her, and the interior of my car.

I imagine ringing. For a moment you look daggers at me, not letting go of the door, and say:

'I want children. Two children.'

I can't think of anything more desirable or urgent. If we start straight away we can do much better than that: surround ourselves with cordons of our own miniature reproductions and in doing so insure ourselves against old age. I lift you in my arms and carry you out to the car. There we make the family nest. Beyond the coordinates of contemporary residential technology, true, and sometimes it's crowded until the eldest of the brood are fully fledged and leave the nest. But we lack nothing because nothing material and nothing earthbound can harm us, let alone pollute our spirit. The ethereal refuge of love and pure spirituality we built in ourselves is resurrected to the letter in our progeny, and they in theirs, and so forth.

Oh, if it could only be...

At Easter, the caretaker brings me two coloured eggs, which we hang from the rear-view mirror, and a poppyseed cake. We eat it while listening to Mass on the radio.

I ring the doorbell.

'The only way for me to accept this, the only thing keeping me alive, is the hope that this is only a dream which will dissipate sooner or later,' I say. 'I'll see your face and realise with indescribable relief that it was all just my subconscious mind playing a cruel trick on me. Without certainty in that, I wouldn't want to live an hour longer.'

Not a word. But that's not as terrible as your smile, its sarcastic pre-eminence, and the yawning chasm it opens between us. Not even the blackest nightmare could create a horror equivalent to the reflection I see mirrored in your eyes, something like a sarcoma or a dung-beetle.

I climb to the top of the building. Fourteen storeys – call it overkill. Washing is drying on lines strung between the chimneys: sheets and children's T-shirts with printed balloons, butterflies and little birds. The tar paper beneath my feet is covered in guano-bird droppings. I climb up onto the concrete fence. I breathe deeply, close my eyes and slowly raise my arms until I assume the shape of a human cross. If anyone happens to view the building from the perspective of Zagreb zoo in this instant, I must look like the twin-spired cathedral to them. Various sources concur that my magic lantern now ought to show the highlights of my existential *chef-d'oeuvre*, nostalgically revisiting the most moving sequences. Instead, only the noise of traffic makes it through to my consciousness. Down below, endlessly patient trams crawl from left to right and back again, cars crowd up against one another, mopeds drone in between them, all in the unquestioned faith in some destination, at least as bona fide as necessary to avoid a gridlock. All of a sudden, a gust of wind throws me off balance. I wave my arms in panic to regain it back. My heart wants to leap out of my throat. I get down from the fence and sit with my back against it until the pulses die down.

Aimlessly, like a boat loose from its moorings, I drift along the footpath towards Maksimir Park. Smells of spring in the air interweave with those from the bakery, exhaust pipes and girls now in almost summer clothes. I stand at the traffic lights vis-à-vis the park's entrance. Popcorn and helium-filled dalmatians are on sale there, and a boy is being lifted onto a pony for a ride. A truck with a trailer comes rumbling down the street. The moment it enters the intersection I take a step. Its sign *Horto Fruktić – Potting Soil / Peat / Fertiliser* stays beneath my eyelids forever...

Cottony balls of poplar fluff fall on the car, then yellow birch leaves, then snowflakes. The old Peugeot has a lean and is rickety, and one tyre has gone flat. And the door creaks. But a man's home is his castle, how true is that old adage! Every Christmas Eve I decorate it with branches of fir. There's no longer a caretaker, but the children from the building help me; they bring baubles and little angels from home. I help them with their homework. Almost all of them are lovely. They show me newborn kittens and introduce me to their girlfriend or boyfriend. Having firecrackers or rotten eggs thrown under my car is now a rare occurrence. I made friends with some of them before they started school, and I've just received a postcard from the eldest who's away on military service. Now I have a dozen of them on the windscreen and windows, showing different places on the Adriatic coast...

* * *

Today is 20th March 2006. Tomorrow will be the first day of spring. Tomorrow I won't live here any more. I won't open this notebook again. If I had a little more sense of the theatrical, I'd burn it.

The desire must have been creeping up on me for days. Then, on Christmas Eve, I just snatched my coat and rushed outside, went all the way through the city by tram and then three stops with the bus. I had a lump in my throat when I got out, but the familiar scenes brought not only bitterness but also a pleasant tingling all over my body. The multi-level fountain surrounded by garden gnomes. The terrier which stuck its snout through the bars and waved its stumpy tail as if it recognised me. The crucifix with a dozen lanterns glowing at its base. Just the palm tree was missing from the courtyard, probably the work of last winter's frosts.

A heartbeat away from the house I was abruptly slowed by the question of what exactly I was doing, as if I'd been out of its range until then. The idea of ringing you had seemed wrong. After all, it wasn't based on real desire or feelings. It was a whim, the fruit of curiosity and a long period of loneliness. But what I would say when you opened, and what pain I would perhaps cause you with this frivolous gesture, didn't enter my consciousness even in the last few metres.

It's easy now to claim that I wouldn't have rung at all and would have got exactly what I needed by simply walking past the house. All I know for sure is that I stood thunderstruck, staring at the man who was hanging up little light bulbs on the stunted pine tree out the front. From the top of the ladder, without rudeness but also without much kindness, he asked me if I needed any help. He was balding, with a big moustache, around fifty. Nor could he give me even the vaguest idea where you'd left for after selling him the house.

It was probably that shock and the sudden emptiness it created which impelled me to write. I began that same evening, in a hurry to set down all I hadn't said to you. Not that there was any spark of life in the deadness of our relationship. Ever since I aborted it, the desire for a fresh start with you couldn't be reborn. But coming to terms with that total and evidently final disappearance did stir my vanity somewhere deep inside. Had it really been that worthless? And had it become so obnoxious for you that you needed to flee? Or was that all just a hallucination of mine?

I wrote and wrote for two months, extracting everything, maybe in the hope that I would see things more clearly on paper, but it didn't lead to any great enlightenment. What's more, I then forgot about the notebook and didn't return to it for weeks. After all, there were real things which demanded my attention: two exhibitions, for example, one of them abroad. I was also awarded a prize. Now my pictures are being sold. The galleries want more and more every day, and the prices are going up. It seems I can sell anything. As an experiment, I tried making pieces as rubbishy as possible and interspersing them among the others: the gallery sold them all within three days. But let's not worry about that. It's taking its course, wherever it leads.

Hardly a week after I stopped writing, Ines came to see me. She brought along her problem, hoping it would become mine too. I hadn't seen her in such exaltation for at least decade, ever since she got off the dope. Was that it?

'No, I'm in love,' she exclaimed.

'Wow, that's great news –,' I said, 'I guess it was time for a new life after cluttering this one up so much, what with a gaggle of kids up to your eyeballs.'

'Hey, thanks for your sympathy. But do you know what the trouble is?' she sighed, and went on to tell me of her quandary.

Just when her therapy had really started to work and her world began to look acceptable and she really felt she belonged to it, just when Marko had been approved a loan for a flat and Dora had stopped wetting the bed, she went out for coffee with this guy she'd met a few times in the waiting room of the psychiatrist they both went to – without any particular intention, out of pure curiosity – and it clicked.

'You can't believe what spiritual kinship we've discovered. No one else can imagine the feeling born when we spoke: like we've always known each other and are kindred, twin spirits. I can't say I didn't love Marko in a certain way, we had our moments, but now I've discovered a completely different dimension. Now I know what it means to be in love.'

'How about you chill out a bit? Have you really weighed things up?'

'You think I haven't? It's just that I'm afraid it's too late, that life without it is no longer possible, that I wouldn't survive the return to earth...'

'All right,' I said. 'Then you should do what you have to in order to stay alive.'

'Oh, if only it were like that if I split up with Marko. But I think that would pretty much kill me.'

She sat there mutely, entrenched in the armchair, not releasing me with her gaze, which was at once imploring, red-hot and despairing.

'Can't you help me make this decision –,' she pleaded, 'or at least tip the scales in one direction...'

'Talk about a tall order!' I grumbled. 'Look, don't be angry, but I've got a meeting and I'm running late.'

That didn't pass through me as smoothly as I described. But Father was due in for surgery a few days later. His cataracts didn't permit any further delay. Although there's no great danger in that operation, the very thought of going under the knife must have prompted him to hold a confessional. And what was the deeply buried thing which absolutely had to be revealed before the operation *in case something happened*? What realisation could I not live without? He beat around the bush for fifteen minutes before I learnt that I'm 'probably' not his biological daughter. 'Probably' was a euphemism because there had been a time when he and Mother *didn't live as husband and wife*, while her episode with another man lasted. He said he'd tell me who it was if I wanted to know – he was still alive. I declined. In brief, Mother ended the extramarital adventure and was forgiven. Father accepted the fruit of that affair as his own.

The fruit took the news fairly stoically. Although the realisation put something of a dent in my genealogical mythology. But what was the goal of that confessional? For whose benefit was it intended if not to arouse in me the consciousness of his sacrifice and the gratitude he deserved? The altruism of the elderly is notorious.

Father survived the scalpel, but it didn't produce the desired results. After a week, it was indisputable that he saw less than before, in fact almost nothing. Allegedly it wasn't their fault – his eyes simply didn't respond well. Another operation was scheduled, although they warned us not to get our expectations up. In other words, we would probably have to get used to the idea of him being blind.

Since then I've spent most of the time with him; I virtually only come back here to sleep. Now I've decided to put an end to the toing and froing and am moving back. What awaits me is barely imaginable. It took so much time and energy to get his suffering out of my system. But I have no doubt that I'll get used to it again. I'm sure it looks worse than it really is, like going to the dentist's. The pain in the dentist's chair hurts less than the mental picture of that chair.

In the autumn I approached the Boss and requested that he find me a job in Germany – any job – I just needed to leave and would be grateful if he didn't ask any questions. I went to him as a friend, which he'd been for all those nine years, and told him frankly that I had no one but him. And that I thought I'd worked more than diligently and given all of myself. Now I asked him for that favour; I couldn't express how much it meant to me, and with the reputation he'd acquired over the many years of doing business in Germany it ought not to be a big problem for him.

He flinched, reflected for a moment and muttered that he hadn't expected this. A silence followed, obviously levelled at my resoluteness, intended to enlighten me as to how insulting the very thought of betraying him like this was, and also to make me repent while there was still time. Since nothing of the kind was forthcoming, he attacked once more with an intensive gaze and the question if I was sure, and for an instant he cloaked himself in regret for the bright future which had been in store for me at the firm. Then he almost shoved me out of his office with a semi-promise: 'We'll see. I haven't been to Germany for a long time and the old friendships are gone.'

For two weeks I went to the office on edge until he announced to me, reluctantly, scrutinising me for any signs of me coming to reason, that the acquaintance of an acquaintance, who he'd never met in person, was willing to take me on probation in his trading firm in Canada. That was all he could offer. Great, I said, I was eternally obliged and hoped I would be able to repay the favour one day.

The house proved much easier to sell than its condition had led me to expect. I had several substantial offers, but they were all from entrepreneurs who looked through the house as if it wasn't there; they were purely interested in the block, which would be cleansed and would soon sport a beautiful multi-story building. Sentimentality was the current enemy, that truculent demon; the vision made me feel most uncomfortable and became an ongoing thorn in my conscience. I decided in favour of a machinist and his family from Travnik in Bosnia, who judged these climes to be more beneficial, above all for the children's sake. So it was that they and I each made a modest contribution to global migration trends, evacuating the South and East to the benefit of the North and West.

So there would be no lack of the random and incidental, in the middle of the conveyancing period a phone call came from my paternal uncle, who I didn't even know I had. But I learnt straight away that I wouldn't have him for much longer. That was the real reason for the respect he accorded me by getting in touch: the doctors had announced that his life had entered the finishing straight. Did he therefore want to meet me before reaching the tape? So as to enhance his luggage for the Other world with the knowledge of what his 33-year-old nephew looked like? Moreover, he also wanted to give me letters his brother had sent him from abroad, among them one addressed specifically to me, in a separate, unopened envelope. My father (he stopped for a second, doubtlessly smarting from the acoustic fiasco of that word) had asked him to give it to me when the time came. I was overwhelmed by my father's touching attentiveness. But how did Uncle know the time had come? Did the envelope mention a date of maturity? Or had Father finally given him his blessing? Actually, and much more understandably, he'd since fallen out with my father (also by correspondence – we're a very epistolary family) and lost all track of him. And I knew how it was: work without end at the farm, one worry after another... To be honest, he'd forgotten the letter.

That gentle uncle, today probably six feet under, lived in the country. Unlike my cosmopolitan father, he stayed in the house our ancestors had built a good many generations ago. Following his directions, I found the village at the end of a track leading off the country road where the bus dropped me. Just a few muddy metres' walk were enough to make me long for my old car (I'd flogged it off to a snotty-nosed kid for almost nothing), and after several hundred steps my soles were most unwilling to be separated from the ground; the track wound in between wooded hills sodden by the autumn rain. And now it drizzled something more like liquid mould, smelling strongly of mushrooms, rotting leaves and millennial decay. Distant generations of my family hunted wild boars here until they were taught to keep them in sties. Porcine dwellings took up a significant part of every farmyard, along with a barn and dungheap as their necessary complement, adorned with chickens scratching around. Our farmhouse didn't deviate from that model in any way; it was pointed out to me by a man who turned up on the doorstep of the next-door house, cleared his throat loudly and emptied the contents of his nose on the ground.

Although riveted to his bed, weak and yellow, my uncle was visibly and obviously moved by our meeting; a tear even rolled down his swollen, unshaven cheek. He too had an only child, about ten years older than me, who was also a bachelor – it looked bad for our line. My cousin and aunt showed endemic conversational restraint and didn't let my presence distract them much from their daily preoccupations. When my uncle and I were left alone to talk in confidence, he fell to evoking his childhood and youth: he emphasised the deeds and character of my father, skipping his short-lived marital episode, and succinctly touching on later stages and the countries where he'd lived and worked. Although he was at his strength's end, he even wanted his wife to get out the old photographs. I declined, promising to come again; the main thing was that we'd found each other. I said goodbye, took my father's letter, and threw it into one of the dungheaps on the way out of the village.

One more interesting thing happened before I set off across the ocean, although perhaps I'm seeking meaning in it which it doesn't have: Goran, my childhood friend and walking landmark of the neighbourhood, winked at me in passing the same day as I bought my ticket. He winked like you do at a kid or a younger colleague as a sign of sympathy and support. Although he didn't look back when I called his name, I'm sure it wasn't just my imagination.

In my first Canadian home, Toronto, I was taken in as part of the family and even went on family excursions. Ante Grmusha, my Croatian host and sponsor, had come to Canada in the mid 1980s after high school with a three-month visa, which he promptly upgraded to a permanent one by marrying an emigrant's daughter. First he got a job as a car salesman and a year later he was a self-employed businessman, whose activities rapidly spread. He mentioned some of them in very general terms, and I needed no telling that it would have been imprudent to ask more. After all, I was a complete stranger and he'd been kind enough to sign the sponsorship form for my visa and provide me with food and lodging. I was given a bed in a room which served as a store for merchandise, between Korean sneakers, Indian shirts and German vacuum cleaners. In return, I proved myself to be readily utilisable labour, cheaper than local workers. He couldn't pay me more because he was already exposing himself to a great risk – he'd really be in hot water if they caught me working off the books. He felt pretty awkward about it, but needlessly so; I didn't really care how much I was paid.

Sunday breakfast with the Grmushas, without exception, was an overture to going to Mass. Belonging to the family had to be confirmed by participation. Missing out on the patriotic sit-togethers which took place at their house at least once a week was out of the question. These were attended by very picturesque figures; some of them, enfeebled with old age, were actually carried in and laid on the couch. Everyone wanted to make my acquaintance and hear the news from back home, and I made superhuman efforts not to disappoint them, either in content or interpretation. They tried hard to speak some kind of Croatian, broken and confusing, until they got stuck and switched to English, to everyone's relief. They found it hard to follow my descriptions, even when vastly simplified; their eyes would soon wander off to the mythical picture of the Croatian Fatherland sealed in their soul, an image which no current events could displace or challenge. Occasionally the concept of *going back* would flit through the room, unburdened by sincere intent: it was an incantation to arouse the spirit in the lamp, but only for domestic use. They didn't demand anything more of the old country than that it stay where it was. The evenings typically ended with the murmuring of old songs; when they were all sung, they put on cassettes with ballads by Ivo Robić or Thompson's nationalist refrains.

Ante invests a lot of effort in maintaining Croatian folk traditions – and also in assimilating: he never misses an occasion to emphasise his pride at being a Canadian citizen. He hasn't been back to the old country for years; the Bahamas are better for holidays. He isn't a romantic but an investor and a paragon citizen of the New World; the immigrant community enabled him to establish a business network, and his foster-country gilded its strands.

Less than a month after I'd moved in, he strode radiant up to the stand where I was showing a demonstration video for selling a weight-loss ring. He'd just concluded a record wholesale deal for the stain remover Didi Seven. We quickly crammed my things into the van, picked up his wife and two daughters, and zoomed off towards the Niagara Falls to mark the joyous event. It was inhumanly cold: the dusk had turned to black by the time we arrived, but the place where the river plunged downwards shone brightly in the beam of mighty floodlights. A huge, icy monolith reared up above us; fine liquid dust rose out of the cauldron below, merging with the misty air and congealing in a cloud of rainbow crystals. From the edge, secured by a high fence, one could look down into the chasm. We stood there gazing for a time and then headed back towards the van. But not before Ante had immortalised us with his digital camera. On the photo, a little removed from the embracing female triangle and looking away, glum, wet and pinkish, I was visibly out of place and called for editing out.

That same evening, I found a few interesting offers in the nationwide advertiser, went for a walk and made arrangements in a telephone box. I stole out before dawn and the coach left at seven. Winnipeg sounded ideal: far away from the colonies of Croatian emigrants, in the middle of one of the most sparsely populated countries on earth.

It took my body quite some time to adapt to the hard, physical work in harsh weather conditions; but mentally the effect was quite therapeutic – anaesthetic to be precise. I've liked the boss from our very first conversation, and that impression has constantly been reinforced. He treats us all respectfully, without racial prejudice; in fact, the four of us whites who are currently employed do our friendly best to make up for not belonging to the Wong family. The firm prospers owing to good management and market conditions, like a harvest where the produce leaps into the hopper all by itself. The manager, Mr Wong, buys up nineteenth-century colonial buildings like tanneries and steelmills in order to do them over, or demolish them and erect new ones, which he then sells, mostly to new Canadians imported from China. And there's no discernible tendency for demand to slacken.

All of Wong's four sons are employed in the firm. The eldest is his right-hand man, while the youngest does the hard and dusty work together with us, without reprieve; he too will get a place in management when he's earned it. Theoretically he's already a millionaire, but he doesn't show it in any way. He doesn't drive a sports car and doesn't even wear a watch. He's full of enthusiasm but unobtrusive – a nice, regular and sociable guy who never says no when we go for a drink after work. He's mad about songs by Shakira, Anastacia and whatever their names are; he's constantly humming to himself in falsetto, with choreography added when he thinks no one's watching. Nor with any of the other Wongs did I detect the slightest trace of gloominess or anxiety. For sure, there's simply no room for such concepts in their mental make-up.

Jeremy and I are part of the demolition team; we operate in buildings which aren't earmarked for the wrecker's ball but are stripped of everything except the load-bearing walls. We use jackhammers, mallets and crowbars to knock down ceilings and partitions; we pull up floorboards, remove carpentry, rip out wires and pipes, and throw everything into the truck, large and small pieces alike, and sweep out the bare skeleton. Then the construction guys take over and convert the building into a shrimp house, laundrette or TV shop; we're not involved in that bit.

I was actually in no hurry to find work, but when Jeremy suggested I join him, I said *Why not*. And so for three months now we've been getting into his chevy five days a week at seven thirty and driving to the firm's office, where we change into our gear and are taken to the current worksite. In the evenings, one of us fries up something for dinner and the other does the washing up, and the next day vice versa. There's almost nothing I haven't told him about. His perpetual, sphinxlike smile intrigued me at first, and got mightily on my nerves, till I accepted it as part of the decor. The guy has just got it right.

The days pass, and I must say I'm also starting to find a certain satisfaction in reducing buildings to rubble, and the fatigue the strenuous work fills my body with, and also in thinking of the quiet, industrious, reliable Chinese families who arrive here and build a different world amidst the ruins, multiply and spread, and take over continent after continent.

It all now seems very distant; that time of pure pain pervading everything around me, down to the very last detail of my surroundings, when going on for just one more day seemed impossible and pointless, when the only conceivable thing after getting back from the office was to crash into bed without dinner or a shower. My body demanded nourishment, gave warning signals by way of spasms and trembling, but after the first mouthful of food my hunger would disappear. The nights bore me away to painful chasms; still, they recharged a minimum of energy, sufficient for me to get to my feet in the morning and grasp some object, something *real and existing*. But it wasn't enough for me to free myself from the pain which unfailingly woke up with me and held me firmly in its grip, unable to be silenced. It would inevitably break through fitfully in howls and screams for help, or I would scratch at my skin or slash myself with a razor – enough for a little blood to flow; that would calm it for a while. But any word, sight,

248

smell or taste could become an association, a cruel allusion; everywhere was a minefield and everything led to that same place – the one which would never be. When my rational mind capitulated and stopped inventing straws to clutch at, my dreams took over; your face would appear for a fleeting instant, faint as a watermark, or I'd hear words like *I'll be a bit late but don't worry, I'm coming.* And I'd wake up with a pounding heart and tears which never stopped.

Now I feel much better. When I'm at work, hours can pass without me thinking of you. I no longer recognise you in every single woman I see. I don't study the details of their bodies any more, their gestures or facial expressions, the invisible aura etched around them, just to create the sweet pain brought by the comparison with what I held for a moment in my hand. I'm convinced the day will come when a cup won't evoke your hand and the way you hold it and raise it to your mouth, when a toothbrush won't remind me that you're perhaps now brushing your teeth on the opposite side of the planet; I'll be able to speak your name again and also come to live with the thought of it being spoken by another.

istrosbooks

ISTROS BOOKS, an independent publisher with an eye on
contemporary literature from South East Europe, brings you
Best Balkan Books 2013
our series featuring the very best titles from the region.

Sun Alley
Cecilia Ştefănescu
ISBN 978-1-908236-06-7
A novel about the roots of adultery and the destiny of an
exceptional young boy with the power to foresee his
own future.
MARCH 2013

The Fairground Magician
Jelena Lengold
ISBN 978-1-908236-10-4
Winner of the European Prize for Literature, 2011
JUNE 2013

The Son
Andrej Nikolaidis
ISBN 978-1-908236-12-8
Winner of the European Prize for Literature, 2011
SEPTEMBER 2013

Ekaterini
Marija Knežević
ISBN 978-1-908236-13-5
A story of human survival told through the female gaze.
OCTOBER 2013